I0690301

BEYOND THE
GREAT SOUTH WALL

Robert Mason '01

BEYOND THE GREAT SOUTH WALL

THE SECRET OF THE ANTARCTIC

Frank Savile

Coachwhip Publications
Landisville, Pennsylvania

Beyond the Great South Wall, by Frank Savile
First published 1901, New York (New Amsterdam Book Co.)
Published 2008, Coachwhip Publications, with minimal editing.
All rights reserved.

ISBN 1-930585-52-7
ISBN-13 978-1-930585-52-2

Coachwhipbooks.com

Images: Front cover (Antarctic glacial wall), Laurel Stewart.
  Back image and Frontispiece from Robert Mason illustrations included
  in the original publication of *Beyond the Great South Wall*.

CONTENTS

1. A Great Depression 7

2. The Tale of a Coincidence 18

3. The Testimony of Sir John Dorinecourte, Knt. 26

4. What Baines Knew 35

5. Professor Lessaution's Opinion 45

6. We Sail South 57

7. A Light in the Darkness 66

8. Before the Gale 76

9. The Leaping of the Wall 88

10. Behind the Barrier 102

11. A Glacier Cave and What Lay Therein 112

12. The Great God Cay 124

13. A Closed Door 133

14. In the Ninth Circle 144

15. The Mountain Wakes 157

16. The Temple and the Lair of Cay 167

17. A Little Dog's Stumble 177

18. A Desperate Betrothal 188

19. A Wondrous Breaching of the Wall 201

1

A GREAT DEPRESSION

The purr and throb of London was quivering in stuffily through the open windows. The squeals of the "special" newsboys and the hansom-whistles of the early diners-out splashed across the blur and din, standing out against the immeasurable roar as against a silence. The heat of a London summer lay heavily over us; the undying rattle of wheels beat up to us wearily, the mid-season blare and hurry of town echoing irritatingly in their jingle and clatter as they streamed ceaselessly by. The stew and hubbub of the afternoon enclosed us as with a pall of depression.

By us I mean Gerry and myself. Flung back listlessly was I in my club chair, and watching him as he strolled monotonously up and down before the great bow-window that gave upon Pall Mall. His hands were scabbarded hilt high in his pockets. His brows and the corners of his eyes were hard and wrinkled. His gaze was cast steadfastly before his toes. He did a very sentry-go of moody vexation.

Each time he paused, as he turned against the light, every wrinkle and line was silhouetted mercilessly. Wretchedness covered his face as with a mask. My heart began to go out to him, bursting through its own crust of dejection. Wretched we both were, but I was seven years his senior. I began to commune with myself, seeking comfort for him out of my own hard-won store of disappointment, and trying to forget that our sorrows sat upon an even base.

Suddenly he turned towards me and broke the silence that had lasted between us the greater part of the afternoon.

"Well," he said harshly, "that's the end of most things for me."

"Possibly," answered I, "but probably not. The future's very spacious yet, my dear boy. I don't say it in any patronizing spirit,

7

but you're only twenty-four. Try to forget the 'might-have-been,' and buck yourself up into imagining the 'may-be.' It's not all over yet."

He grunted contemptuously, tramping off again upon his beat. A waiter who chanced in with the evening papers coughed ostentatiously, and with obvious intention towards the cloud of dust that followed hard upon his track. Gerry stared him down, and as the door closed behind him, brought himself to anchor before me again.

"That's all rot, and you know it, Jack," he said dogmatically. "Do you think I'm going to stay here and see Vi come back another man's wife? I'm sick of it all—sick of the work, sick of the play. Deathly sick of the utter sameness of what we call life. I'm going to chuck it, I tell you. Hausa Police, Egyptian Army, Hong Kong Regiment—something of the kind I'm going to try. There's nothing most assuredly to keep me any longer in her Majesty's Foot Guards. I'm dipped, and I've lost the one thing that might have kept me to the collar. Great Heavens! what in the name of goodness *should* I stay for?"

I stared back at him answerless. I knew he was talking a cheap sentiment which a month or two later he would be the first to despise. I too was feeling in a modified form all he felt. To me had also come the animal desire for action that follows hard upon mental stress. But that seven years made the difference. Though that day had brought me the supreme discontent of my life, I was still aware that the world continued to wag, and that we should swing along with it. Yet how could I comfort without offending?

Now the reason of all this affliction was simple enough and old as time. To each of us had come the desire of his life, and to each had it been denied. That morning we had spent at the Albert Docks, and had seen a tall ship sail out for foreign lands, hearing upon her decks two maidens who were taking with them our hearts to the world's end.

I never was much of a chap for lover's rhapsodies, so I will make no effort to explain to you how sweet a girl was Gwen Delahay, nor why she held my heart in the hollow of her hand. She was one of the many good and beautiful women—God bless them—who walk this earth, and are to their lovers peerless. And as I worshipped her, so did Gerry worship Vi, her sister—a thing perhaps inexplicable, in that he had seen Gwen, but one to be truly thankful for, seeing that we were friends beyond the ordinary sympathies of life. And now were we left hopeless.

Plain Captain Dorinecourte was I, with a slender six hundred pounds beyond my pay, and Gerry, poor lad, had less. You will not exhaust yourself with wonder then, when I relate the fact that Lady Delahay declined on behalf of her daughters our attentions, contemned our eligibility, and hated poisonously the sight of our ingenuous faces. For all these things, I take it, a Society mother is bound by her allegiance to Society to do. Yet though we felt that she played the game as we understood it, none the less did we cry out upon our luck in being the losers. And now it seemed that we might well throw down our cards.

The fond mother's fears of the blight which our undivided attentions might throw upon her daughters' careers had culminated that morning. A month before an announcement in the *Morning Post* had spurred her to an action which her fear alone would never have conceived. It ran as follows—

"Among the passengers by the s.s. *Madagascar*, which sails on August 4 for her winter's cruise around the world, will be the Earl of Denvarre. His lordship will be accompanied by his brother the Hon. Stephen Garlicke."

This item of intelligence had caught the dutiful mother's eye, and taken vigorous root in her somewhat languid intelligence. Two eligible young men were to be shut up for eight or nine months in a space not more than one hundred yards long by twenty wide. Walking lawlessly in London were two extremely ineligible youths, unchained, ready and willing to wreck her daughters' happiness. Why not extract the victims from this hazardous propinquity, placing them at the same time in the financially commendable vicinitude of a live earl and his brother. Action was born only too rapidly from reflection. We had seen them off that very morning.

So there sat we in the desolation of a mere club, disconsolate amid the roar of the city, while the sunset became the twilight, the shadows of the lamp-posts lengthened, and darkness fell

upon the town even as upon our hearts. And out of the pleni-
tude of my regret I failed to find the word of sympathetic comfort
for Gerry.

Lost in our heavy-hearted musings, it was past eight when
we realized that food was yet a distasteful necessity of existence, and sought the club dinner. Silently we entered the dining-
room, Gerry with the air of one who approached poisoned
dishes, and chose a table apart. Though the soup and sherry
warmed my companion to conversation, it had a bias of marked
contempt.

Clubs, he showed beyond dispute, were traps for the unwary,
committees were things of naught, secretaries insolent and over-
paid. Waiters were plucked from the gutter to be trained in pot-
houses, and cooks cherished the idea that to evolve a savoury it
was but necessary to taint an olive with a decayed anchovy.
Women who were guests of brother members—it was Wednes-
day night—were all dressed in seventeen tints of garish atrocity,
and were of a mediocrity of feature which he plainly condemned.
He mentioned the names of no less than six social resorts off
which he purposed to take his name in the morning. This, of
course, preparatory to stirring activities which would remove
him beyond their sphere of usefulness. Still soured, but evidently relieved, he then retired behind the sheets of the
Westminster, with which he screened himself from further inter-
course with his fellows. Apathetically I proceeded with my repast.

Suddenly the decorum of the room received a shock. A sound
burst from Gerry's throat which I can only term a crow. He endeavored frantically and indecently to masticate the portion which
he had placed between his teeth, beating the paper at me furiously. The sounds which continued to issue from his lips were
such as no one could approve. He mouthed unutterable things.

Hastily I rose and thumped him on the back, and noticed
that his finger continued to tap viciously upon a headline which
he thrust into my face. As the distressing symptoms modified
themselves he gradually found his breath, but ceased not to
bulge his eyes upon me.

"Look, old man, look," he insisted faintly, and I took the
paper from his hand.

"We regret to announce the death of Viscount Heatherslie at Greytown, Central America. His lordship had lately been travelling in the vicinity, and his death is ascribed to malarial fever. As yet no details can be ascertained." —*Reuter.*

The words turned red before my eyes as they danced up and down the green columns. Uncle Leonard was dead—was dead. And I—well, I had to think it very hard indeed before I dared repeat it silently even to myself—I was Lord Heatherslie. Only one thought had possession of my mind. Not a regret did I spare for the dead, not a single reflection as to what this thing meant to me or my prospects did I give beyond the fact that my luck—my cursed Irish luck—had been too late. That one idea had hold of me. A week earlier—a few hours earlier, and what might have been?—what might have been? A curse snarled from between my teeth as I sat down again to stare white-faced across at Gerry.

The excitement had died from his face. His sympathy was quicker than mine had been. He stretched his hand across the table and gripped mine hard.

"Frightful luck, old chap," he murmured; "I know what you're thinking. But—but it needn't be too late yet, Jack."

I shook my head. Things had become blurred in my brain, but one fact stood out bright as a search-light to my mind's eye. Gwen was going out of my life, going away from me as fast as breeze and steam would take her. And the thing that might have stayed our separation—have given her to me—was a week—nay, only a day—too late. I could have smitten my head against the wall in my agony of disappointment.

And yet I had resigned Gwen as fatalistically as any son of Islam. I had schooled myself to think of her as already belonging to another. I had bidden her good-bye without a quiver. Even the look she had given me at the last—a tender, questioning look it was too, and straight from her heart through her dear eyes—I had met with a smile that told of nothing. To me the hopelessness of it all had come home long days before, and I simply wouldn't sadden the poor child and prolong the pain of parting. I meant that parting to be the absolute separation of our lives—one that should leave no dropped threads to be gathered up in future days of further hopelessness.

And now—now I had the right to win her, and honourably. Only a soldier I might be, but I had a place of my own to take a wife to. Nor would she come to me to sink into a nobody. Half a county would welcome Lady Heatherslie, though half that county might be in rags. Poor we should always have been, but not desperately. Modestly we should have had to live, but we could have kept our rank befittingly. And now the chance was gone. Away beyond the seas she would set herself to forget me, and Denvarre would show her how. The black curses fell over each other in their haste to reach my tongue, and the salt tears nigh fled out along with them. I made an effort and pulled myself together.

"Come along," said I hoarsely to Gerry in a voice that I hardly knew myself, and blundered out of the room. Without another word I crept into the hansom the commissionaire called, and together we drove down the glaring streets to my rooms, Gerry offering no sympathy but a silence which I understood and was grateful for.

You know the heavy, choking pain that lies leaden in your throat when one you love has gone out into the emptiness—the desperate unbelief in your torture—the mad hope that insists that this thing is too horrible to bear. My suffering came home to me like that. I could only think of Gwen as of one dead and gone from me, but with the added agony of knowing that to me she might have been life and love itself. I felt that I could beat the air, wrestling with my fate for my desire. I gasped, unmanned with wretchedness.

Then Gerry rose and put his hand upon my shoulder. Here again his selfishness was seven years younger than mine. He could lose his sorrow in sympathy.

"God he good to you, dear old chap," he said; "it's desperate, desperate luck, but after all is it too late? You've the place, the title, and all that—and after all, you know, the old boy might have come home and married any day—why can't you follow them? Surely you might drop in with them somewhere."

"Too late? Of course it's too late," said I bitterly. "Is a girl to wait for ever? Besides, they can't hear of it for weeks—very likely not at all. By then Denvarre will have settled matters, if he isn't the most consummate idiot on earth."

"That may be all very well about Denvarre," quoth Gerry wisely, "though I don't see that it is for certain, all the same. But what about Gwen? You don't allow her much independence of thought. Why should he happen to meet her fancy? Do you think she doesn't *know* you worship the ground she walks on?"

I stared at him, gnawing uneasily at my moustache, and with the sense that he spoke the truth. Gwen knew it—must know it, but she must have seen, as did I, the hopelessness of the business— must have known that the farewell of that morning was to be the end. And yet—and yet that look she gave me. Was it merely question- ing, or did it tell me something? I fell into that moody, unhealthy mind when one forbids oneself to hope for very hope of being mis- taken—assuring myself that I knew there could be nothing but despair for me in the future, trusting all the same that wanton fate would prove me wrong. Which is a phase of unreason, I take it, more wearing than an utter yielding to desperation.

"Now, old chap," went on Gerry soberly, "if you begin to muse and wonder you'll never sleep to-night. I believe this thing comes in the light of luck for both of us. I feel twice the man I did half-an-hour ago, and I'm going to whine no more. How- ever matters go you're very much better off than you were this morning, and, as I said before, what's to prove that either Gwen or Vi may not come back to us again? Heaps of things may happen in a year. Why," he went on smiling, "with the influence of the Heatherslies at my back I mean to get an *attachéship* and marry Vi myself. At any rate I believe now that the game's *not* over. I'll be your best man yet, unless we're both married together, and I won't say that's not possible."

It was good to hear him say it, but all the time I was telling myself frantically that it was rot—that I mustn't listen to him, and I backed my inward despondency with the spoken word.

"But even now," I demurred, "what am I but a pauper peer? Fifty thousand acres of bog are mine, and a few English farms. What's that to Denvarre's forty thousand pounds a year and Gleivdon? I'd take an offer of five thousand pounds a year for all I possess."

He rose and slapped me on the back cheerily, smiling as he reached for his hat.

"There, there," said he, "that's quite enough, Jack. I'm off, and you're going to tumble in. You'll be twice the man in the morning. You're upset with it all, and to-morrow when you're a bit steadied you'll see it all in another light. We'll have a long collogue about it then, and you'll know what you're going to do. Night-night, old man, and don't dream if you can help it," and he passed across to his rooms whistling, though I could but notice it was a very reedy, quivering attempt.

In spite of Gerry's veto I did dream that night, seeing Denvarre in many a heroic attitude save Gwen from desperate perils by flood and field—masterful deeds which I could only watch in restless helplessness. I rode a nightmare which trampled my every aspiration in the mud of desolation, leaving me to awake heavy-eyed and low-spirited, but yet, as Gerry predicted, with some of the hope that each new day brings. And after my bath—and what a mental as well as bodily tonic a cold bath is—I was chastened, maybe, but myself again. I filled my clothes without feeling three sizes too small for them, and ate my breakfast with appetite. As I was at it, Barker brought in a telegram. I ripped the dirty orange-colored paper and read, "Please call at your earliest convenience. Meadows and Crum."

They are our lawyers—have been for generations. My former meetings with them had been, for the most part, embarrassing. Hunted by some pertinacious dun, I had occasionally fled to their chambers in Lincoln's Inn Fields as to a sanctuary, and they had always responded nobly to my appeals. I smiled to think how continually and tactfully they had warned me against backing other men's bills and such-like futilities.

Well, at any rate that sort of thing was over. As a bachelor—I still assured myself that I should live and die celibate, with an eye to the possible fate which might be listening—I should not be so badly off. I could look forward to commanding the regiment some day without beggaring myself. Little rifts of sunlight like this began to break through the fog of my depression, and when I strolled forth to call upon my solicitors, I had pretty well regained the self-possession which that sudden announcement of a tardy good-luck had knocked completely out of my system.

Crum received me. Meadows is an anachronistic figment of the imagination long deposited in a Hampstead vault. His partner continues the business with other partners, who are considered to be sufficiently dignified by the title of Co. He is a benignant old man, with an unblemished bald head and character. I believe a warm heart beats under his deliberation, and he has shown good faith and personal service to my family for more years than I dare say he cares to count. He welcomed me with a quaint subdued tolerance hovering on the outskirts of the chastened air he thought befitting the mournful occasion. For myself I will say frankly and at once that I could pretend no regret for the accident which led to my being Crum's future client. I had never even seen my uncle since I was at Eton. In point of fact I felt the matter to be, personally, only one for self-gratulation.

"Desperately sudden, my lord," quoth the old gentleman, making me twitch in my chair as I heard myself addressed by my title for the first time, "desperately sudden. We received advices from his late lordship on financial matters only a week ago, and now—it's come like a thunderclap, I assure you."

"These are matters of fate, my dear Mr. Crum," said I piously. "I suppose there's no doubt about the report?"

"None whatever, as I learn this morning. We cabled his lordship's valet last night and got the press message confirmed. Death took place up-country, it seems. Baines, his man, talks of bringing the body to the coast and sailing next week by the Pacific Mail Steamer."

"That of course is the only decent and orderly thing to do," said I, "and no doubt you'll kindly see to all these matters—arranging for the funeral and so forth. But what about funds now? I expect this horrible succession duty will make me as poor as a rat for the first year or two, won't it?"

He lifted his pince-nez, regarding me with a curious expression. I immediately divined by a sort of intuition that he purposed giving himself the pleasure of surprising me. There was a decorously cunning light in the corner of his eye that made him appear not unlike a respectable and intelligent magpie.

"I think you and your uncle were comparatively strangers to each other, were you not? Ah, I thought so. You have the impression, doubtless, that he was restless by choice and temperament alone? I can assure you, in that case, that you are mistaken. Your uncle, for the last few years of his life at any rate, has been dominated by a very determined purpose."

"Philanthropic or personal?" I queried. "Not the former I sincerely trust, or the pickings will be even less than I hope for. I know he's been roaming the wide world mysteriously ever since I can remember, but I thought it was the inherited taint of travel. We've had a lot of sailors in the family, Mr. Crum."

"That is very true," answered the man of law impressively, "and in a certain indirect sense I won't say you are altogether wrong. But the simplest way will be to put the whole matter before you as I learned it from your uncle. Excuse me a moment."

He turned to where a row of tin boxes, shiny and white-lettered, lined the walls along a broad shelf. Taking down one labelled "Viscount Heatherslie," he took up a key that had been lying handy upon the desk and opened it. He extracted a bundle of papers tied in red tape, and began sorting them with neat precision. I occupied myself in wondering with unaffected curiosity what on earth was coming next.

Of course Uncle Leonard had been a wanderer on the wide earth, but he had always been to me not so much a man as an impression. My poor dear mother used to remark occasionally, "I see your uncle's wintering in Egypt," or "Leonard's in Japan again," wondering always, as women do, what could induce him to leave the comforts of his native isle for such outlandish realms. But I had paid but slight attention. Uncle Leonard was nothing to me—I was his heir-at-law, of course, but then he had always been expected to marry late in life, as most of his ancestors had done, and I had never troubled about him. I remember his coming down one Fourth at Eton and stumbling across me, more by accident than intention, and tipping me a fiver. But that was a feat he had never followed up and improved upon in later life, so I had let him drop out of my calculations, and he—well, he never spent three weeks of the year in England, I suppose. Some men have the regular gypsy taint in the blood. They must move in aimless joy of moving, or they absolutely shrivel up for want of occupation. The mania in his case was more or less inherited, I knew. Half-a-dozen of our forebears have been adventurers—not to say buccaneers—in the past. They pop up in various capacities all across the pages of Elizabethan and eighteenth century history. So the fact that in my late uncle's case there was more behind this activity than was his by birth and ancestry came to me truly as a surprise. I awaited developments pondering many possibilities.

Old Crum found what he wanted at last. Replacing all the papers but one—rather a musty-looking document—he kennelled his legs comfortably beneath his writing-table and began his revelation, tapping his fingers upon the dusty law books before him to emphasize his remarks.

I'll give you the tale as he gave it to me. Then judge me if I was a consummate fool or not, in that I followed in the footsteps of my uncle.

2

THE TALE OF A COINCIDENCE

"The late Viscount Heatherslie," said Mr. Crum, tapping the desk before him like a schoolmaster demanding silence for a lecture, "was a collector, and at the same time an economist. These you will probably think are walks in life entirely incompatible one with the other. I will explain further. Though he lived far within his income, he had the mania for collection and gratified it. But he did this by making it a rule never to buy what had a merely temporary or sentimental value, but only what was likely to be intrinsically marketable. I never knew a man with a sounder sense of finance or one who, without professional knowledge, made such use of unprofessional experience. I doubt if he ever struck a bad bargain in his life. You will to-day reap the benefit of his judgment. I do not think I exaggerate when I say that you may safely count on his treasures fetching a sum of not less than one hundred thousand pounds."

I gasped in amazement, nearly bouncing from my chair. My excited shuffling upset a blob of ink from the inkstand before me. With an air of respectful deprecation Crum began to mop it up methodically, before answering the questions I fired at him like bullets.

"Great Heavens!" I exclaimed, "the leery old dog! You mean to tell me in sober earnest that he has amassed all that money by simple grubbing after curios, when we thought he just roamed around for mere amusement and love of travel. Where has he stuck them all? Not at Kilberran, I sincerely hope, or they're all rotten with mildew by now. And what are they? Pictures, bronzes, china? Why, neither my mother nor my poor old dad had an inkling of it. Great Scott! One hundred thousand pounds. Now really, don't you think you may be exaggerating, my dear Mr. Crum?"

"I may say that it is not a habit to which I am given, my lord," he answered dryly, "but it will not be hard to convince you. The collection has been valued by more than one expert, and the lowest figure rendered by these gentlemen was a hundred and thirty thousand pounds, and the collection has been added to since then."

"But what in the name of goodness can be worth all that money? Why, it would take a large gallery to house pictures up to that figure."

"Certainly. But I may as well explain at once that the whole collection is within these walls. It is in a large safe in my cellars. It consists wholly of coins."

"Coins!" I bawled delightedly, "then I hope the half of them have her majesty's face on them, God bless her. I see what you're getting at. You mean the old boy was a miser."

He drew himself back into his chair with an air of offence.

"I am not given to jest on business matters," he said in his stateliest manner. "No; your uncle was simply one of the first numismatists of the century. His is the finest harvest of ancient coins ever made by any private individual. If you see fit to turn it to its marketable worth, you will create an excitement among collectors unparalleled for the last five decades. And till the catalogues are published, not one of them will have an idea of the treasures they will find listed there."

"Well, as far as I am concerned, I don't mind how soon they're gratified and surprised," said I; "but I should like to have a look at the lot now, if it's not seriously inconveniencing you. Can we descend to visit them?" for I itched to view this astounding hoard with my very own eyes.

"Of course, my lord. It would be only natural that you should wish to inspect such an important part of your inheritance. But I have something more to say. It was not in mere zeal for collecting that your uncle had lately travelled so widely. I have another astonishment in store for you—not so entirely agreeable, no doubt, but out of the common, I think I may say absolutely out of the common."

"Well, as we're out of the range of coins this time then, I trust it's nothing less than bank-notes," I answered. "But for goodness

sake what is it?" I added impatiently, for his self-important deliberation began to get on my nerves.

He did not suffer himself to be in the slightest degree flur-
ried by my impatience. His sentences, in fact, seemed to gather
a yet more leisurely accent as he unfolded his tale.

"You must let me tell the thing in my own way, my lord. It
will be far more conclusive than jerking it out at you in scraps.
The facts in sequence were as follows—

"Among the family treasures which have come down the centuries—and I sincerely wish there had been more of then—was
a certain amount of old coins which have been in the custody of
my firm for at least five generations. They comprised for the most
part specimens of the gold and silver coinage of most European
countries during the fifteenth and sixteenth centuries. Some
were of great value. Some were by no means rare. Evidently one
of your ancestors—probably, I should say, Sir John Dorinecourte, the famous Elizabethan admiral—had the craze of collection, which has since broken out in your late uncle's case. At
any rate the box contained moidores, zecchins, pesos, crowns,
and every sort of currency of every known land—known to our
ancestors of that time, at least—to a very considerable amount.
The mere bullion, I should say, would be worth a considerable
sum. Among them were, however, a couple of gold pieces placed
apart, and these had no signification placed opposite them in
the catalogue, and bore no sign either on the face or the reverse
in any language known at the present day."

"It sounds charmingly mysterious, my dear Mr. Crum," I
interrupted. "Now, you aren't going to tell me that the secret
still remains unfathomed?"

"My lord, my lord," said the old fellow entreatingly, "you
must allow me to tell you the thing methodically, or not at all.
If I'm hurried I shall forget some detail, and I have given time
and effort to memorize the matter completely."

I apologized humbly, settling myself back in my chair resignedly to hear the thing out with no further interruption. Crum
continued in his slow, modulated tones.

"I think that it was the sight of that hoard, when your uncle
saw it at his accession to the title, which first woke in him the

craze for collecting. He no doubt reflected that here was the nucleus of an exceedingly fine numismatic museum, and from that day he set himself steadily to add to it, with an increasing knowledge of his subject, of which you are now reaping the benefit. But those two unknown coins were always a sore mystery to him. Many a time have I seen him take them up—he used to visit me two or three times every year to place what he had possessed himself of in that time with the rest—and turn them over and over in his fingers wistfully, studying every line and figure as if there must be some concealed clue which he had missed. But it was only last year that he gained the trace which put him on the road to success, and also, as it has unfortunately turned out, to death as well."

"What!" I shouted, nearly jumping out of my chair. "Do you mean to say—"

He held up his hand deprecatingly.

"Please, my lord, please restrain your impatience. You shall have every detail in good time, I assure you. I only mean to say that it was in pursuit of his intense desire to solve the origin of those coins that he was travelling in Central America, where he caught the fever which has been fatal to him. The rest I will tell you as shortly as possible.

"It was last year, as I was saying, that the first trace came to his hand by the merest accident. His lordship was in Portugal. From there I got a letter from him on business matters, and at the end—his lordship was aware that, of course in a modified form, I was interested in his quest—he remarked, 'A most extraordinary thing has happened. I have found a dozen more of the unknown coins, and what is more an ancient document—no less than a letter written by Sir John Dorinecourte, my ancestor. I will tell you more on my return.' It was some three weeks after that that his lordship came to see me.

"Nearly his first words to me were, 'Well, Mr. Crum, the mystery of the coins is pretty well solved, but a greater mystery has arisen on the ashes of the first. The gold pieces are Mayan.' The word Mayan, I must confess, conveyed nothing to me at the time, but he very soon explained it. The Mayans inhabit—though perhaps your lordship knows as much—the land of

Yucatan to the south of Mexico. They are a wild and savage race, but there is every reason to believe that centuries ago theirs was a mighty empire. The coins dated from this extinct civilization of long ago. And now for the method by which your uncle ascertained as much.

"He was wandering along the side-streets of Lisbon one afternoon, when he espied a small curio shop. Outside the window were displayed various articles of furniture, china, etc., for sale, and among these was a curious cameo brooch which rather took his fancy. He entered to make a bid for it, and managed to secure it for what he considered a fair price. He wandered listlessly about the shop, as the woman in charge was placing it in a box for him, and suddenly came upon a glass-covered box full of coins. You may imagine his surprise when, among the rows of copper and silver pieces, he saw staring up at him no less than twelve gold replicas of these mysterious coins of his own. His astonishment was great, but he managed to conceal it from the shop-keeper when he asked her the price she demanded for these 'medals,' as he prudently called them.

"She named one very little higher than their simple worth as bullion, intimating at the same time that as they did not seem to commemorate any special event, customers for them had been few. She went on to relate how she came to possess them. A strange story indeed. With some pride she told your uncle that her husband was really of noble blood, but sunk to a narrow pittance beyond the keeping up of his title. Ruined by the failure of vintage after vintage, he had at last compounded with his creditors by giving up his landed possessions, and she and he were now living by the sale of art curios, a good proportion of which she sadly explained was from their own dwindling inheritance.

"Further inquiry elicited the fact that the 'medals' had been discovered in an ancient box of cedar wood, which had been left to rot and moulder in an attic of their former mansion, where, wrapped in papers covered with writing in a foreign tongue, nigh fifty of them had been found strung together on a slender chain. She pointed out that all of them had a small hole beside the rim, and your uncle remembered that the same thing was noticeable in those he possessed himself.

"The first and most natural thing was to inquire for the paper wrappings, but for some time these could not be discovered, and it was feared they were lost. However, the next day his lordship received a message from the woman to the effect that she had found them thrust away among a heap of similar refuse and that they were at his service if he chose to purchase them for a small sum. Your uncle did not dally in returning to the shop, as you may suppose. You may also imagine his surprise when he found that one of the documents was not only in English, but absolutely signed by his own ancestor. You shall see the original, so I will not stop to describe it. It is of the other document that I wish particularly to speak.

"It was inscribed on a peculiar yellow-looking fabric, more of the nature of linen than of paper or parchment, and experts have since decided that the coloring matter used as ink is the fluid emitted by the octopus. But the most curious part was the writing, if writing it can properly be called. It consisted of squares, oblongs, parallels, and other geometric figures ranged in a sequence which was not easy to understand, but the chief point of interest was that these figures resembled in every particular the figures on the coins. His lordship immediately and willingly paid what was asked for them, took his passage straightway home to England, and armed with his document paid a visit to the British Museum to get what expert help he could in translating them.

"It is an extraordinary thing how circumstances dovetail into one another. No sooner had he entered the department, where he had so often been before to get light on his coins, than he was greeted with the following question by Professor Barstock, the head, before he had even mentioned his errand.

"'I am particularly pleased to see you, Lord Heatherslie,' said the Professor, 'because information has lately come to hand which I think will settle the origin of your coins, which we have so often pored over. Monsieur Lessaution of Paris, the well-known Egyptologist, has discovered that there is a connecting link between the ancient Egyptian script and that on the monuments of Yucatan. It seems absurd, considering that they are divided by five thousand miles of sea, but he puts his points very plausibly, and I think you should see him.'

"When you have seen the other paper which your uncle dis-covered—the one in English—I think you will understand that these words came as a most astounding confirmation of his suspi-cion that he was on the right track at last. He simply opened his bag and spread the mysterious scroll before Professor Barstock, laying one of the coins beside it.

"You may imagine the astonishment of the latter on seeing not only the coin with which he was familiar, but the scroll covered with similar symbols. Nor did he fail to astonish your uncle in his turn. Taking him to another part of the building he showed him some grey, fibrous-looking slabs of dried pulp, and they too were covered with the oblong, square, and parallel figures of the document, only that instead of being raised they were indented. They were, as Mr. Barstock explained, squeezings, taken from the temple *facade* at Chichitza, where M. Lessaution was now conducting his investigations.

"The Frenchman's theory was that by comparing the Egyp-tian symbol with that in Yucatan, and using the grammar and accidence of the former language as a guide to the latter, these inscriptions, which have as yet been undecipherable, would be made clear, and much would be learned about the Mayan civili-zation of long ago.

"This was quite enough for your uncle. He decided that he would not wait for M. Lessaution's return, which was not expected for another six months, but would cross the Atlantic and inter-view him on the spot where he was conducting his experiments. After reading the letter left by your ancestor, I can quite under-stand that to a man of leisure like his lordship, and a man with a taste for wandering to boot, the fascination of such a quest would be great. At any rate he sailed for Greytown about five months ago, and with the exception of a single letter purely on business matters I have heard no word from him since. You can imagine that his death has come as a shock."

"Well," said I, "I am certainly astonished, but I cannot say I am greatly moved by your tale, Mr. Crum. It would certainly never have occurred to me to cross three or four thousand miles of ocean to interview a foreign savant about a coin or a docu-ment. But then, you see, I am not made that way."

"Very likely, my lord," submitted the lawyer, "but you will pardon me if I say that you have not seen the letter by Admiral Sir John. That sheds a very curious light on the question, and certainly adds vastly to the interest one of your family must take in it. But I will show it to you at your leisure."

"I am as leisured now as I am likely to be for the rest of time," said I, "but before I see the letter I should just like to squint at the coins, if you are not particularly occupied for the next hour."

He rose at once and preceded me to the outer office, where a door opened on to a flight of stone steps. Down these he guided me, ushering me at last into a broad, whitewashed cellar, wherein not less than half-a-dozen great safes faced each other from wall to wall. He clicked a key in the lock of one, and turned a handle. The great door swung back and showed row upon row of numbered sliding drawers, lined with velvet, and covered— every square inch of them—with coins of every degree of dirt, ancientry, and denomination. One drawer alone was nearly empty, and this held two gold pieces, and placed beside them on the velvet a sheet of ancient paper, covered with crabbed writing and faint with the dust of ages. The lawyer took it up and unfolded it carefully, and then I saw for the first time the screed that sent my uncle speeding across the ocean at its behest, and which was to leave its mark on my life also.

3

THE TEſTIMONY OF ſIR JOHN DORINECOURTE, KNT.

The lawyer pushed back the drawers methodically, clanged to the safe door, and turned to me as I laboured toilsomely to decipher the faint scratchy handwriting. He held the two coins in his hand.

"I think," he said slowly, "if you will permit me to read this document out to you, you will find it much easier to interpret if you desire to read it yourself a second time. I may say that I have conned it pretty thoroughly—it took time to master it, I confess—and faint and yellow as it is, I can decipher it at sight."

I was only too glad to accept this benevolent offer, and we returned to the upper office again. Here I settled myself back in my chair, old Crum found and very deliberately donned his spectacles, unfolded and smoothed the sheets of dirty parchment, and then began to expound the writing as follows—

"I, John Dorinecourte, of the parish of Sellwood, in the county of Somerset, here make oath and declare that the writing hereto, to which I have set my hand and seal, is the very truth, so help me God.

"On the seventeenth day of August, in the year of our Lord one thousand five hundred and seventy-eight, being in command of the ship *Pride of Barnstaple*, and Captain Fowler of that port and Dom Pedro da Suhares of Maceira being my fellow adventurers, we were in mid-ocean, having passed the straits discovered by the Admiral Magellan about two days, and were bearing north along the coasts of the Indies. It happened then that one of the ship's company at mast-head hailed the deck, declaring a ship to approach; whereat we, as was but reasonable, supposed the same to be some Spanish craft, and beat to

26

quarters, tricing up boarding nettings and getting powder on
deck. But as we approached nearer to the strange sail, we perceived it to be a lateen and under no control of steering, for she
yawed and came about, and then of a sudden fell away upon the
other tack, being water-logged, and as it seemed deserted. So,
calling to me the crew of the pinnace, I set to board her, which,
the day being calm, we accomplished easily enough. Then were
we horribly astonished to find upon her decks no living man
save one, and him at the point of death. Six bodies there were,
and one living soul, and the men were a fair and noble company, but like to no other men whom I have seen. Now Da
Suhares, who hath been in Mexico—for being renegade he joined
our vessel at La Guayra after slaying the nephew of the governor
in duello—protested that in most respects these unfortunates
resembled the inhabitants of that ill-fated empire, now ravished
and enslaved by the devil-serving Spaniards. Which might be
like enough, for the men were covered with gold ornaments, and
bedecked with the plumage of bright tropic birds, such as is the
custom of these tribes as I have always understood. 'Twas evidently thirst that had brought them all to their death, for no
drop of sweet water could we find upon the craft, and the tongue
of the living man swelled forth from his lips, forcing his jaws
asunder, and his sweatless skin cracked as tense parchment. We
hasted therefore to bring our surgeon, and water with a little
wine. With difficulty he swallowed it and revived, though but
slightly. He gazed upon us as one affrighted, and shuddered,
placing his hand upon his breast as if holding there what he
would fain conceal. By which, I take it, he imagined us Spaniards, and expected their deviltries, as well he might. But we
spoke to him gently, and tended him, taking sails to make him
a couch to lie upon. Yet he rallied but little, murmuring we knew
not what, nor could Da Suhares understand him, though he had
knowledge of some few words of Mexican.

"Then the poor wretch raised his finger slowly and pointed
towards us, and afterward held up his open hand many times,
which we took to mean that he had been of a numerous company; making gesture also to our ship which swung, heaved to,
some quarter of a mile away, he swept his hands abroad wildly

towards the waste of waters, implying doubtless that his was one of a great fleet of vessels.

"As in a flash came to me then the tale which was at that time a by-word in the South Seas, of the great expedition of the natives which had set sail from the coasts of Southern Mexico, the which was witnessed by the Spanish forces advancing from the north, yet could in no way be prevented of them. Mayax is the name of the land whence they sailed, and the fiendish warfare of the Spaniards—ravishers of women and slaughterers of babes as they be—had so prevailed by terror upon these simple folk, that they had committed themselves to the deep to escape their villainies, and had vanished, forty sail or more, no man knew whither.

"The memory of this tale came back to me, as I say, vividly—and indeed it had been the common talk of every port along the coasts of the Southern Indies this two months past—and I pointed inquiringly to the poor fellow as he languished and lay dying at my feet, and then swept my finger northward as if determining that to be the direction whence he came. Whereat he nodded, and then swung his hard southward again, as if to say that now he sailed from the opposite direction. Then reluctantly, as it were, he drew from his breast the scroll which I have here set aside for your care and consideration, and I beheld for the first time those symbols and the presentation of that wondrous beast which are to me now as the alphabet for familiarity. As he gave me the relic, he feebly took from his wrist the golden bracelet which hung haggard thereon, and from his neck a string of gold pieces. The armlet he gave to me, and the necklet to Da Suhares, as if in thanks for our consideration which came thus too late. Then with the last throb of strength left in his withered frame he raised himself from the loins, and turning, faced the sun which sank cloud-free and ruddy into the open main. Bowing himself towards its fading glories, he spread abroad his hands with a single word and fell back and died, unconquered remnant of a conquered race. And for a space we stared silently at the dumb dead, wondering, half afraid, but full of pity for his sad case, and of admiration for his uncomplaining end.

"Then did Da Suhares, Master Fowler, and I take counsel together upon the matter to imagine what this might mean. For

I called to their memory the tale of the escaping Mayans, and Da Suhares vouched for the truth of the same. For his own brother had been of the company of conquistadores that had advanced south from Mexico, had seen the men of the escaping fleet fare out into the deep, and had with others made strenuous effort to overtake and capture them before they launched forth to sea. For report went that they carried with them the ancient treasures of that hapless race for centuries back. Adding that within a month an expedition of adventurers had set forth to track them along the southern coasts, but had returned empty and rewardless. And common talk held that he who should find that company would also find wealth beyond desire or conception. Here he doubted not that we had one of them. For when we came to examine their barque there was great store of gold upon her, not as treasure indeed for the most part, but put to plain uses; for though the ornaments upon each corpse were of gold, yet were the very baling vessels made of wood shod with golden bands and held with strips of golden metal. Upon each man's breast also was a medal, or some such decoration, bearing upon it the similitude of the same wondrous beast that appears upon the mystic scroll which you have herewith. So we reasoned upon the matter, and in much thought the solution thereof came to us.

"The expedition had sailed, and had come to some secure sanctuary as they had desired. Now they sent back this small company to advise their fellows left in bondage of the same, that they too might leave their own land, over-run by the Spaniards, and come also to safety and a sure dwelling-place. And the more we thought on this, the more the truth of it came home to our minds.

"Now this I write in the glorious year of our Lord, one thousand five hundred and eighty-eight, when the Lord hath, by the destruction of the Spanish oppressor, so signally shown His favour to His children who hope in Him. The news of which final deliverance hath come to us long months after by chance of our meeting Captain Bostock of Bristol, who saileth in the Guinea and West India Trade. Ten years have I and my comrades, Da Suhares and Captain Fowler, sought wearily for this people, and naught hath come to us in reward. Yet have we gotten to ourselves sufficient of this world's goods, in that we have taken more than one of his Catholic Majesty's treasure galleons, and three years agone five of his pearling fleet which we fell upon when they were storm-sundered from their fellows. Rich are we therefore in possessions, but not yet in knowledge, and the madness of the quest hath bitten into the souls of all of us. Not an island, not a bay, not a single river's mouth, have we missed for nigh two thousand weary miles, but unavailingly. And now I draw into years, but I cannot rest from it.

"Thus have I put down the matter plainly for my children to wot of, and if I come not back to them, a charge do I lay upon them. Ten years have I sought, and wrought, and toiled, sparing none of mine and least of all myself, and it may well be that from this last adventure I come not back. Ten years, therefore, do I lay upon you that come after me, ten years each of you unto the tenth generation, and the blessing of the Almighty be with you in your search. Do the matter diligently, but in secret, lest it come to the ears of the Spanish folk, and they triumph at the last. If ye find this people (and of a verity I know in my soul that they still walk God's earth) be to them a safeguard from their enemies, using the might of England to bulwark them from their foes, and get to your race and family great honour. So do, and my blessing be upon you. Forego this quest, any one of you, and my curse rest with you unceasingly. To which charge I put my hand and seal this nineteenth day of December in the Annus Mirabilis, one thousand five hundred and eighty-eight.

"John Dorinecourte, Knt."

Crum placed the musty sheets of lettering on the table before him, solemnly took off his spectacles and wiped them, and then stared across quietly at me without a word, as if he would let this astonishing balderdash sink deeply into my all too shallow soul. There was a silence in the office, unbroken save by the buzzing of the blue-bottles at the windows and the distant roar of the Strand, filtered by intervening acres of brickwork. For my part I found no words to express my emotions. For really it came upon me as a shock to think what crack-brained enthusiasts our fathers were. Here was a sound, apparently intelligent, old British seaman, who had knocked about the world more than a little, worrying himself to set curses on the heads of his unborn descendants if they should fail to be just such fools as himself. He meets a half-dozen of forlorn savages in mid-ocean, by purely circumstantial evidence connects them with another band of whom he has only got word by hearsay, and proceeds to spend ten years of his life in tracking the latter to a lair which probably never existed. And not satisfied, as I say, with this astounding waste of time and energy, but he expects ten other fools to do the same. I stared, therefore, at the good Crum with these unvoiced musings extremely vivid in my brain, the while I thanked God softly below my breath for civilization and common-sense.

It was the lawyer who broke the silence before it got strained.

"I may say, my lord," he remarked, "that we have compared this writing with the signature of your ancestor's marriage record in Sellwood church. It is identical, and there seems to be no doubt that it is authentic. I would remind you that it is beyond question that he spent many years in what was called 'The Indies' at that date—the Southern Seas of America, in point of fact—where he left the reputation of a valiant sailor—I'm afraid I must say buccaneer. But you must remember that times were different," he added hastily, feeling that as a supporter of the law he must not seem to favour equivocal methods.

"That I believe is entirely true," I conceded. "Tradition has it that he was one of the most energetic old pirates of his day. But may I ask how you propose to explain his document getting to Lisbon into the shop of the local rubbish dealer, or whatever he may have been? Why did it not come home to those for whom it was intended? My unfortunate forefathers for twelve generations have had these curses hanging over them, and have lived in comfortable ignorance."

"I don't think there is much difficulty in finding explanation," he replied deliberately. "You know that Sir John *did* perish out there, and to this day no news has been heard of his ultimate fate. My own suspicions are that Da Suhares—by the way, the people from whom your uncle purchased these documents bore the name of Soares—very possibly brought him treacherously

to his death to possess the wealth that they had reaped in company. It is a very possible solution of the mystery, and we are
not likely at this time of day to find a better one. But I must say,
my lord, that to my mind the authenticity of the document is
absolutely determined, and I have had experience of similar
matters, I may say, for over half-a-century."

"It's plausible enough," said I, shifting my ground, "but not
good enough in my discretion to send a man fussing over to
Yucatan for further explanations. Supposing the thing is absolutely correct, both in itself and in its deductions, what good is
to be made of it at this time of day? Surely my uncle did not
expect to find this unknown race after they have been lost three
centuries or more? At any rate I shouldn't have thought it of
him. He showed no signs of brain softening ten years ago—or
twelve, was it?—when I last interviewed him."

He leant his elbows on the table, and drew the tips of his
fingers together in a judicial attitude before he made answer in
his intolerably cautious accent. Then he delivered himself of his
opinions weightily.

"I think you are forgetting the other scroll—the one in symbol
which was purchased with the one now before you. Recollect that
if this could be interpreted, the mystery in all probability was one
no longer. Your uncle was a man of leisure, fond of travel, and with
the collecting mania. I am bound to say that under these circumstances I can understand his attitude. He knew that in Central
America was the one man who could translate—if anybody could—
this extremely recondite document. He also knew that in any case
at his journey's end he would find a vast field of interest in the
lately discovered monuments of Yucatan. I must say that considering these things I should have been surprised if he had *not* gone. If
you think of the astounding possibilities opened up to him in
discovery if he *did* find a meaning to this scroll, and remember
the enthusiastic nature of his temperament on matters of this
kind, no room for wonder is left—at any rate not to my mind."

I was fairly dumfounded. To think that a little cut-and-dried
old solicitor could absolutely find, not only excuses for this absurd
conduct, but a positive encouragement, was more than I could
have believed possible. I gaped upon him.

"My dear Mr. Crum," said I pityingly, "we are not in the sixteenth century. I can conceive a rampant adventurer like Sir Walter Raleigh, let us say—a man with the heart of a lion and the brains of a four-year-old child—setting out on some such wild-goose chase, but that a British peer, of good health and wealth, nigh threescore years of age—"

He interrupted. His spectacles were tilted rakishly on the bridge of his nose, and his eyes positively glinted behind them. He absolutely barked an exclamation at me.

"Yes, my lord; he was all you say. And I am not ashamed to add, that in his case, and with his opportunity, I should have done the same!"

"You!" I shouted—veiled, in fact, so taken aback was I. "You would have gone to this unspeakable climate, to seek out a forsaken French adventurer, to get a clue to a fudged-up cryptogram three musty centuries old! Mr. Crum, Mr. Crum, I should have as soon believed it of the Lord Chancellor."

He had regained his *aplomb* by now, and arranged his papers methodically in front of him before he ventured another word. Then he looked up again, his calm and judicial air entirely regained.

"I have no wish to pose as a sentimentalist, or to have it thought that the mere glamour of a mystery would carry me outside the realms of common-sense. But I must say, my lord, with all due deference, that it seems to me that your uncle was simply guided by weight of evidence in what he did. From the facts connected with its finding and those since elicited, I should say there can be no doubt that the document before you was written by Sir John Dorinecourte, and that the matters detailed in it were true. The good knight's supposition about the identity of the persons he encountered seems to me extremely reasonable. Your uncle had nothing in his life to check his desires for adventure and discovery. It would have been marvellous to me if he had let such an opportunity escape him. I can see too," he went on with a smile, "that our temperaments differ, my lord, and that though you are the soldier and I the lawyer, our blood flows with an irregularity that is not in sympathy with our professions."

It is not pleasant to be called a coward by your own lawyer, I confess, and I will own that I flew into a rage. I rose and took my hat.

"Thanks, Mr. Crum," I said coldly, "it is more than probable that I am in every particular the absolute inferior of my late uncle. However, I fear I am using your valuable time for reflections and deductions which are not professional" (put him back in his place there, thinks I). "Is there any other business you wish to see me about this morning?"

The old chap flushed as he rose in his turn.

"I—I'm sure I trust I have not been offensive or indiscreet, my lord," he stammered. "I only wished to prove that in my poor opinion your uncle was justified in the course he took. There is naturally much I should like to talk over with your lordship in connection with the estate, but it can wait till the will is proved. But perhaps you will not consider it necessary to employ me further."

I saw I had hurt the worthy old chap badly, and could do no less than make immediate amends.

"Is thy servant a dog," said I, holding out my hand, "that he should do this thing? No, my dear Mr. Crum, though I may be of a slow-blooded, not to say poltroon-like spirit, and you are still in the midst of the middle ages, if you will excuse my saying so, as far as the practicalities of life go, I'm sure we shall get on together as well as two thorough opposites always do, and I can't say more than that." Then I wrung his hand heartily, and fled, but for the life of me I couldn't say for certain that I was right and he was wrong.

4

WHAT BAINES KNEW

It was three weeks after my first interview with Crum that I found myself travelling down to Liverpool to meet Baines, my uncle's man, who was bringing home his body. It was a dull, rainy, depressing day as I stood upon the dock-side above the landing-stage, and watched the tender come sidling up with the crowd of umbrellaed passengers upon her deck, and my errand was not of a kind to elevate the spirits. Beyond the mournful circumstances that had brought me there, I had a sense of foreboding as if undefined evil was coming to me with the dead, though, considering my very slender acquaintanceship with my uncle, it seemed extremely unreasonable. But there it was all the same. I put it down to the weather and the worry of the last three weeks. For really I had had a very trying time. Gerry was more or less at the bottom of it, and Crum and my own conscience helped largely. The fact was that in a moment of weakness I had detailed to Gerry the story of the screed and the two mysterious coins left by my old buccaneer ancestor. He had fastened upon the thing like a dog chewing a meaty bone, and rested not day nor night dinning into me his opinion that my bounden duty was to investigate the affair "up to the hilt," as he inappositely remarked. And in another astoundingly weak phase of absent-mindedness I had taken him with me on one of my visits to Crum. The two had managed somehow to get on the subject of the mystery, and then had started in full cry together to brow-beat me for my lack of enthusiasm, proving—Gerry with terse vulgarity and the lawyer with deliberate decorum—that I was throwing away the chance of a lifetime, failing in my duty to myself, my honor, and my nation, and showing forth a pusilla-nimity and poverty of imagination which was a disgrace to the name of Dorinecourte. And out of their badgerings a wild and hasty promise had grown—wrung from me by pure bullying—that should any further news of the ancient scroll of hieroglyphics come to hand, or perchance the scroll itself, I would not fail to do my utmost to obtain translation for the same, even to the extent of crossing the Atlantic myself and interviewing Professor Lessaution. Pondering, therefore, this rash mortgaging of my future happiness and freedom of movement, I stared down upon the snapping little steamboat with melancholy eyes, reflecting that she possibly bore to me a cargo of worry and unrest which would shadow my life with unmerited discontent.

There was the usual fuss when the dripping passengers landed, the usual rush for the customs, the grating of the rolling-luggage stage, the interchange of impudence between the dock porters and the crowd, in fact the everyday burly-burly of a liner's incoming, and it was not till after an hour's patient toil and the signing of various detestable documents, that Baines and I were permitted to load our burden upon the hearse that waited, and get it to the railway-station. I had no chance in the crowded train of conversing with the man in any sort of privacy, so arranged that he should call at my rooms that evening, and that there he should tell me all there was to tell. Fortunately Crum had notified a firm of undertakers to meet us at Euston, and there take charge of the coffin, and finally I was at liberty to make my way home, change, and eat with what appetite I could. Then lighting my pipe I set myself to await Baines and his revelations with all the apathy I could command.

And then Gerry saw fit to drop in. He was brimful of inquiry and investigation regarding the day's doings, and showed unbounded disappointment that as yet no further developments had ensued. He hinted, in fact, that I was burking all further knowledge of the subject, and sat arguing and discussing like an embodied British Association. It was in vain that I tacitly agreed to all his premises, and passed over his insults. He sat and sat, and there he was when Baines arrived, and then I knew that the game was fairly up. Under Gerry's encouraging cross-examination I felt sure that the worthy valet would have seen and heard marvels which no man could gainsay, and would be guided into revelations of my uncle's last words and messages which might bear any sort of meaning that Gerry chose to apply to them. I groaned as the smooth-faced, dapper little chap was ushered in by Barker, and Gerry's face of enthusiastic delight was a picture.

Baines stood in an uncertain sort of attitude near the door, fingering his hat, and waiting, after the first good-evening had passed between us, for me to speak. I motioned him to sit down, and as he deposited himself gingerly on the edge of a chair I rose, and straddling across the hearthrug, began my interrogation.

"Well, Baines," said I, "it has been a sad time for you. Can you give us any details of your master's illness?"

"It was very short and sudden, my lord," said Baines, with a terseness for which I blessed him. "It came on at 'Uanac, where we were camped; his lordship went about much as usual for the first day; the second he was very bad, and we sent on down to Greytown for a doctor, but by the next day 'is lordship was delirious, and died the day after. The doctor came too late. I nursed him all the time, my lord," and Baines's eyes shone mistily for a moment in the candle-light, "and I think all was done that could be done, but there was no help for it. They tell me these malarial fevers always are like that, but 'is lordship was never what I should call robust, my lord."

"Do you think he knew that he was dying?" I queried, as he paused. "At least, was he delirious all the time, or was there an interval of consciousness?" I added hopefully.

"Oh yes, my lord. He was quite calm at the last, and knew he was going. I think what vexed him most was that he hadn't finished the business he'd come for."

"And what was that?" demanded Gerry and I as with a single voice.

Baines looked at Gerry a little uncertainly, shuffling his hat between his hands, and glanced at me interrogatively before he made answer. I understood what he meant, and hastened to put him at his case.

"You can speak freely before Mr. Carver," said I. "I have no secrets from him."

"Well, my lord," said Baines, with a sort of apologetic hesitation, "I cannot think that 'is lordship was altogether himself these last two or three months. He had possessed himself of a piece of paper covered with what you'd call 'jommetry'—at least that's what I believe it's called, my lord—when we were in Lisbon, and for hours together he would pore over this when we were going out to Greytown, and mutter away to himself in a really most extraordinary manner. Then when we got to Greytown he wouldn't stop there a day—and they say you should always take a day or two to get acclimatized before you go up-country—but got mules together and started at once for Chichitza—"

"Chichitza?" I exclaimed, remembering Crum's story, "are you quite sure that was the name?"

"I know it only too well, my lord, considering we spent nigh a month there. A horrible place too. Uncanny, I called it."

"Uncanny. Why?"

"Oh, it was all shut in with trees, my lord, and there was nothing but great ruins all covered with figures and carving that looked diabolical I thought, even in the day-time, and as for night—well, I never dared stir from my tent. There was moans and rustlings going on in them all the time. 'Is lordship used to say that it was only the monkeys and sloths that lodged among them, but I didn't care to go and find out. I kept pretty close in camp after dark, I can tell you."

"And what did my uncle do all the time?"

"His company and conversation was reserved pretty much all the time for the French gentleman we found there," said Baines, with an air of some contempt. "He seemed to find a good deal to say to him, my lord. Then when they weren't examining and digging among the temples and things, they used to press lumps of squashy stuff on the carvings, and pick them off when they dried. Really, my lord, without meaning any offence, I think I should have had to give notice if we'd stayed there much longer. The dullness and the bad food, and one thing and another, was too much for any ordinary Christian as wasn't concerned in carvings and such like."

"When did they give up?"

"Just about six days before 'is lordship was taken ill. They'd packed up and were going down-country to camp a little way—about two days' journey, I think they said—outside Greytown. There they wanted to stay another three weeks or month, I understood, to see something of the natives. And what there was to see, I can't say at all, my lord. A dirtier, horrider set of ruffians I never come across, and I've been with 'is late lordship in a good many countries before now."

"What was the cause of the illness, d'you think?" I queried. "Bad food? Bad water? Anything of that kind?"

"Just the pure reek and stink of the places, I consider," said Baines impressively. "There was a white mist that rose at night which fairly got one in the chest, my lord. And up at the ruins it was worse than anywhere. I only wonder I didn't go down with it too. Only I was more careful at night than 'is lordship."

"Well, Baines, what did his lordship say when he was conscious? Did he send any message to any one, or give any directions?"

"Yes, my lord," replied Baines with a promptitude that made Gerry heave in his chair with unrestrained excitement, "he sent your lordship a message which perhaps you'll understand, for I must confess I didn't."

It is not advisable to wear your emotions upon your sleeve before a servant, and it was a stonily indifferent face I turned to Baines and an unquivering voice in which I bade him deliver his word from the dead, but I will own that discomfort and nervous expectancy had me by the throat. Gerry's face expressed nothing but unstinted and tremulous glee and triumph.

"'Go and see Captain Dorinecourte;' he said, 'when you get home, Baines. Mr. Crum will have told him why I'm out here. Then say to him from me that if he's worthy of the name he bears'—I'm only repeating it as he said it, my lord," interposed Baines apologetically— "'that he'll continue with Monsieur Lessaution what I've begun, and what's nearly done too,' he added. He was getting weaker all the time, my lord, and I don't think I caught all he said, but there was a lot about the alphabet, and the ruins at Chichitza, and that the French gentleman had nearly got it all—all of *what* I don't know, my lord—and things of that kind, when I think he must have been wandering, but just at the last he sat up on his cot and spoke quite loud and clear. 'After all these generations, when I had it in my grasp, it's gone to Jack. It's the cursedest luck in the world, Baines,' he said, turning to me very wild-like and passionate, 'the cursedest luck, and if Jack throws away his chance, I'll—I'll—' and then a sort of cough or sob took him sudden in the throat, and he fell back gasping. I held his head, my lord," went on Baines, his voice getting perceptibly unsteadier, "but it was no use. He turned his eyes to me, and I'm sure he took me for some one else, for he smiled so beautiful and glad that it made him look quite different and like some other person. His lips moved again, but I couldn't hear any sound. He just breathed deep and quiet-like two or three times, and then was still, and I'm sure he had no pain," and as he concluded his simple tragedy a large tear rolled over the brim of the faithful valet's eye and fell with quite a sparkle on the carpet.

The silence held complete possession of the room for a good minute after Baines had finished speaking. I ruminated sadly over the confirmation and support that would be given to the wild theories of Crum and Gerry by this unfortunate testimony from the dead. Baines was lost in pathetic reminiscence of the end of a master whom in his way he had loved, and to whom he had given nigh a score of years of faithful service; while Gerry a single glance showed to be indulging in fantastic dreams of triumph which only a certain feeble sense of decency prevented him divulging to us on the moment.

"What about Monsieur Lessaution, Baines?" I queried to break a silence which was getting heavy with foreboding. "Did he stay in Greytown, as he didn't cross with you?"

Baines flushed suddenly and looked yet unhappier.

"No, my lord, he went back to Chichitza—at least so I understood."

"Why?"

Baines stammered, and fumbled his hat diffidently before he answered, striving evidently to use chosen words in describing a disagreeable incident. At last he burst forth incontinent, forbearing circumlocutions.

"He was very impudent to me, my lord—I can't describe it in any other way. He wanted to possess himself of one or two of his lordship's papers—particularly the one with the signs on it, that I've spoken of—and was quite passionate to me about it. Of course I knew my duty, and wouldn't let him have it, and he used dreadful language to me in French—at least I'm not a scholar, my lord, but it sounded almost devilish. At the end he rounded on me. 'Well, pig of pigs,' he said, 'take it to England then. It but remains for you to bring it back when you get there. Tell the new Lord Heatherslie that I await him at Chichitza till Christmas. After that I shall work on my own account,' and that was all I got out of him after that, my lord."

There was a gurgle of unrepressed delight from Gerry's corner, followed by a murmur of "No getting out of it, my boy." I quelled him with a glance, and proceeded with my interrogation.

"And that was the last word you had with him, Baines?"

"That was the last word he spoke to me, my lord," answered Baines guiltily.

I understood. "You should not have answered a gentleman back," said I severely. "What did *you* say to *him*, Baines?"

He grew perceptibly hotter, but answered honestly.

"Well, my lord, I didn't expect ever to see the gentleman again, and he was very outrageous about the papers. I only said that you came of an obliging family, my lord, and if he meant to wait all that time in America, your lordship was just the man to do as much in England. He didn't make any answer, my lord, but just bit at his knuckles, and went away dancing."

Gerry walked to the window and looked gravely into the night. I assumed a sphinx-like expression, answering with sedateness.

"It was an unpardonable reply, Baines," said I sadly, "but it cannot be helped now. I must write and apologize to M. Lessaution for it. I think that will do for the present. Of course I shall continue to pay your wages till affairs are settled, and shall probably want to see you again more than once. Lodge as near as you can. My man will give you a glass of wine," and I rang the hell and delivered him into Barker's hands, the latter's usual impassivity being marred by a bubbling excitement as he

received this travelled *confrère*, who might be expected to enter-
tain him with astounding histories of adventure by flood and field.

"A peculiarly pleasant gentleman, Mr. Baines," said Gerry,
turning pink-complexioned from the window as the door closed.
"So versatile and gifted in the lighter arts of conversation and
repartee. Now, old chap, do you realize that you've got to go
through with this thing? Not only is it proved beyond a doubt
that there *is* something to be looked into, but it appears more
than likely that the investigation thereof may become amusing.
What more could any reasonable person desire? We're both of
us down in the mouth, and require relaxation and a tonic for
diseased minds. Here is an unexampled chance ready to our
hands. Apply, therefore, for leave; run over to Chichitza, and
interview the good Lessaution before he is tired of waiting. And
I tell you what I'll do—I'll come and look after you."

"You overwhelm me with your consideration," I sneered, "I
can't possibly permit myself to trespass on your kindness."

"Don't trouble yourself to be sarcastic, old man," said Gerry
composedly. "If you desire it, I'll openly avow that I'm crazy to
go and forget all the brooding and whining of the last month,
and therefore I mean to make your life a burden till you consent. That's all for tonight; but to-morrow we'll go and see Crum
again, and hear what he has to say. So goodnight, old man."

I suffered myself to be led an unwilling captive to Crum's
office the next day, and the old man heard our version of
Baines's story patiently. And thus he made answer, speaking
didactically.

"I must say," said he, leaning forward and tapping the points
of his fingers ceaselessly together, "that what Baines has to tell
us seems to me to be most conclusive that your uncle, in con-
junction with M. Lessaution, has lighted on some further clue to
this mysterious document. Though apparently they have not solved
it in its entirety, they have satisfied themselves that it is Mayan
in character, and has some bearing on the adventure described
by Sir John Dorinecourte. The French gentleman evidently has
accumulated knowledge which makes him the only authority on
this subject, and it is to him you must address yourself if you
would go further in the matter. I think, my lord, that you would

very possibly find it interesting so to do, but it rests with you. It is regrettable that M. Lessaution is not returning to Europe at once, and that he remains at Chichitza. It is also evident that he has—or thinks he has—information which may make him independent of you in this question, or, on the other hand, his threat of working without you may be merely a piece of bluff to induce you to go and interview him. In conclusion, I must say, that all things considered, it is the only course I see open to you, my lord, if, as I say, you think the matter of sufficient interest to be inquired into."

"And of that there is no possible, probable doubt, no shadow of doubt whatever," interposed Gerry. "But don't you think we should have a look at the thing which has been at the bottom of all the excitement? It's among the boxes which have been deposited here, Mr. Crum."

Cruin smiled. "I have so far expected this visit, that I made bold—in my character of executor—to open your late uncle's dispatch-box, which was deposited here last night. I have found the thing in question, and, speaking for myself, am of the opinion that there can be no question but that the coins and the document are in the same symbol," and opening his writing-table drawer he produced a tin case. Out of it he took a sheet of yellow, rough-looking material wrapped in tissue paper. He spread it out before us.

It was mouldering and musty, and emitted a faint, incense-like odour of perfumed wax. It was covered, as Baines had described, with "geometry" of sorts, namely squares, and oblongs twisted and welded together with intricacy, but with apparent method. The long lines of them ran across it in ordered rows from top to bottom, though which was the beginning, it would have been hard to say, except that at the end appeared a drawing—the presentment of as diabolical a looking monster as I have ever seen. It was of the nature of a huge lizard, with a long, sinuous neck doubled into terrifying contortions and flung back upon its thick and lumpish body. The lines which radiated from its eye evidently represented the baleful glare which was supposed to proceed from that organ. But it was portrayed with a rough skill which was more or less admirable.

"Well," said I after a pause, when we had ceased to gape upon this absurdity, "I think you are driving me into an escapade worthy of the worst kind of lunatic, but as you are all against me I give in. We sail for Chichitza, but while I say it, I am calling myself fool, fool, and again fool, and there is no other word to characterize every one of us."

And so amid Gerry's shouts of acclamation was set on foot that outrageous adventure which brought us to the Great South Wall.

5

PROFESSOR LESSAUTION'S OPINION

It was a hot, damp, oppressive October evening when our little coasting steamer deposited us at Greytown, whither we had come after being landed by the Pacific Mail at Colon. Gerry and I fought our way ashore amid the crowd of colors and half-castes of varying degree, while the melancholy Baines brought up the rear, eyeing doubtfully the all too easy porterage afforded our baggage by the long-shore loafers who had annexed it tumultuously.

Baines had accompanied us under strong compulsion, and only by the promise of a stipend that many a weary curate would have deemed beyond the dreams of avarice. When the point was mooted—and we felt that his experience was a thing worth struggling for—he had met our proposals with a flat refusal. He had explained emphatically that he had already had sufficient, for one life at least, of irruptions into the tangle of primeval forests where the dark green abyss of jungle made twilight eternally. Where, as he forcibly expressed it, the crawling beasts of peculiar noisomeness were thick as flies upon a butcher's stall; where the water was soup and the soup water; where the grey mists of malaria enveloped one as with a blanket of ague germs. All these things, as I say, were contrary to him. But the financial allurements held out to him, and the magic of Gerry's silver tongue had prevailed, and now he conducted us personally, though lugubriously. He it was who hustled a way eventually for us to the wretched inn, and set himself to prepare our morrow's transport.

Nothing, we ascertained, had been seen or heard of M. Lessaution, and it was therefore to be supposed that he was still encamped amid the ruins of Chichitza. By noon the next day we had accumulated our carriers, and set forth a half-day's stage in that direction before evening, full of excitement in our quest, and of hopes of adventure in the attaining of it. For now that we found ourselves in these tropic wilds, visions of encounters with savage man and beast loomed largely before our mind's eye.

A greater disappointment than the reality I have seldom, if ever, had to undergo. Instead of varied and delightful travel, enlivened by brilliant experiences of peril at the hands of the aborigines, or the claws of the forest denizens, the advance was simply one long, perpetual grind. Eternally we hewed our devious way through the thickest brush which exists, as I believe, on this earth. Every moment of the day and night were we devoured by mosquitoes and other noxious beasts, including "jiggers," which lamed us both for the best part of a week. Nothing did we eat save cassava bread and the perpetual monkey and porcupine steak, and over every portion of our bodies were we covered with enormous tropical boils, by reason of which we rested not day nor night. So in stupendous misery did we proceed to Chichitza, seeing neither man nor beast of the slightest import during the whole ten days we spent in the transit.

Well do I remember our arrival at the ruins. The last few miles we had stumbled on a faint track among the creeping lianas and spiky aloes, and Gerry and I, hearing that the end of our quest was only a matter of an hour or two, had begun to head the party with some small show of *élan*. Thus as we strode hopefully through the endless gloom, we saw a ray of blessed sunlight flicker down between the masses of dense foliage about a quarter of a mile ahead, and yelled with pure delight at the sight, the monkeys and parrots answering back defiantly. Then we took to our heels and ran like lamplighters down the aisles of rotting logs that lay between us and the gladsome shaft of brightness, shouting uproariously.

Still sprinting we emerged suddenly into an encampment where white civilized tents gleamed in the noon-day sun—oh, the loveliness of open skies—and tripped with startled outcry upon their pegs, rolling at the feet of a little wan, wizened, black-bearded man, who stared down upon us with timorous amazement.

It did not take his invocation of the sacred name of a pig to convince me that we had in very truth stumbled upon our man. I rose and bowed to him with dignity.

"I believe," said I in French, "that I have the honour to address M. le Professeur Lessaution? Allow me to introduce myself as Lord Heatherslie, and this gentleman as Mr. Gerald Carver, of her Majesty's Regiment of Foot Guards."

He flung up his arms ecstatically. "But what a joy!" he shrieked in his native tongue. "Monsieur has not failed me. But I convinced myself that a gentleman of monsieur's blood would not. I said no, it is not possible that any Englishman with his native love of adventure will forsake this so great quest. Monsieur, I have the honor to embrace you with all my heart," and he'd have done it too, not only with his heart, but with his lean little arms, if I had not dexterously caught his tempestuous hands and wrung them with an effusion that left him too exhausted for more familiar demonstrations.

When Gerry had also evaded the luscious raptures that the good little man in the fullness of his soul would have inflicted on him also, and the ingenuous *abandon* had somewhat subsided, we proceeded to explain ourselves, detailing under what circumstances we had received his message, how we had been affected thereby, and how our purpose to visit him had grown into fulfilment. Then tremblingly he demanded if we had with us the original document, and satisfied about this by its exhibition beneath his sparkling eyes, turned to evolve an entertainment worthy of the occasion. Meanwhile we sought changes of raiment—by this time our carriers had overtaken us—baths, and suchlike luxuries which we had been without for ten long and weary days.

As we emerged again into the sunlight—and how we revelled in it, hot as it was—we found our host in the full ardour of hospitality. He was dashing about from tent to tent, cuffing relentlessly those of his servants who failed exactly to meet his behests, personally superintending the cook, and flitting from saucepan to saucepan with strange bottles and jars of piquancies like a very *cordon-bleu*. The result, when we sat ourselves down before it half-an-hour later, was in every way a success.

Finally, as the coffee circulated in choice little cups, and pipes and cigars were lit, and contentment sat upon every brow, the little chap proceeded to open the conference, speaking as one who conducted a very rite, rather than a mere discussion.

"In the first place," said the little man, speaking in French, "I have to ask your pardon, M. de Heatherslie, for the attempt I made to deprive your uncle's servant, the good Baines, of the contents of the dispatch-box with which he charged himself so rigorously. My action was inexcusable, I admit. But, on the other hand, put yourself in my place. Look you that your uncle and I together had toiled months—weeks, at the least—to elucidate the symbol of this document—this so ancient document in which many things of the most curious may be recorded. And understand also that we are very near the conclusion of the matter. At this precise moment Monsieur Baines takes from beneath my eyes the prize for which I have toiled so laboriously. Do you not imagine, therefore, that I feel a distress that is cruel—that I bemoan his obstinacy—that I endeavour by any means to alter his decision? Tell me this, and at the same time accord me your forgiveness for my hastiness."

"I think," said I, beaming upon him benignantly, "that you must have exercised great restraint, my dear Monsieur Lessaution, in refraining from destroying him and rifling his body. Let us forget this absurd incident. Happily we have returned to you the means of doing so. Here is the paper, and here are we, boiling over with curiosity to get a translation. Are you now in a position to give it?"

He bowed impressively, his soft little brown eyes gleaming gratefully at me from behind his spectacles. Then he continued his discourse.

"It may have come to your ears, my friends, that I have for some time convinced myself that the interpretation of the Mayan cabalistics, which you see here graven upon these mighty ruins"— and he waved his arms solemnly towards the grey walls that showed dimly through the foliage— "is to be found by comparing them with the ancient Egyptian symbol. This I have now proved beyond a doubt to be correct. But this being so, only half the battle is won. I arrive at the language spoken some centuries ago by the inhabitants of the Mayan Empire. To translate this language I must find its connecting link with the Mayan of the present day—and this is but a bastard *patois* of the original, being corrupted with Indian. But by familiarizing myself with Mayan, as the people of the country speak it to-day, I have made long strides in solving the twisted carvings of these ancient monuments. It was at the point where your late uncle and I had decided that some knowledge of colloquial Mayan was necessary to further our plans that he unfortunately contracted the illness which proved fatal to him. During the last two months I have familiarized myself with this language. I say it with due humility, but I believe with some certainty that in the course of a short time I shall decipher the document. But supposing this done, shall you be guided by the result?"

"That's just a little too previous a question," said I. "Don't you think you had better get the answer to the Mayan conundrum before you embarrass us with plans which have as yet no basis to start from?"

"But surely you have seen the letter of your great ancestor, who was the original discoverer of this document? Naturally the translation will show us where to seek this lost people."

He was so serious about it, not to say so cock-sure, that I nearly imperilled our friendship by laughing in his face. To my stolid British mind, the conclusive way in which he took my romancing old ancestor's yarn as gospel truth struck me as humorous. But I preserved a staid demeanor as I answered.

"Let me assure you, monsieur," said I, "that I shall feel it my duty to be guided in this matter by your advice. But before we discuss hypothetical questions, let us endeavour to deal with facts. Take then this paper and apply to it your knowledge. I have great pleasure in handing it over to your care."

It might have been an insignia of knighthood at the least, judging by the reverence with which he received the musty relic. In a very fury of grateful protestation he bore it to his tent and surrounded himself with a mass of papers, books, and references. And there through the live-long day he continued to sit amid his piled accumulations of literary matter. The door of his tent was ever open, and our view of his actions unimpeded. Fatigued by

the stress of ten days' marching, Gerry and I were only too glad
to rest beneath the shade of a great granadillo tree and smoke
the pipe of peace, and the sight of the little man's energy was a
restful tonic to our jaded constitutions. He flung himself upon
his task like a navvy. From book to book he flew, and from note to
note. He dodged about from one heap of manuscript to another
like a little robin picking crumbs in the snow. He jerked his little
head from side to side as he annotated and compared with the
eager, intelligent air of a fox-terrier before a rabbit-hole. He
sweated, he tore his hair, he seized his head between his hands
in a very travail of mental effort. The sheets of foolscap flew
beneath the touch of his practised fingers. Symbol after symbol
gave up its secret as he travelled down the lines of interwoven
cabalistics. The copper-plate of his translation grew in volume
steadily; the pace increased rapidly as he neared the end. Not a
word did we offer, not a suggestion did we make. Apathetically
we listened to his curses or smiled at his squeals of triumph as
the figures alternately obstructed or fell before him. Finally, as
the tropic night closed in with the swiftness of a curtain's dropping, he gave a yell of frantic joy and bounded out of his lair,
waving the completed copy with terrific gesticulation. He thrust
it into my hand, still shouting.

"Aha, aha! it is done, it is complete. I have them, the great
race of Maya. Before the world we shall present them. We shall
say, Behold the glories of so long ago, and to us will be the
honour—the so great honor of the discovery. Read, then, read,
and say if I have not succeeded," and with his eyes aflame he
hovered round me, waving his ten fingers ecstatically.

Here is what I found writ down in artistic French, and render into my own bald native tongue:

"From Huanhac, leader of the migration of the people of Cay,
greeting to Camazmag, priest of Cay and overlord of the people
who remain in the land of Mayax.

"This to inform you that to the people of the migration is
come prosperity and great honour, for indeed we have found
the habitation of the god Cay himself. For having put out into
the deep after our departure, behold a great tempest arose

swiftly bearing us south, and for the space of fifteen days we saw naught but water and a sky of doom. On the sixteenth day, when both water and victual were vanished from among us, we came to regions of much ice—ice in comparison with which that upon the mountains of the Northland is as naught, at the which were we dismayed, expecting death by cold and hunger, but the purpose of the god was upon us. For as we drifted through the lanes of ice, a great wall rose before us, high and implacable, nor could we anywhere perceive a break therein. So for some hours we were tossed by changing currents, fearing instant destruction against the frowning crags. Then of a sudden Carfag, of the tribe of Xibalab, being in the leading ship, called aloud, saying that round a jutting peak of rock before him a bay was opening, which passage was exceeding intricate, and might pass unnoticed. So following Carfag we rounded the cape and found still water and a sandy sloping beach. There we landed amidst a crowd of sitting seabirds and sea-beasts of surprising magnitude, the which were not scaled as fish, but furred as foxes. Yet all was rock and pebbles, nor had we means to light a fire, save with such lumber from the ships as we could spare.

"But as we wandered further up the foreshore, there ran ridge-like across the face of rock a line of black stone having the similitude of wood, and with the marks of ferns therein. This some of us knew would burn, having seen the like in the Northland.

"Then lit we fires, and smote over unresisting some of the great birds which without fear sat upon the sand, and roasted them to make a meal therefrom. As the fume of their roasting went up savorily upon the air, and all prepared to satisfy their hunger, behold one lifted up his eyes towards the land and cried aloud in awe and great terror, for thence came down towards us the god Cay himself in flesh apparent, his mouth agape as if demanding sacrifice. Then consulted we hurriedly upon the honor which had thus befallen us of the migration—shown now of a surety to be in direct favor of the god—and selecting Alfa, daughter of Halmac, as fairest, bound her for sacrifice. Her we thrust forth into the path of the god, though Hardal, to whom the maid was promised, would have stayed us. Then came Cay in his bodily shape, and did take the maid, and did eat her in token of blessing and acceptance to us his faithful people, and Hardal, seeing his bride rent and dismembered, ran forth to the feet of the god, and was himself devoured also. After which did Cay withdraw himself from our reverent and astonished eyes, and we gave thanks that he in his mercy had guided us to his own abode, though verily the land is passing savage and barren of every growing thing.

"So we hasted and collected of our stores and put them on our best ship, and have sent unto you Migdal and six of our bravest youth, that you too may come to the land which Cay himself hath deigned to bless. In witness whereof hereunto I subscribe the sign of the god, fervently desiring that to you may be given his protection until you also come to his own seat.

"Huanhac, priest of Cay, and chief of the migration."

I handed the paper on to Gerry without a word of comment, and then turned to Lessaution with questioning eyes. He was sitting opposite me chuckling and bubbling away in an indescribable manner. He beat his little hands together, digging at the soft earth with his restless heels while Gerry also digested this astounding rigmarole, evidently bursting with the desire to speak, but restraining himself till he could spring his fatuous surprises upon us both together. For the next five minutes he made the most hideous and unconscious faces at me, winking and smirking meaningly as he caught the emotions flitting swiftly across Gerry's features, and finally, as the latter laid down the paper with a low whistle of astonishment and incredulity, he poured forth his abounding triumph boisterously.

"You see, my friends, you see?" he shouted. "It is as plain— but yes—as plain as the great temple behind you. You have heard, you have read of the great wall of the unknown lands of the Antarctic? You have remembered what M. Borchgrevink has told? Of the great cliff that stands up unclimbable from the ocean? There they have gone. It is there they have founded their new empire in the land that no man has discovered. It is all in one with the letter of the good Sir Dorinecourte of long ago. Where but there could it be? Where is the ice? Where else the great cliffs? We will go to them. We will discover them again. To the world we will present this ancient race, and to us will be a glory that we cannot as yet dream of. We shall be the great ones of the century. The discoverers of the peoples of yesterday. What do you say? Hein? Hein? Hein?" and he grunted like an inquiring pig.

"My dear Professor," said I patiently, "you don't really mean to imply that you believe that this race exists to the present day? Why, they've perished long ago by cold and hunger; or been eaten by their god. I must say that I think I may safely take this document to be—let us say—an allegory, written by some mendacious old priest for wicked purposes of his own. The story of the god Cay is quite sufficient to show the absurdity of it. How on earth could such a monstrous impossibility have ever walked the earth either in the Antarctic or anywhere else?"

"My friend, my friend," he babbled, his words nearly tripping over each other in his hurry, "it is not so; I assure you of it. Let us even allow that the race is dead. But the remains of the wonderful people exist. We can go, we can dig, we can find the traces. And remember the gold. We go not for honor alone—though for me, I am French, and it is enough—but there will be the gold. Think of the very baling-vessels made of gold in the letter of the great Sir Dorinecourte. There will be wealth, and the fame—oh, the very great, magnificent fame."

I tried to be tolerant with the enthusiastic little ass, but I will own that his credulity was altogether too much for me.

"You have not yet answered my question about the god Cay," I replied. "How do you propose to explain that very obvious falsehood?"

"And you think all this is a lie," he bawled, "just because this priest wove a little religion into his message? And who are we to say that it is not true? Have we been behind that wall of rock where these people remain either alive or dead? How then can we decide what is there or has been there? It will be time enough to say what exists or does not exist when we have made examination."

Now did one ever hear such nonsense? There may be a queer thing or two loose about the earth, but to ask one to believe that a terror such as that depicted at the foot of the Mayan scroll was alive and being worshipped not much more than three centuries ago was a trifle too much. I said so with no uncertain sound.

"M. de Heatherslie," answered the little man gravely, "you speak of what you do not know. What is that your poet says? There are more things in heaven and earth than your poor little philosophy thinks of. Why, tell me, are you convinced that such a monster cannot have existed? You but repeat what the ignorant said to M. de Chaillu about the gorilla."

"Humbug," said I, getting warm. "Monkeys there always have been, and monkeys there always will be. If this monster was like anything that nature ever invented there might possibly be something in it. But it's a thing utterly outrageous. Who ever saw a hippopotamus with the neck of a giraffe and the legs of a lizard? and that is practically what the mythological god Cay is, both on the scroll and on the ruins here," for we had found more representations of the loathsome divinity studded into the twisted inscriptions on the facades and walls of the temples.

As the discussion grew he began to light up as well. "Monsieur," he squealed, with glowing eyes, "I endeavor to say it with courtesy, but you are ignorant and obstinate. You have slept away your life in the fogs of England; you think that there is nothing worth considering in the world that has not the *cachet* of Piccadilly. I tell you—I affirm to you—that I believe that far away in the unknown South much may have happened—much may still be happening. We are ignorant, you and I, but there is no reason that we should not learn. I have translated to you this document. I give to you my opinions on it. I say that it should be investigated, and to your family is due the first chance of investigation, if only out of respect to the honour of your uncle, who is unfortunately dead. But if you throw away this chance, then I claim the right to give this honor to France—my country. But I beg you to remember that I beseech you to make use of your knowledge first, that afterwards there may be no recriminations."

I bowed sneeringly. "You do me too much honor," I replied sarcastically, "for I can imagine that every savant in France is yearning to stand in my shoes. Why, heavens, man! do you think there's a fool big enough to back you anywhere between Dunkirk and Marseilles?"

He glowered at me malignantly, flapping his hands against the turf. "Monsieur wishes me to infer then that I am a fool?" he queried coldly. "I accept monsieur's compliment in the spirit in which it is dealt to me. But let me tell monsieur this. He may have the wealth, he may have the courage, he may think he has the wisdom of the century at his back, but he has no spirituality, and, I say it with assurance, but little intellectuality. He is crusted in conservative unbelief like an oyster in his shell. With all his practical qualities I pity him," and he swept his hands abroad with a wave of disdain that was dramatic in its haughtiness.

You will perceive that the makings of a good quarrel were here, however absurd the subject. A sentence or two more and I and the little ass would have been, figuratively, at each other's throats. Here Gerry stepped into the breach.

"Jack, you're in the wrong; and what's more, when you're cool, you'll own it. What's the good of looking black at another gentleman simply because he differs from you in a matter of opinion? The remedy lies in your own hands. M. Lessaution tells you that if you sail in a certain direction he has good reason to believe that you will find certain things, or the remains of certain things, which he judges to be of importance. Well, sail there. We've a very great desire for something exciting to do just at present, and here you have an ancient family quest ready to your hand. I can't imagine anything that could possibly improve upon such a providentially given chance. You've got the money for it, and the health, and last, but not least, you've got two companions ready to accompany you. If you've any spirit left in you, go," and as he concluded his lecture he smote me resoundingly on the back.

I failed to see sense in this any more than in the Frenchman's hare-brained purposes, but a sudden thought had come with glowing swiftness into my mind. I turned hastily to Lessaution, who was regarding me with anxious inquiry, and asked him a question.

"Supposing," said I, "only supposing, we were to sail due south to the land which you believe to exist beyond Cape Horn, how should we proceed?"

"We should of course make the Falkland Islands our base, and steer a directly southern course from there. They would be the nearest inhabited land."

I pondered this information silently, ruminating various matters in my mind. Finally I turned benignantly towards the Professor, and seized his hand.

"Monsieur Lessaution," said I, "I will say frankly that I do not believe that we shall find a vestige of this extinct race, and I am inclined to think that both the English letter and the Mayan document are frauds. But I want relaxation and excitement, and I believe the cruise may possibly do me all the good in the world. We will return to England and find out the cost of equipping a yacht for sailing in these latitudes. If my man of business advises me that I am in a position to undertake it, I shall do so. And I request the pleasure of your company if this proposal becomes an accomplished fact."

His sallow little cheeks flushed up with pleasure, and he shook my proffered hand violently. "I was not mistaken in you, Monsieur de Heatherslie," he said, with dignity. "I felt that no man of your adventurous race would fail at a chance like this. Receive my congratulations on your decision, and my regrets that I used unpardonable adjectives to goad you into it. You will find me, I trust, not unworthy of the honour you have done me."

Gerry used less set terms in his address. "Thanks, old man," he remarked complacently; "I should like to come, though you haven't asked me. And now all's settled peacefully, let's have a drink," and he headed the procession which advanced with much unanimity upon the dining tent.

But I felt a hypocrite and a pretender. For what had influenced my decision was simply a sentence culled from the published itinerary of the s.s. *Madagascar*'s winter's cruise. And it ran thus—

"On or about February 6, Port Lewis in the Falkland Isles, previous to her return home."

6

WE SAIL SOUTH

It was the end of October before we were back in London again, and had begun our preparations for the expedition to which I had pledged myself. Crum gave me no financial excuse for departing from my promise. In his management things had looked up during my uncle's tenure of the title, and I was a deal better off than I had believed possible. Farms were in good condition and well let. Bog and heather in Ireland had found tenants for shooting, if not for grazing. Investments of accumulations had prospered marvellously. And above all was the wonderful collection of coins which was to be sold as soon as it could be accurately catalogued. I was well to do, it seemed, when all I had expected was a bare escape from penury.

"Your lordship need have no fear of lack of funds," said the old man, as he finished listening to the tale which I had to tell on our return from America. "The twentieth part of what the collection will fetch in the open market will be ample to meet every expense. And if your lordship will permit me, I should be glad to help you in your choice of a ship. This is no case for a mere yacht."

"You, Mr. Crum!' I questioned amazedly, "pardon my surprise; but the practice of the law does not as usual induce experience in ship-rigging or building."

"No," said the old fellow meekly, "not as a rule. But in this particular instance it has been one old lawyer's hobby. My pleasure all my life has been yachting, my lord, and I have many friends who go down to the sea in ships."

This was a bolt from the blue and no mistake, and a blessing which I was not slow to avail myself of. I gave Crum a free hand with the greatest delight, and the result was in every way admirable. Not only did he bring to his task a wealth of finicky little details such as are dear to the yachtsman's heart, but took to him retired master mariners and other sea-going veterans of his acquaintance, who possessed more than his amateur capacity for judging good lines and fittings. And thus did they bring their kindly toil to a conclusion.

The *Raccoon*, formerly of the American whaling trade, barque built, and with stout timbers and bulkheads to resist ice, was for sale. With cautious advances Crum became her purchaser. She was of five hundred tons burden, had an auxiliary screw with one hundred and eighty indicated horse-power, and was reputed a first-class sea-boat. We had the greasy try-works swept from her decks, and a skylight fixed therein, which gave light to a spacious saloon partitioned out of the barrel deck below. Aft this we fashioned a cosy smoke-room, round which were four cabins for ourselves and the captain. Other cabins below the main-deck housed the mates and the engineer, while forward the crew and stokers had the best of quarters. We took aboard much provision, supplied us by a famous firm of caterers, together with liquid in due proportion. Coal we took a large stock of; not that we expected to steam more than we could help, but we wished to be independent of coaling stations. Mr. Waller of the R.N.R. and the merchant marine came with many certificates of various sorts to be our captain, and Mr. Janson of the same service to be his second in command. Mr. Rafferty, sometime of Cork City, was boatswain, and the engineer, stokers, and deck-hands were all British; the first whole-colored, single-tongued crew that Waller had ever commanded, as he feelingly remarked.

Under these favorable auspices we sailed from Southampton on November 22nd, and thus the adventure to the Great South Wall was fairly started.

I am not going to give you the wearisome repetitions which my log shows as indications of what monotonous things we did during the next six weeks. We had the usual toss as we threshed our way across the Bay, we took the usual pleasure in sighting the Canaries and Madeira, and we shipped the usual turtle at Ascension. After the fogs we had left in England, we found the eternal heat of the line bearable for about six hours, and then cursed it with the usual malevolence after experiencing it for six hours more. We got very much bored with each other's company, and found conversation languish after the first week. We got huffy with one another more than once, and finally settled down to the voyage, shaking, each of us, into his allotted place automatically. And we grew fat and bilious.

Lessaution was by far the most energetic. His curiosity was abnormal, and he left no inquiry unmade that would tend to satisfy it. He was as sick as it is possible for a full-bodied Frenchman to be sick for the first three or four days, and after that seemed to renew his youth. Not that he was by any means daunted during the period named. He crawled about the deck in paroxysms of the most terrible description, interrupting the crew with queries on every and any conceivable subject; he attempted to mount the bridge, and was hurled back disconsolate as a green sea thundered aboard; he ventured into the cook's department and endeavored to complete that worthy's education during the height of a gale; finally he was rescued from imminent death on the bed-plates of the engine-room, where he was explaining the superiority of French boilers to the contemptuous chief, Eccles. When the winds and the sea had calmed down, he proceeded to bring out his gear which he had accumulated for the adventure, and overhaul it with pardonable pride.

He had certainly not forgotten anything that was likely to be of any possible use. Ice-axes there were in profusion. Climbing-irons, portable ladders, ropes, chisels. These to be used in the attack upon the precipice of rock or ice which he convinced himself would lie between us and our desire. He had also provided for further feats when the first difficulties had been surmounted. Toboggans or sleds he had two or three of; no less than six pairs of snowshoes, and, wonder of wonders, a pair of skates!

He explained when taken to task on the subject that he belonged to that gathering of the elect the *Cercle des Patineurs*, though as yet he had not attained the style which he desired to affect, and was in consequence unable to cut the figure he would like in the *beau monde*. Now he thought an opportunity of instructing himself in this health-giving and aristocratic pursuit would be afforded him. He would be able to gain the plaudits of all on his return, for, let us mark, he had brought with him a book of self-instruction on the subject, and would perfect himself in intricacies unbelievable. Yes, it would not do to spend the whole of the time on industry; we must not let our search deprive us of all thoughts of relaxation. At times he would unbend—he would sport. As an exercise this skating, let us remember, was without a peer.

Careless of our rude pleasantries, he proceeded to unveil further treasures. He had a perfect armory of offensive and defensive weapons. Bowie-knives were sown throughout his baggage like plums in a pudding. Revolvers decorated his cabin walls in pairs. A rifle flanked a shot-gun on each side of his cot. A tomahawk was precariously affixed to the deck above, whence it fell perilously every time we broached to between the great Atlantic surges. It was evident he was prepared for the worst that the future might have in store.

We rallied him gently on his warlike preparations, but he met us with logical arguments. It was understood, was it not, that we went to discover a new people. Let the memory of the old conquistadores be in our hearts. By the magic of their perfected weapons they had prevailed upon the ancestors of this very people we went to seek, and from them we might learn a lesson. It was not to be expected that we should be greeted peacefully at first. A display of force—only a display, let us certainly hope—would be necessary. He, Emil Saiger Lessaution, would give that display, and inaugurate a reconstruction of their medieval empire. Met by a dispute of his data, in that we refused to acknowledge the possibility of any such race surviving in the desolation of the Antarctic, he turned our flank by remarking happily, that at any rate animals of a ferocious disposition would abound, and would need to he captured or quelled. He promised himself many trophies of fur and feather, which would make the eyes of members of the shooting club he patronized bulge out with envy.

Gerry had brought a pair of guns and a rifle, with some vague idea of sealing, and found encouragement therein from Mr. Rafferty, who had sailed in whalers. I gave it to be understood, however, that I did not purpose wasting time in the chase, and should not allow us to stay our course short of our destination. One circumstance, however, came to light, which turned the laugh strongly against the Frenchman. It was while he was examining with a depreciatory air Gerry's guns, that it suddenly occurred to him that with all his store of weapons, he had no means of loading them. In the excitement of departure he had left all such practicalities as cartridges to the last, being filled with the loftiest ideas for using them. The consequence was that he was absolutely dependent on Gerry's slender store, and Gerry, with all the good nature in the world, found that the barrels were of different bore, his being twelve and the Professor's sixteen. After which discovery we had a morning's unavailing gnashing of teeth, and then the little man forgot his troubles in a new excitement.

This was the first ice. We had sighted Bovet's Island a few days before, when we saw it—a solemn, stately ice-hill, floating along island-like on a calm and unrippled sea. There's something rather overpowering and awesome about a big berg. The deathly blue-whiteness of it, the silence that broods about it, the great grottoes that pierce its sides like tombs of the lost, the glassy radiance that does not cheer but repels one—these things have a very depressing effect on me. I realized for the first time the sort of business we were going in for, and confessed to myself that a very little of this sort of thing would go a very long way. But it acted on the Professor's spirits in quite another manner.

We had rigged the crow's-nest the day before, and he was up in it before you could wink an eye. He leaned out over the edge of this eyrie, waggling his hands ecstatically, and singing songs of victory, welcoming this indication that we were approaching our goal with a hubbub that resounded indecently among the echoes of the bergs.

That was the only one we saw that evening, but next morning there were rows and rows of them, great pyramids of sheeny white, coming along in stately columns and companies, overhanging the blue sea, crashing now and again against each other, and hustling and grinding the floe-ice that clotted the wide sea-lanes between.

We steamed cautiously down the aisles, dodging from one sheet of open water to another. Now and again some unsteady pinnacle, loosening from the side of its parent berg in the heat of the sun, would plunge thunderously down the smooth slopes, and roar into the sea, sending great waves of curling foam to right and left, the rainbow rays dancing in the flying spray. The cascades poured continually from basin to basin in the laps of the ice-hills, tinkling and plashing as they fell. Here and there, on the bare, smooth base of some mighty piece of glacier, rows of seals lay and basked in the sun, staring at us as we slid by them with stupid, curious, brown eyes. Every now and again a sea-lion rose with a snort from some pool beneath the shadow of the shining crags, and played and tossed happily among the ripples. The birds, tame as chickens, unaccustomed to the sight of men, flew and swung and whirled and circled above us in clouds, tern wailing to tern, and gull to gull in plaintive outcry. And over all the sun shone with the strength of the Antarctic summer, now just beginning in its full vigor and brightness.

It certainly was an uplifting day, and quite swept out of my head the despondent horrors of the evening before. I climbed to the crow's-nest with Lessaution, and stayed beside him there hour after hour, drinking in all the glories of the scene, and listening lazily to his babble, taking pleasure in the mere joy of living.

We rolled slowly down the lessening passages all that day, and at sunset lay to with springs on our cables, for the floe-ice surged upon us ceaselessly, making it too dangerous to charge in among the pack without the help of daylight. In fact, we had to keep watch and watch about and fend off with poles, as the great splinters tangled round us, and ride out and back more than once as a berg moved upon us ponderously.

With the dawn we were under steam again, and wound our way in and out and about till, at mid-day, a shout from aloft proclaimed land in sight. And then we saw it. Far away, gray and shadowy through the haze it ran across the horizon, a long wall of rock or ice-faced cliff, reaching from east to west and dying into the dimness of the ice-strewn sea.

As we drew nearer, down the long corridors between the floes, it seemed to grow higher and more implacable at every mile. Sheer, ledgeless, and ice-smooth it was, never an approach or opening to its summit visible.

The shadows beneath hung duskily over the ripples, making the blue of the outer ocean seem to have an edge of mourning on its brightness. Here and there a berg clanged and butted against it restlessly, grinding away huge masses of its flanks in showers of twinkling splinters.

Along its sea-level the pack-ice heaved, eternally smoothing and planing its surface. About its face the sea-birds swirled, dipping and shrilling in their clouds. From many a little channel on its summit the rivulets from the melting glaciers fell in sparkling cascades, like the swishing tails of a stabled squadron. And far beyond it, smiting up haughtily into the empty blue, a giant range of mountains reared their heads, grim, white, and glancing in the sunlight.

We slowed when we were within a mile of it, and then began to wear a way slowly along parallel to the land, waiting till we should see some sign of a break or cranny in the relentless cliff. But never a sign of one was there. Early in the afternoon we raised islands to the north-east, and threw the lead, finding fifteen fathoms. We crept into the channel which ran between this archipelago and the mainland, and found a larger space of open water. Here, then, at Lessaution's earnest request I anchored, and dropped a boat down for him; with a crew of six we put off, and rowed down the narrow, changing passages towards the crags.

The little Frenchman was sanguine that a nearer investigation would show a means of scaling the heights, but try as we would, and strain our eyes, as we did, to the uttermost, no vestige of a split or crevice in those endless walls of rock could we see. We rowed and rowed, but the result was ever the same. The sea-lanes between the floating lumps of floe stretched endlessly across the sea like the meshes of a spider's web. We seemed to grope in an eternal maze, which had no appointed outlet. Only now and again could we approach the wall of ice and stone that overhung us. We had to be on guard continuously. The pack would spring and close like the jaws of a trap, and we had to back and row, and row and back, without cessation, to avoid its ever-waiting grip. One very sharp escape we had. We were lying on our oars, while the Professor examined some of the lichen which covered the cliff in patches, when we were suddenly aware, that what a moment before had been a sheet of water, clear for an acre around, was a fast thinning streak of sea. There was a yell from Rafferty, who steered, and then by backing furiously we managed to crawl into a pool between two sturdy bergs, and wind our way out into the less crowded channels. But as we saw the floe surge down upon the rock, and grate and grind upon it lingeringly, scoring away its own edges by the ton, we shuddered to think what an eggshell our boat would have been between that mighty hammer and that granite anvil.

That day was but the precursor of many. The yacht, with banked fires, perpetually corkscrewed her way along about a mile from shore, and day by day we took our boat and wandered continually in the shadow of the frowning wall. In Lessaution's breast hope burnt eternally, but only to be quenched at night. His plans were numerous, and some of them ludicrously ingenious. He suggested that a kite should be flown with a knotted rope attached, which might perchance catch in some crevice on the top, and permit him to give us a gymnastic display. He wondered if the carpenter could not manufacture a hundred-foot ladder, and then anchoring the good ship *Raccoon* below the precipice, enable us to place the highest rung against the top. He even proposed that Gerry should throw his cartridges into the common stock—this I am convinced was partly from jealousy at Gerry's owning these useful articles, which he had forgotten—that they should be opened, and that the resulting powder should be used to blast a way from point to point, and thus a path be won over these disgraceful rocks at which he shook his fist perpetually.

These futile proposals meeting the contempt they deserved, he became gloomy and morose, hinting strongly that our hearts were not really in this quest, and affirming that he, with his unquenchable French valor, was perfectly prepared to be left upon an iceberg with such provision as we could spare, if we thought it advisable to give up the adventure through our want of spirit.

After about three weeks of this sort of thing I ventured to interpose. I explained to him carefully that I did not purpose giving up the expectation altogether, but that I must plead for an interval in it. I affirmed mendaciously that I had arranged with the worthy Crum to call at the Falkland Isles in case there should be matters of importance to be telegraphed or otherwise sent—I had not the least idea if there was a telegraph station, and had a notion the post went once a year—and I must beg to be allowed to proceed there for this purpose, to re-coal, and to get further store of provision.

The unfortunate little man lamented desperately. Once let us get away when we were thus on the spot, and it was inevitable that we should never return. Might we not have one more week: nay, a day? That very evening as we knocked off work he had viewed a break in the top-line of these unbending crags, of which he had the brightest hopes. How could we find the spot again? He must implore—he must entreat.

For once I was adamant. I explained that if we were to be detained here by any accident with our slender supply of fuel and provision, things might be very awkward. I showed how necessary it was for a man in my position to be in touch with his lawyer every few months. I reiterated my assurance that we should return, using every oath and affirmation that I thought convincing. But it was a sorrow-stricken face that the poor little man hung over the stern the next morning as we turned our prow northwards, and the cliffs drew down into the veil of the haze.

Gerry had at first shown unbounded astonishment at this sudden change of plan, but during my discussion with the Professor a light seemed to strike him. He retired to the saloon, and through the skylight I saw him consulting a manuscript note or two which I could have sworn were in a feminine hand. He came on deck with an unclouded brow.

"To-day's the 29th, isn't it?" he queried cheerily. Then turning to Waller he demanded, "How long shall we take to steam to Port Lewis, captain?"

"About a week, sir," responded that functionary readily, and my young friend faced me with a grin splitting his ingenuous countenance.

"You old humbug," he chuckled. "Coal indeed; provisions running short, are they? *Go* on," and on we went.

7

A LIGHT IN THE DARKNESS

I received Gerry's more explicit congratulations in private. The poor little Professor continued to bemoan our desertion of the quest with such heart-breaking insistence, that the merest suspicion that it was no stern necessity that bade us sail north would, we felt sure, induce paroxysms of fury. We cheered him to the best of our ability, by picturing our early return refreshed for deeds of high emprise in rock climbing, and with perfected means for their accomplishment. But he continued to bewail himself.

It was about six days after we had turned our backs upon the great rock wall, that the wind began to get up strongly from the north, and we had to thrust our way slowly enough through the great surges that rolled down upon us mercilessly from the Atlantic, with four thousand miles of gathered impact at their back.

Our good little boat cleft her way through their white manes with a sturdy shove and shake of her prow, sending the spray swinging in jets before her cutwater, and flooding her decks as she dipped to the rollers and sent them roaring down beneath the bridge.

Two men had to be lashed to the wheel, and the crew took their stations between watch and watch, only by the activity with which they dodged the incoming billows. Two of our boats were swept from the davits, and half the deck-house windows were smashed before we got them battened over. The cook kept a fire in the galley by the display of the most extraordinary agility, and our meals were snappy and disconnected. Nor did we take much pleasure in them. Gerry and I had found our sea-legs to a certain extent, but poor little Lessaution was a terrible sufferer, and we found it hard to take a neighborly interest in his behavior—

he would insist in coming on deck, though he had to be lashed there—and afterwards find appetite for the cook's hastily improvised dainties.

We had twenty-four hours of this sort of thing, and then it began to get monotonous. The wind dropped little by little, but the sea was nearly as high as ever, and the evening closed down upon us with our wretchedness still supreme, and the waves pervading everything from the cabins to the stokehole. We joined Eccles in the engine-room, where, if not dry, we were at least warm, and toasted our steaming clothes before the red glow of the furnaces, while we took exercise by bracing ourselves to avoid being dashed into the heart of the machinery by the great heaves and struggles of the fighting ship. It was a way of passing an evening which came with some originality and freshness to both Gerry and myself, and we stayed there late confabulating over our prospects, and wondering whether our attempt at an interview with our young women would be successful, and what sort of greeting we should receive.

"It's all very well for you now," said Gerry despondently, "you're all right. You've got your title and an income, which might be worse by a long way, but where do I come in? I'm as badly off as ever. You'll have to work your new-found influence pretty vigorously to get me any sort of billet to satisfy my ma-in-law."

"That sort of thing'll have to come later," I answered. "Probably we shan't get more than an hour with them, if that. Port Lewis isn't such an enticing sort of place, from what I've heard, that the *Madagascar*'s likely to stay there long. They'll just coal and that's about all. But if Denvarre and his brother haven't settled matters by now—which the Lord forbid!—I think it won't do us any harm to remind our young women that we're alive and still taking an interest in them. But with Denvarre for competitor I don't see that you're worse of than I am. Don't let's brood, though, old chap, but let what will betide. If our chances are gone from us completely, then we've got the best possible counter-irritant to depression handy. We can turn back and find our excitement still waiting for us at the foot of that stupendous wall."

Gerry smiled hopefully, bending forward for a light for his pipe. A dreamy look crossed his face as he swayed apathetically to the roll of the ship, and as he rose and braced himself with his arm around a stanchion I could see that he was musing mistily over the future. I felt a little that way myself, and there was a silence between us for a time, broken only by the regular beat and clang as the great piston rods thrust themselves backwards and forwards, and the eccentrics jolted round clamorously.

Suddenly from the deck above came a hail, and Janson thrust his face, glistening with salt-foam flecks, into the disc of light where the man-hole gave upon the darkness.

"Light on the starboard bow, my lord," he bellowed, to make himself heard above the jar of the machinery and the shriek of the storm. "The skipper thinks there must be a whaler a-fire."

Gerry and I snatched at our oilskins, which we had doffed when we had descended from the sousings of the deck, and climbed the little iron ladder unsteadily. We were still ploughing our way into the trough of the head-sea, we found, when we gained the deck, but the great rollers did not come shooting over the bow and down the slippery planks as they had done an hour or two before. The sea was evidently going down, but was heavy enough yet to make us pity from the bottom of our hearts any poor wretches who had to battle with it in open boats.

Far away, very dimly and intermittently as we rose on the crest of wave after wave, a light flickered now and again away to starboard, shooting up occasionally into brightness as we and the burning craft stood out on the top of a sea together, lost utterly when both of us sank back into the trough between the seas, and evidently drifting towards us rapidly before the force of the northern gale.

I clambered up on to the bridge beside Waller, and bawled into his ear.

"Shall we be able to help," I questioned stentoriously, "or is it too late?"

"Too late to do anything for her," he shrieked back, shaking his dripping head, "but we ought to stand by for her boats, if they can live with them, poor wretches."

The stress of conversation was too great to indulge in further. I grasped the rail before me and stood at Waller's right hand, straining my eyes into the night. We needed all our strength, really, for the screw, but at Janson's suggestion the dynamo was set going, and our little searchlight streamed out in a thin shaft of light into the darkness. It tinged the frothy breakers with a dead white glow as of hoarfrost.

So we rode forward into the storm, the wind shrieking through our strained cordage, the spray falling like the lash of whips on our glistening decks, and the thud and swish of the surges against our bows answering the regular thump and rattle of the anchor-chains in the hawse-pipe, and the racket of the groaning machinery that echoed up from below.

Far ahead the little zone of golden light flashed before us, dancing and winking amid the tossing of the seas, darting here and there, pulsing quiveringly down the shaft of brightness that fed it from our top, flitting like some brilliant petrel of the night from crest to crest, spurning the foam, glittering through the veils of hissing spray that fell behind it like cascades of radiant jewels. And after it we waddled along steadily, fighting the rollers, flinching before the sting of the flipping drift, nosing into the depths of the green combs of angry water, rolling, pitching, jarring and quivering, but ever following like some trustworthy and attentive duck trailing after an evasive hummingbird.

The sheen of the furnace upon the sea was gleaming nearer. At times the glimmer of its flames was hid from us, as some mountain-like wall of water flung itself in between, but the glow of it was never lost to us. We could see the sparks stream up like puny rockets, as the gale planed them off the edge of the blaze, flinging them in clouds to leeward, as the ungoverned hulk swung heavily between the seas. The masts were pillars of living flame, that streamed into the night in bannerets of fire. Out of the main hatchway a solid white-hot glow of light was projected, shot with red streaks as burning splinters floated up in the strong sea-draught. From stem to stern the unfortunate bark was wrapped in a fiery sheet as the conflagration leaped and roared about it, devouring the seas that broke aboard into clouds of rosy steam.

"God help the poor wretches," I shouted to Waller; "there's no one left alive on that."

"No, my lord, not this half-hour back. It's their boats I'm watching for," he answered, as, with the peak of his cap pressed over his eyes, he strained his gaze into the night. "It's a ten to one chance against any boat living in this sea, but—well, there's always a but, my lord."

Janson was flirting the searchlight about and about the blazing hulk, like a very will-o'-the-wisp. It fled round it questioningly, picking at and dipping to every floating piece of wreckage, but never a one showed the sign of boat or human being. With our steam to help us, there was no danger in approaching the floating furnace as near as we thought well, and we slid up towards it as it lurched past us, till the heat of it blistered across the red seas on to our salt-cracked faces smartingly. The sparks skipped by us, and hissed like little adders on our streaming planks, but gaze as we would, nothing but charred timbers and leaping breakers met our eyes. We plunged forward into the darkness again, as she lumbered by before the wind.

"We ought to hang about in the direction she came from," explained Waller thunderously. "The boats, if they lived, wouldn't keep her pace. They aren't so much exposed to the gale."

I nodded, still gripping the rail before me, not wishing to waste breath that was twisted from one's very lips by the wind, before it could frame a single intelligent word.

So we plodded on for a quarter of an hour or more, seeing nothing. I could but remember what agonies the unfortunate victims of this mischance must be suffering, if by any terrible hap they were swinging near us on those hungry seas, seeing help and safety at hand, and yet without a hope of rescue save by utter chance. And I thanked God for the wet deck below me that I had been cursing but a short hour back.

"I suppose the oil caught fire?" I asked Waller, as a slight lull gave one a chance to make oneself heard. "I shouldn't have thought any ship could have flared like that in this sea."

"She's no whaler, my lord," returned the skipper decidedly; "I can't quite make out her build. More like a liner, only no liner would be down this far south. She had big engines, judging by her funnels. Looked for all the world like one of the old Black Cross Line."

"The Black Cross Line!" I repeated wonderingly; "why, that's a funny thing. Some friends of mine have gone cruising in one of their steamers round—" and then the frightful horror of it took me by the throat, and I could have shrieked aloud. The Black Cross Line! The *Madagascar* was one of their boats, yacht-fitted for cruising. Oh! the thing was impossible. It was some coincidence that fate had raised up to frighten me. Waller just spoke in the hap-hazard way men do when they make comparisons. Of course, he had served on some vessel of the fleet, and his thoughts strayed back to it. And yet—and yet—no ordinary liner would be sailing these seas. And the *Madagascar* was expected in these latitudes. My God! it was a thing too wanton for even my luck to have conceived and brought about. No fate could be so devilish as to drag me out these weary thousands of miles to see my love's agony of death in these desolate southern seas. No; no God that ruled the universe could allow it. I wrestled with the cold reason that insisted that these things could be, and that it was stretching the limits of mere coincidence to say they were not.

Into my tortures of despair a hail from Janson broke, and he swung the leaping flash-light from before our bow like a lightning streak. It streamed, a path of light across the billows, to port, and centred there on a tumbling, reeling object, buffeted by the bluster of the breakers, half hidden by the curtain of the spin-drift. Together Waller and I tore at the wheel, and slewed the ship towards it. Slowly, ever so languidly, the bows came round, and began to edge across to where the disc of light hovered unblinkingly. The dark object leaped up ever and anon, poised upon the dancing surge, only to drop back as if engulfed absolutely in the dark abyss behind the roll of the breaker. A white object fluttered, as we could see between these intermittent eclipses, streaming out against the yellow light daringly. Round this, as we drew near, we could distinguish a huddle of misty outlines, animate or inanimate we could not tell.

We circled heavily to windward, and Waller roared his orders to the crew. The oil-bags were hung outboard, and as they dribbled lingeringly across the surface of the foam, the tossing died down as by magic. Half-a-dozen seamen clustered at the side, and with uplifted hands, swayed coils of rope above their heads. The engines slowed as the engine-room bells clanged, and we half stayed. Then with the blow of a great roller upon our lifting keel we staggered on again.

Still nearer we floundered, drifting broadside on, to the round yellow patch wherein the dim mass still danced uncertainly. Nearer still, and we hovered over it, reeling under the thunderous blows that the windward waves hammered upon us, and rolling nigh bulwarks under into the oily calm to leeward. Nearer again, and the ropes lashed out like whip-cords across the interval from the waiting crew, and were caught and hauled at desperately by the eager wretches aboard the pitching boat. Nearer now, almost under the churn of our wash, and the searchlight stared down unquiveringly into every crevice of its wild confusion, swathing each face in its glare. And white and set, silhouetted haggardly against the blackness of the outer night, the face of my love—my own dear love—looked up into my unbelieving eyes.

I heard an exclamation from Waller as I flung myself from the wheel, and heard him grip his breath as he braced himself to meet the plunge of the ship alone. I was but human, and who was I to stand unmoved beside him there when the light of my eyes was swayed in the grasp of death before me? I took a leap on to the wet and slanting deck, and fell upon my hands, but rose beside the bulwark unhurt and panting. Then a hail from the boat reached across to us above the raving of the wind, and I saw our men tug frantically at a rope that tautened suddenly. A dark body came swiftly flying up to the bulwarks as the men hauled, and with eager hands we seized it, fending it from the jumping list of the timbers. A single glance showed me Lady Delahay's face, sunken and shrivelled with fifty new lines of haunting fear. Another hail, another strenuous pull, and Violet fell into the arms that Gerry held out to receive her. And then—ay, then, and till I go out into the eternal beyond, the memory of it will be vivid in my inmost soul—out of the swirl and uproar of that black, yeasty whirlpool came my love into my embrace, and lay upon my breast.

We bore them into the cabin, and poured cordials between their white lips. We chafed their frozen hands and fetched hot bricks from the engine-room to place beneath their feet. We tore off their outer garments—for ceremony flies through the port-hole when death is knocking at the door—and wrapped blankets round them and rubbed their limbs furiously. We did everything that men can do, of a good purpose but unhandily, to bring them back from the edge of the eternal sleep whereon they hovered, and soon—in the younger women's case at least—with success. Then as their eyes opened, and the color began to creep back lan-guidly into their cheeks, and they sat up in utter wonder at their surroundings, we left them, with every appliance we could fur-nish forth, to revive in her turn their mother, giving them but little explanation of their whereabouts, and being eyed by them with a surprise that we could but hope had pleasure at its back. But this was no time for sentimental musings, and we hurried on deck to see what had betided to the others.

Eight men had been hauled by main force from the tumbling boat, which had reeled more and more tempestuously as her living ballast lightened, and the last poor fellow, with no restrain-ing hand on the far end of the line, had been bumped fearfully against the bulge of the hull as we rolled back. But bruises were the worst that any man had received, and we hustled them into the smoke-room unceremoniously.

Janson was still flinging the searchlight rays across the tum-bling waste of water, but a word from one of the half-drowned mariners made us stay him.

"Not another two spars are afloat together of the other boats," he gasped, as the blood began to flow again in his fro-zen veins. "Every one was matchwooded against the side as they left. Ours was carried off half full by a wave that broke the painter, or I shouldn't be here, and thank God for it."

"How many aboard you?" I asked, shuddering to think what a toll the night had taken; "you're the *Madagascar*, aren't you?"

"Yes, we're the *Madagascar*," he answered slowly and with surprise, "though I don't know how you know it, seeing you've let the boat drift. An hour ago she was the finest pleasure craft afloat, with a hundred and twenty passengers and fifty crew as jolly as could be. And now there's *us*," and he flung his hands out towards his fellows with a gesture of weak despair.

"An hour ago!" I demurred, "more than that, my man, surely. She could never have blazed up to a bon-fire like that in the time."

"I tell you, sir," he answered obstinately, "that less than an hour ago six score of happy men and women were feeding themselves as contented as could be in her saloon. And now," he added grimly, "they're feeding the fishes. And in that boat for three-quarters of an hour we've been tossing over their dead, drowned carcasses, reckoning that every minute would see us join them. And Captain—my captain, what I've sailed with this ten years past—he's down there among them, and I'm here, and ought to be thankin' God, and I keep cursin' every time I give myself leave to think. And that's what comes of followin' the sea, sir," and he laid his rough, damp, grizzled head upon the table, and burst into a storm of hysterical tears.

The others were coming back to consciousness one by one. Baines touched me on the shoulder.

"There's one here that won't last long, my lord, I fear," he said, leading me towards the other end of the saloon, where another limp body was stretched across the table. "We can't bring him round at all."

It came as no shock of surprise to recognize Denvarre's face and drooping yellow moustache. His eyes were closed; his cheeks fell in limply against his jaws; the breath came in a thin wheezy hiss from between his white lips. He was in the last stages of cold and exhaustion. They tried in vain to force brandy between his set teeth. He had not the muscular power of swallowing left. It did indeed look as if Baines was right.

I won't stop to tell you the thoughts that seethed and ran riot in my brain as I saw him fighting for his life with the cold that had nigh mastered his pulses. They belong to the category of devilish inspirations that come to a man when some wild battle with nature furnishes forth a throw back to pure animalism; when self is uttermost and honor unborn. They are monstrous phantasms of the brain too dark to materialize into wholesome words, and best forgotten save when the system needs a purge of shame. God forgive me my desires at that single moment—for a space of mere seconds saw me myself again.

Suffice it to say that with every aid we could devise we joined him in his wrestle with the death that was gripping him for the final throw. We fetched spirits, and rasped every part of his body with rough towels soaked in whisky. We smote with our palms upon his rigid limbs, and bent and kneaded his unyielding joints; we thrust heated bricks against his feet and hands; finally, at Janson's suggestion, we collected handfuls of the sleet that was falling on the decks, and grated them furiously upon his skin. And at last the life began to flicker in him.

A tinge—faint and barely perceptible at first, but growing in strength—began to filter into his cheeks. A sigh burst from his throat and the tense lips parted. We tilted brandy drop by drop into his mouth, and heard his spluttering cough with joy. And then of his own effort he stirred and whispered faintly.

"Gwen?" he queried in a faint, far-away voice, and it was for me to answer him.

"Safe, and on board," said I cheerily, as my heart sledge-hammered at my ribs, and my hands twitched to grasp his throat and tear the chords of speech away from him eternally.

"Quite safe, old man, and coming round nicely."

He smiled a happy, drowsy smile that stayed and slept upon his face as he wandered back into consciousness. And then I left him to his brother—who was among the rescued—and to Baines, and went stolidly up on deck, the fires of hell burning in my heart, and rage—the insane, unreasoning rage of disappointment—astir in my blood.

"Gwen, Gwen," I repeated to myself, as I flung myself out into the gale that still slashed cuttingly down the deck. "Gwen she is to him, and, curse him, she's Gwen no longer to me."

8

BEFORE THE GALE

I stood beneath the bridge holding on to a friendly stanchion, and gazing apathetically before me. I could see Waller's brawny figure outlined upon the bridge, every movement of his muscles showing up against the moonlit sky. He wrestled strenuously with the bucking wheel as it fought in his grasp, while above him the ragged clouds scudded fiercely, giving him the effect of rushing violently backward into space as they passed swiftly over him. The wind had increased with the rise of the waning moon, and the lull, which mercifully allowed us to rescue the derelict boat, was blotted out in a turmoil of foam and fury. The tumult of the night found an echo in my heart.

For, unlike my usual custom, I had allowed myself to hope. In my conceit of my plan for gaining an interview with Gwen—in my hopes and fears of our meeting coming off—I had not dwelt much on the fact that it might end in failure—in despair. Gerry was partly responsible for this. For the last week he had continually dinned his sanguine reassurances into my ears till they had almost ousted my natural pessimism. I had forgotten to deceive Fate with a pretence of despondency, and she had turned to sneer wickedly in my face and to flout me for my inattention. I gripped the stanchion savagely as I thought of these things, I turned a silent face to the hubbub of the night, while every passion of my body rioted in my brain. I took an infuriate comfort in the thunderous grapple of the elements.

For, look at it how I would, I was condemned to hours—if not days—of smiling torture. Here was I cooped up in the same ship with the woman to whom I had utterly given over my heart, and honor—bare courtesy, in fact—forbade me to so much as hint to her my love. Mere common kindness bade me further the wooing of my rival. And he—I gnashed my teeth as I remembered it—if my luck had only allowed, might have been a thousand fathoms deep in this shrieking whirlpool of a sea. If ever the temptations of Cain filled a man's heart, they crowded mine that tempest-ridden night.

I fought with my passion, thrusting these ideas back from me, conjuring up to myself every thought of chivalry that my upbringing could give birth to. I remembered my apathetic renunciation of Gwen when we parted six months before—my calm and fatalistic determination to live down dispassionately the desire of my life. None the more did it bring comfort as I told myself that now I had the right and the means to win her—that as before God, and not before a sordid, money-worshipping world, we were just man and maid, and had looked upon each other in natural love and liking. I cursed the narrow world of Society with an insistence that gained power from the fact that I stood in the very cradle of nature's wrath, and Society was dimmed by the distance of three thousand miles—veiled behind a curtain of storm and dancing spray. Thus during the long hours of the night I battled with myself in disjointed, hopeless argument, and the storm rattled round, me with growing clamor.

It was about three in the morning when the climax of the tempest came. A shock quivered up from our stern, vibrating through every timber of our hull as if by electricity—a tremor such as no mere breaking wave could have caused. It was as if we had been smitten by some Titan sledge-hammer. Above the bellow of the storm I heard Waller's cry of dismay, and saw the wheel spin uselessly through his hands. He came headlong down from the bridge.

I sprang forward to steady him as he half stepped, half fell from the ladder, and he lurched into my arms. As the unguided ship swung round before the impact of the rollers, the deck stood up at an angle that shed our footing from it. We gripped each other unhandily. The bow leaped, and shook itself as if in pain. A ponderous surge charged into it. The ship gave before the shock, throbbing through every timber. It swayed, hesitated, and then, defeated in the unequal struggle, broached to, and, lay in the trough of the sea. A great flood roared down the deck,

snatching up the captain and myself in its green mane and dashing us stunningly against the deck-house. We spluttered and
choked, gasping for breath.

"The rudder-chains are broken," exclaimed Waller hoarsely,
as he gulped and crowed, and he made a dash for the foc'sle,
roaring aloud for the watch below. They never heard him till he
thrust his face into the very door. Unsteadily they came tum-
bling out to scramble along the listed deck, and find and splice
the sundered links. The rattle of their intermitting hammerings and
draggings could only be heard if you stood within a foot of them.

The seas boiled over us eternally while this was doing, and
for half-an-hour we were practically beneath the waves, the ship
settling under the weight of water as she rolled broadside into
the seas. The engine still thrashed wearily round, but ungoverned as we were, our leeway was twice our speed of steam. We
only butted our prow more and more under the combs of the
great rollers. Finally six men were stationed with ropes spliced
to the broken chains, and Waller mounted the bridge again. By
strenuous tugs they hauled upon the tiller as his hand motioned
to them, and slowly we came round to face the gale again. As we
did there was a clang and a jar. The white wake faded from behind
us, and came flying up past the sides. We were sidling back with
gathering speed into our sternway. The cover was flung off the
engine-room man-hole, and Eccles's grizzled head appeared.

"The propeller-shaft, my lord," he bawled, his voice rising
screamingly in his excitement, "the propeller-shaft's split. I
daren't give her another turn in this sea."

As our way lost itself in the force of the contending waters,
and died down into nothingness, we slowed, stopped, and a huge
mass of ocean roared against our prow. It lifted, lifted, lifted,
soaring towards the very heavens. I saw it eclipse a red, angry
planet that I had noticed high above the bowsprit-stays a moment
before. It hovered a single tense instant, and then with a swirl
and heave came flying round, reeling and staggering. There was
a rush of the crew to gain some hold or to brace themselves
against some shelter. Then with a frightful roll we swung over,
and lay on our beam ends, the hungry waves licking along our
submerged decks like wolves ravening for their quarry.

Out of this hopelessness Waller led us like the brave man he was. After infinite research the carpenter produced a storm-sail, which had not been buried beneath the weight of superincumbent wreckage. Under the captain's skilful supervision this was bent as a jib. Slowly, as the wind gained force upon it, we dragged from under the weight of the waves that were thrusting us deeper and deeper under their piled thronging, and drew round to show our stern to the wind. As we ploughed our way out of the trough of the sea, the waters rushed more and more from off our streaming decks. We rose; the ship shaking itself like a dog. We gained speed. The men took up the rudder ropes they had flung aside, and in another two minutes we were riding—racing, before the gale, back—straight back—to the regions of the Great South Wall.

As we gained way the ship steadied herself. The ponderous lurch and roll grew less. The keel sat more evenly in the hollow between the seas, cutting through their crests like a knife as the sail bellied out and tautened. We managed to get another piece of canvas spread, and then like a thing endowed with sudden life the *Raccoon* began to tear before the wind, bursting aside the surges as she overtook them, as if she would revenge haughtily the shame they had put upon her helplessness. There was an exhilaration about the fury of our rushing. It was like riding a mettled and tireless steed.

I left the crew to their work of re-connecting the broken rudder-chain and went below. The saloon was a desolation. Every movable thing had been swept to port by the list of our sudden broach to. The table was leaning with its top against the side. A litter of glass and crockery filled the port corners. A mass of pantry gear had been shot across the floor. Smears of various sauces from the same locality stained the carpets. Water had forced itself down through the hatchway—though this had been battened—and sparkled in puddles beneath the electric light. The knives and forks and splinters of glass jingled as they clustered and broke apart again at each heave of the ship. And in the midst of this conglomerate desolation sat poor Lady Delahay and her daughters.

The former rose hastily as I swung myself off the stairs into the doorway. She staggered towards me, her face white with anxiety. Her hand trembled as she dropped it unsteadily on my arm.

"Lord Denvarre?" she questioned, tugging insistently at my sleeve. "He's recovering?"

"Right as the mail," answered I; "he was a bit knocked out of time at first, but we've brought him round famously between us. And you?" I queried, "I hope you have been ministered to properly?"

"I could think of nothing—absolutely nothing," she answered, "while we were without news of him. Oh, Lord Heatherslie, supposing my darling had been practically widowed before my eyes?"

"It's been a terrible night for you," said I, "but I'm glad you were spared that crowning sorrow. Then I suppose I'm to congratulate Miss Gwendoline on her engagement?" I went on, looking across to where the two girls were trying to tidy up some of the worst of the jumbled disorder of the floor. "I'm sure she has the best wishes for luck and happiness from me."

"It's not announced at all yet," said the good lady hurriedly, "in fact, you see there was no one to announce it to. There were no people of any position on board, and it has only really been seriously taken into consideration the last few days. A little awkward, you know, under the circumstances, our being fellow-travellers for so long. So we have decided that it shall not be recognized just yet. Just an understanding, you see, not a formal betrothal till we return to England, if we ever do," added the poor old thing doubtfully. "Oh, my dear Lord Heatherslie, shall we ever reach any port alive?" and she sank back on to the cushions of the locker seats with a groan.

"Well, at present," said I, "I must confess that we're flying away from the nearest port at the rate of about twenty miles an hour. Our engine's broken down, and we have to run before the gale. But it'll only be the case of an hour or two, I hope, and then we shall be able to beat up for the Falklands. But it'll be a long business at the best. You will have to put up with our bachelor quarters and our rough accommodation."

"Lord Heatherslie," she said brokenly, "when I think what might have happened, I should be less than Christian if I didn't

give thanks with a full heart. Even though we have lost everything in the way of clothes and property, I have my darlings
safe, and their happiness is secured. That is sufficient for me."

"Oh," I said, "then I have to congratulate Miss Violet also.
Mr. Garlicke, I presume?" I inquired with an air of savage festivity.
Poor Gerry, his optimism was to get felled to earth along with
mine. Well, I felt there was something in both being in the same
boat. We could make our moans in company.

"Quite on a par with Gwendoline's affair," answered Lady
Delahay, holding up a warning finger. "Nothing to be said about
it yet, please. Is it possible I recognized Mr. Carver on the deck?"

"Quite possible," I replied dryly, "you did. He and I and the
Professor Lessaution—who is helping him tend the rescued
men—are the only passengers aboard," and as the girls gave over
their useless competition with the litter of the crockery, and
came and sat beside their mother, I began to give them the whole
story.

For a girl who had just been dragged by main force out of
the blackest shadow of death, I never saw anything to equal
Gwen. Her eyes were bright, her complexion was pink and shining, the sparkle of the salt spray was on her hair. She looked as
smiling and content as if she had found the desire of her heart,
instead of having just seen five-score of fellow-beings consigned
to a frightful end. Her gaze dwelt upon my face as she listened
intently to my story. She looked as complacent as if we were at
anchor off Monaco, instead of driving Lord knows where into
an uncharted sea, before one of the fiercest gales that ever
started a ringbolt. I reflected with internal wretchedness that a
girl's horizon is bounded very narrowly when she is in love, and
envied Denvarre under my breath furiously.

In their turn they told me of their adventure, and what had
befallen them on that night of horror. How in the midst of light
and life, and the friendly converse of the yacht's saloon, a dishevelled lampman had appeared, grimy, hot, and with fear of death
writ largely on his face, and beckoned out the captain from
amidst the throng. How, restless in his continued absence, one
or two unquiet passengers had followed him, and returned with
vague reports of a fire in the lamp-room forward, and how on

the word the whole mob of passengers had surged on deck. That then the iron sea discipline of a well-ordered British merchant vessel had been closed around them instantly, and they had been marshalled in parties to the boats to which they had been assigned. But the fire continuing to gain, and the sea to rise, they had been confronted by an awful death on either hand. When the captain had been obliged to abandon hope, he had lowered away the first boat, and within seconds they had seen it dashed to pieces like an eggshell on their bulwarks. The second and third boats had shared the same fate, and two more had been swamped in sight of the vessel. Then as a last chance the captain had had a boat swung from the bow with a long tether, and they had been transferred to it one by one as the seas swung it backward and forward between their passing and repassing, but when but a dozen of them were aboard, the painter had parted—worn with the constant to and fro against the timbers—and they had been swept to leeward as in a flash. Five minutes later the flames had covered the ship from stem to stern, and they shuddered when they told what they had seen, as dark forms began to drop from her red-hot decks into the merciful cold of the sea. And they ended the tale with the tears that are the due of utter terror and long despair, and I made no effort to stay this gracious relief of nature's pity.

As the ship began to steady her plunging, we made efforts to find accommodation for the ladies, to whom, of course, we gave up our cabins. They were absolutely destitute of everything beyond what they stood up in, and were robed as it was in such rugs and blankets as had been collected while their outer garments were dried in the stoke-hole. We got them at last to retire and find a much-needed repose, a thing that their terror had forbidden so far, for the rolling of the masterless ship had been enough to make any one believe that she would only find a resting-place on the bottom of the furious sea.

I left them with good wishes for sleep and for forgetfulness of the horrors they had experienced. I sought the smoke-room to make inquiry for the rescued men, and found that they had all lapsed into unconsciousness, tucked up in the blankets which the crew had surrendered to their use. Lessaution and Gerry were stretched upon the floor, sleeping heavily after their strenuous attendance on the half-frozen folk, and I left them to their slumbers; amid my own misery I had a heartache to spare for Gerry's awakening of sorrow.

I climbed up upon the bridge again and stood beside Waller. White-faced and haggard with the anxieties of the night, he was still at his post. He watched with hopeful eyes the coming of the dawn, which was already tingeing the east with an angry, lurid crimson. Still racing before the billows that hunted us we were plunging ever southward, returning swiftly down the track up which we had fought so ploddingly the last six days. The captain's clothes hung about him in limp sodden clingings; he leaned wearily upon the wheel, guiding it delicately in the strong grip of Rafferty, who shared the toil of restraining it. There was weariness and exhaustion in his every pose, but his eye was still bright and his face set steadfastly upon his duty. I watched him with admiration—the strong, confident sailor who held our lives resourcefully in his unshaken grip. A glow of pride pulsed through my veins as I recognized that this was the type of commander who was lifting England's honor high across the seas of two hemispheres, that what this staunch self-reliant man was doing would have been done in like case by unreckoned hundreds of his fellows. I thanked God again for the mercies of the night, with special acknowledgment for the fact that we were manned by a wholesome British crew.

I laid my hand lightly upon his shoulder.

"Take a rest, captain," said I; "let Janson come and have his spell. You've been at it twelve long hours already. Surely there's nothing left but to let her drive."

"Thanks, my lord," he answered, smiling back cheerily into my inquiring eyes. "Janson's only been two hours below. I'll give him an hour longer at least."

"But Rafferty's here, and I can hold the wheel, if that's all," said I reproachfully; "what's the good of killing yourself, man?"

"I've had many a longer bout in weather no better," and he shifted the spokes a point in his deft, unhesitating hands.

"But what's the trouble?" I answered, almost irritated by his unswerving determination. "Why can't we take her from you? We've got the sense not to let her broach to, at any rate."

"Ice is the matter, my lord. Ice—and acres of it. You forget we're racing back into the South at fifteen knots an hour. If the gale doesn't drop before evening, we shall be among the bergs again. We may meet out-lying floes at any moment."

"Then we'd call you," said I argumentatively; "so just you skip along and take a snooze with a clear conscience."

"Thanks, my lord, I shouldn't sleep," he said dryly, wiping the spray from his beard, and there was nothing further to be said. I shrugged my shoulders and left him there, vigilant, alert, eternally craning his eyes into the veil of the spin-drift, a valiant warrior of the deep.

The presage of the lurid sunrise was fulfilled. All day long the gale shrieked and raved behind us, screaming through our taut rigging like some inarticulate storm-spirit's agony. The sullen waves still thundered after us, lifting our stern, and burying our bows now and again in the crest of some laggard comber. They broke thunderously across our bulwarks, dashing themselves into a very dust of spray. It glistened snow-like in the sun-rifts, as they broke now and again through the leaden haze that hid the sky. The scud of the clouds kept pace above us, wreathing and twisting into a thousand fantastic shapes. The gulls screamed and hovered, and the petrels clipped and scurried from crest to crest. The roar of the surges and the shiver of the laboring timbers followed one upon the other monotonously. One got stupefied by their ceaseless, recurrent boom and thud.

About mid-day the stress of the night began to tell upon me. I remembered that during four-and-twenty hours of physical and mental excitement I had had no sleep. I staggered wearily down into the smoke-room, curled myself up beside Gerry's still motionless form, and before I had closed eye a minute, sank off into dreamless unconsciousness.

The dark was falling again as I woke. Both Gerry and Lessaution had disappeared, but I could hear the bellow of the tempest strong as ever.

I scrambled to my feet, and made my way uncertainly to the saloon. The remains of a meal stood uncleared upon the table, and I began to satisfy a hunger which had got stupendous. Then back up the pitching companion-steps I tottered, and strode out upon the deck.

The seas were still leaping along our sides, but not quite so strongly. Up on the bridge I recognized Janson's burly figure, and perceived with thankfulness that Waller had at last surrendered his post. In the bow Gerry and Lessaution were clutching the foremost stays, and pointing excitedly before them. I wormed my way along the deck and joined them.

Standing out blue-white above the froth of the boiling sea a great iceberg was rearing its head. It hung there haughtily and unmoved, despising the rage that made the breakers raven at its feet. The wind shrieked about its pinnacles, thrusting one now and again from its seat upon the ice buttresses, and sending it crashing into the deep. But the main mass of the white mountain stayed motionless, a mighty breakwater sheltering the leeward surface into a rippling pool.

Janson raised his hand to his mouth, and roared some indistinguishable order to the watch on deck. The men came racing forward, and hauled at the sheets. The sails came lumbering down, and as we lost the steadiness of their grip upon the wind we began to pitch and tumble again.

Not for long. The wheel spun in the mate's hands, and with our way still swift upon us we began to turn. We nosed in towards the white pyramid. We swung past its leeward edge. Our cutwater broke a burnished line across the stillness of the sheltered pool. In a very instant the travail of our storm-hunted vessel ceased. We swung, heaved to, upon the calm, gently swaying to the ripples, while outside the storm still bellowed for our lives.

Behind this sudden refuge we lay almost motionless, looking up wonderingly at the shining peaks above. Baines and the cook accepted the altered conditions with surprise and thankfulness, making immediate preparations for a meal which should obliterate the discomforts of the past eight-and-forty hours. The smoke began to curl anew from the galley, and various tinned victuals were disinterred from the pantry wreckage.

Within five minutes of our finding this unexpected harbor the door of the captain's cabin opened, and Waller strode forth, gaping upon our changed surroundings. The sixth sense that lies in the seaman's brain had warned him, sleeping as he was, that we no longer dipped and tossed amid the breakers. A glance to starboard, and he understood, giving Janson a quick nod as the other pointed to the ice. He stayed still a moment, watching the edge of the berg curiously, and then climbed up and joined the mate.

I could not hear the words they exchanged, but I saw a shake of Waller's head as he jerked his thumb over his shoulder. They strode together to one end of the bridge, and the captain gesticulated toward the berg again. A half-smile crossed Janson's face. He was evidently meeting his chief's arguments with a polite incredulity. Following the line of Waller's pointing finger, I was in time to see a strange thing happen.

The edge of the ice rose slowly, but perceptibly, mounting from the water-level with a heavy swish. I looked up in amazement, and saw the topmost pinnacles bow slantingly across the drifting clouds. There was a suck and a wash as the water rolled in toward the ice to fill the vacuum. The berg lurched slowly back again, and a big breaker gathered itself up, and crested out toward us. There was a line of foam across the pool.

An order roared from between Waller's lips, and Janson came at a bound from the bridge to wake the watch below. His face was white with terror. He shrieked into the foc'sle in a shrill, unnatural voice.

The men came leaping up, and at the captain's shout dropped the two port boats over the side. A rope was passed to them, and with furious tugs they passed ahead, towing desperately. The men left on deck set the sails again, waiting for the first breath of the gale to catch them. They stared wide-eyed over their shoulders, watching, staring, gluing their gaze to the mighty ice-cliffs astern.

I scrambled up to Waller, full of unquiet surprise. I felt that something was imminent—some possible disaster that I could not fathom. I demanded explanations.

"Mr. Janson has committed a very serious error of judgment, my lord," said the sailor shortly. "A few minutes will see it repaired, I hope."

"But, good gracious!" said I with some annoyance, "you're taking us out into that whirlpool again just when we were comfortable. What on earth's the matter?"

Before he could answer me the first breath of the gale began to catch upon the sails. The sailors hauled upon the sheets to tauten them as he bawled his orders down, and the boats' crews were beckoned back. As they slipped alongside, and the davit-hooks caught again upon the pulleys, Waller gave a great sigh of relief and turned to me again.

"That iceberg—" he began, and at the words no explanation became necessary.

We were both staring at it when again the edge of it began to lift. But this time there was no return. Up, up, it soared, lifting its dripping flanks into the air, and the seas poured back from it in torrents. The waters boiled behind our stern, heaving as if in the bath of some gigantic geyser. For one single moment we danced haltingly upon the turbulence, the wind fighting with all its strength upon our canvas against the under-currents that tore at our keel. Then, thank God, the gale was victor. We slid away from the grip of the back-flow, out into the riot of the storm again. And behind us one of nature's dramas was enacted awfully. With a roar and a thunderous crash the iceberg slanted, swayed, poised itself one motionless instant, and then rolled completely over, dashing its topmost summit into the heart of the deep, and, heaved up by its mighty fall, a huge wave rose and almost engulfed it. The great rollers came clamoring after our flying hark as if in vindictive disappointment for the escape of their nearly won prey. But their fury defeated them. Their crests thundered on our stern, and flung us with growing force out into the ocean, while behind us the berg slowly emerged among the tossing, to point new pinnacles toward the clouds. And out in the storm again we continued our ceaseless race before the seas, flying anew down the long trail south, buffeted, tempest driven, but safe again by the favor of a brave sailor's quick-witted knowledge.

9

THE LEAPING OF THE WALL

Another night of tempest succeeded, diversified by stinging showers of hail and sleet. I believe neither captain nor mate left the bridge the whole night long, for the floe and berg began to grow around us, tack as we would. But the deeper we got into the heart of the multitude of island ice, the less grew the force of the wind. I rose the next morning after a few hours' restless slumber to find us floating gently in a calm, untroubled sea, while around us, as far as eye could reach, the white pack stretched in uneven masses to the horizon.

We dawdled down the broad lanes of black water between, the little puffs of wind coming fitfully from behind the sheltering masses. Our range of vision got less and less as these increased in size, and about mid-day the sun came out gloriously, and Waller was able to take an observation.

He came toward me, smiling doubtfully, after he had worked out his calculations in the little chart-room.

"M. Lessaution will be enchanted, my lord," said he. "We are within a few miles of our original starting-place. It is an extraordinary thing that we should have been driven back so exactly on the line we had come. I have only steered by the stars and dead reckoning."

"He may be pleased enough," I answered, "but he'll be entirely alone in his gratification. Do you mean to say we've got to wrestle back all those weary miles? What desperate luck! but just the usual kind that dogs my footsteps. Why, it'll take weeks to do it sailing."

"I'm afraid it would," agreed the captain, "and that's why I have another proposal to make. Since we got among the ice, I have been interviewing Mr. Eccles. He thinks that if we were in a dead calm, that he could get the split of the propeller-shaft rivetted, and made tight enough for half-steam. I would suggest, my lord, that we lie to and let him have a try."

"But not in this ice," I objected; "I don't want a repetition of yesterday's performance with a different climax. Suppose one of these great bergs turns turtle?"

"I have thought of that," replied Waller, "but I have a plan. If you remember we were under the lee of some islands when we left on our cruise north. I think I can find them again, my lord. We could probably make them an ice-free harbor."

"Why, certainly, then," said I at once, glad to snatch at half a chance of curtailing a voyage that could be nothing but misery for me. "Search them out, captain, and let Mr. Eccles do his utmost."

He went back to the wheel, and began to nose our bows to starboard, taking advantage of every breath to slip delicately from pool to pool.

About an hour later a thin column of smoke showed suddenly as we rounded the flank of a mighty berg, and there, a short mile to port, the familiar islands showed up, gray and haggard in the sunlight, as we had left them eight or nine stormy days before.

Lessaution had joined me by now, his little eyes agleam with pleasure. As he recognized his surroundings, he turned and seized my hand.

"This time we shall not fail," he declaimed ecstatically. "Before twenty-four hours are over, I shall have scaled the cliffs that keep the mystery of the South. I—Emil Saiger Lessaution—I proclaim it."

"My good sir," I said, "you'll have to be quick about it. We only stay here for repairs. You don't mean to say you imagined we were still pursuing our quest? You certainly are a pretty sanguine personage, if you did."

"M. de Heatherslie," replied the little man with dignity, "do you think that I have such little consideration far the distressed ladies of this party, that I would keep them a moment longer than necessary from returning where they can obtain what is needful for their comfort? No. But I have questioned the good

Eccles, who assures me that not less than forty-eight hours will
he necessary to effect his work upon his engines. By then I shall
have accomplished my desire, and will be able to show you such
proofs that after we have landed the ladies at the Falklands, you
will retrace your course here and pursue this adventure with
me. But to think that I wish to inconvenience the ladies by a
single instant!—I who worship the sex from the bottom of my
heart!" and he twirled his little mustaches fiercely.

I did not attempt to answer these chivalric sentiments, and
we drifted into other by-ways of conversation amicably enough.
The *Raccoon* wound along the irregular canals amid the pack,
and finally swung under the overhanging shadow of the summits.

The isles were high and sugarloaf-like, with great hollows
on the flank that faced the shore cliffs not a mile away. We threw
the lead in the channel between them and the cliff wall, and
about the centre found fourteen fathoms. Here we dropped anchor.

Great lean rocks ran up from the water's edge in buttressing
ribs, crowning the gaunt summits. Here and there deep rifts
showed in their sides. Curious snake-like twistings wound about
them. Scales of molten stones lapped over and about each other
wherever a resting-place was found. It did not need the black
column of smoke that pillared up into the sky to inform me that
these were volcanoes.

That day was given up to tidying the ship, lashing up what
had run adrift of our various impedimenta about the saloon and
smokeroom, and making things ship-shape generally.

About noon the ladies appeared, bright, smiling, and cheerful. Gwen met me with the friendliest interest and unconcern.
She was dressed in a neat skirt of sail-cloth, supplied by the
carpenter, or rather the material for the same. She and her sister, I found, had been fashioning these in the privacy of their
cabins, the dresses in which they came aboard being practically
ragged pulp. They had wound thin strips of blanket about their
shoulders most becomingly, and now wore these impromptu
toilets before us by no means abashed, and with the certainty
of producing a good impression undisturbed upon their faces.

We hastened to congratulate them upon their appearance.

They bowed their thanks, and began to ply us with unceasing questions. They were full of curiosity about their whereabouts, and their chances of a speedy return to civilized regions. I assured them that no efforts of mine should be wanting to swiftly bring them back to the known world at the earliest opportunity, but explained the situation with regard to the engine.

Gwen flashed a look at me I hardly understood.

"You seem anxious to get rid of us," she said. "Is our dishevelled appearance too much for you? We'll endeavor not to obtrude our society upon you more than necessary."

She looked so adorable as she said it, with the little curls just leaning down her forehead to peep into her blue eyes, that I could have seized her in my arms then and there, and dared Denvarre to so much as think of her again. As things were, being at the end of the nineteenth century, and not in the middle of the tenth, I smiled apathetically, and answered with as much emotion in my voice as there is in a phonograph:

"It must be very uncomfortable for you, I fear. No clothes, no luxuries, no anything."

"Neither Vi nor I are made of Italian glass," she answered quaintly, "and mother's tougher than she looks. Truth to tell, I was getting bored on the yacht. This sort of thing suits me excellently—I adore adventure. But I'm sorry, of course, if our coming has put you about," and she smiled again, happily.

I suppose it is the nature of the sweetest of women to be merciless at times. I reflected this in excuse as I gazed seawards without finding an answer, and thrusting back the words that came bubbling to my lips. The wretchedness must have been apparent in my face, for she suddenly changed the conversation as we strolled forward.

"So you're no longer Captain Dorinecourte?"

"Alas, no," said I forgetfully.

She turned quickly to look at me with surprise.

"Good gracious! Lord Heatherslie, aren't you glad to have the title?"

"I only meant," I stammered, "that there have been many responsibilities and—er—disappointments accumulating for me since I succeeded."

"But surely that'll soon be over," she queried. "It's only a matter of lawyer's business, is it?"

"They're terrible people when they get you in their hands," said I vaguely. "But tell me how you have enjoyed your trip so far."

She looked back at me very straight. "I told you when we left London I shouldn't enjoy it, and I can't honestly say I have. The monotony got to be terrible."

I had meant all references to what had happened in London to he forgotten. I did not think it kind to refer to them again in this outspoken way.

"But—but surely Denvarre and—and Garlicke made it pleasant for you," I hazarded. "It must have made it awfully nice for you having them all the time."

"Of course they have been attentive, if that's what you mean," she said, with a slightly contemptuous inflection in her voice. "But one can get tired of even undiluted attention. I'm sure I've done my best to quarrel with Lord Denvarre several times, but he's far too polite."

I didn't know what to think. Did she openly mean to give me to understand that she had accepted Denvarre for the position? Or were they simply indulging in the luxury of their first quarrel? Or was it just her off-hand way of speaking of him? I found no answer.

"Now, if we'd only had the prophetic instinct and known that you were going to start on this delightful trip, we should have waited and come with you. You'd have invited us, wouldn't you?"

I smiled to myself as I reflected that Lady Delahay would have found an extremely polite but explicit refusal to any such proposal. But I answered courteously:

"It would have been too great a privilege. But my luck never permits arrant good fortune like that to be mine."

She looked at me curiously, and sighed a little restlessly, turning away to watch the cloud of mollies that skipped about our stern. There was silence between us for a minute.

"I prefer captains to peers," she said at last, with a little laugh. "I don't think you're improved."

"It's a prejudice you'll have to overcome, won't you?" said I. "Denvarre—" but as I mentioned his name he came on deck, and spying us, walked up and joined us.

The two smiled into each other's eyes pleasantly enough, but—but something was wanting. Gwen never had been what one would call a sentimental girl, though at times—but that was ages ago. I left them to stroll off together, while I marched forward again, musing over the very level-headed way in which she treated her engagement and her *fiancé*. For I had imagined she would look at the matter differently. We had been such old—well, comrades, that I'd expected to be told of her happiness, and by her own lips too. It would have prevented all the sense of strangeness that had somehow got between us. I shouldn't have whined or referred to old times—she must have known that. I could only repeat to myself that women were beyond my finite understanding, and continued to take a miserable and utterly useless pleasure in the fact that at any rate she did not worship the ground that Denvarre trod.

Gerry was smoking a gloomy pipe over the stern, and I joined him. He kept his face studiously averted from mine, and I had to lay my hand upon his shoulder before I spoke.

"Poor old chap," said I sympathetically. "Have they broken it to you?"

"The old woman has," he answered, adding a crisp execration which should never be used in connection with a lady.

"Well," said I, trying to look into his eyes, "it'll soon be over, old man. If Eccles can get steam, we'll be back at the Falklands in ten days' time. And we must buck each other up," I added, trying to be cheerful.

"I didn't think it of Vi," burst out the poor lad with an air of desperate aggrievement. "Not that I believe she cares the flick of a finger for him now. It's that old hag of a mother that's done it."

"My dear boy," said I, "we mustn't put *too* stupendous a value on our fascinations. Denvarre and his brother are good men all through. And you and I are detrimentals—or at any rate I only shave it by a short head," I added, as I thought of the collection which was to bring in a tidy trifle.

Poor Gerry. He just let himself loose upon the word. He cursed wealth and all that wealth brings with a sudden burst of passion that I had never dreamed he was capable of. He railed at Lady Delahay; he condemned the name of Garlicke to the lowest pit; he anathematized every usage of polite Society and every useless luxury that we are bred to consider a necessity, showing the aptest reasons for considering them the true creators of every vice and cruelty that is perpetrated beneath the sun. He swore in a very storm of passionate bitterness, leaving no object of his hatred untouched. He went into comminatory details which were almost superfluous. And I let him rave.

For, mark me, there are masculine moods where oaths and curses are the equivalent of feminine tears, and in neither case should you attempt to restrain them if they are the culmination of some great tribulation. They sweep out the bitterness in their stream, and though the ache be left in the wound, it has no longer a poisoned smart. And that is why Gerry shook my hand a few minutes later, and let less haggard lines pervade his countenance, while he confessed himself a fool. And in this worthier frame of mind I led him aft, and into the conversation of his fellows.

As the dusk drew down—and you must recollect it was nearly mid-summer in those latitudes, and the nights were but an hour or two long—we managed to get some sort of dinner. The cook evolved a meal which he would have considered unbefitting his dignity at another time, but which we ate on our cracked plates with great appreciation. For the first time for over a week we fed at a steady table, and enjoyed the peaceable conversation of our companions. Gerry, under the influence of coffee and chartreuse, even rose to the lengths of chaffing poor little Lessaution.

The latter had spent the afternoon in unavailing effort. Supplied with a boat-and crew he had set forth to fend along the great rock wall which seemed to stretch unbroken to the horizon, seeking, but with an utter want of success, for a means of ascending the same. And the poor little chap was taking it most seriously.

Gerry thought fit to twit him on his futile adventure, and he was furious as a trapped rat. It was suggested to him that the quest was, and ever would be, hopeless, and that we had better give it up before we all got cricks in our necks staring up precipices we were never destined to climb. We declared our conviction that we were in the wrong spot altogether—the responsibility for our position rested in the first place with the Professor, I should explain, who had worked out by some intricate scheme of his own the probable route the storm-driven Mayans must have taken—and that he must have entirely misjudged the wind, or the currents, or something. Finally, that there could not possibly be anything worth seeing if he did happen to claw up the barren crags.

The little *savant* fell upon his adversary, foot, horse, and artillery. He demonstrated that he was a disgrace to the name of Englishman, and had of imagination no single jot. That it did not matter, in effect, what such an unsportsmanlike rascal did think, for fortunately our destinies lay with me—the good earl, let it be understood—who would be guided in this matter by the dictates of sense and practicality. He himself would only give up the quest with his breath, and staked his reputation on his success. Cowards might do and say what they pleased. Finally, in an access of irritation he flung from us to go on deck and compose his vehement mortification with a cigar, and to gaze hungrily at the cliffs which mocked him with cold white serenity.

Small talk and amiability were the order of the hour. Induced by our fervent representation, Gwen even went to the piano and enlivened these desolate solitudes with a song or two. We were settling into a thoroughly pleasant evening, though amongst us two hearts were still throbbing lonelily.

Suddenly a shrill yell resounded from above. There was the sound of hurried footsteps on the companion, and Lessaution burst back into our midst. His eyes were agleam, his hair stuck up like quills in his excitement. He bellowed at us.

"The ice goes, the ice goes!" he hallooed. "It goes, it disappears, it draws itself off. The sea runs away. There will be nothing—nothing at all. You shall see. We sink to the bottom; no water shall remain at all. Name of a pipe! what is to become of us?"

Without exception we all jostled at his heels as he turned and fled up on deck again, even old Lady Delahay being carried away by the prevailing excitement, and when we all poured out of the companion-way, it was a strange sight and no mistake that met our gaze.

The moon shone bright as day, almost, and lit up a scene of cold splendor, the like of which I have never seen equalled. But the strangeness of the matter lay in this. There was not a breath stirring; indeed, a close, dense stillness lay heavy over the sea, but the waters were pouring past our bows like a river in spate. They seethed against our sides like the rush of a mill-stream, purring and rippling oilily.

On the bosom of the dark tide the floe-ice swirled along, crashing as it charged our stem, and butting at our timbers thunderously. Berg thrust at berg like the jostle round a street accident. The pack-ice split and worked in masses one against the other, lump grinding on lump. The crash of their striving was deafening. And at the tail of this turmoil came open water unflecked by the slightest ripple, and pouring past our stern in a steady, unfaltering swirl. Comparing great things with small, it was exactly like the opening of a lock-sluice, and for a moment, in my mind's eye, the tangle of the bergs faded, and I thought of Cliveden Woods and the gay parasols upon the river.

Our hands shook upon the deck-rails as we gaped upon this icy chaos and the hurtle of the floe. The roar of the jostling ice, the ceaseless surge of the current against the bow, the black persistence of the tide flow—all these things seen under the glare—the scorching glare, I may almost call it—of this pitiless moonlight, had an appearance of horrible unreality. I pinched myself as it occurred to me that I might be dreaming, and felt the resultant pain with sorrow.

The whole crew had mustered on deck, and were staring upon this wonder with all their eyes. I strode to Waller's side and fairly had to bawl into his ear to make myself heard above the din of the fighting floes.

"What is it?" I screamed. "What are we to do?"

"Can't say, my lord. Never saw the like before. Nothing we can do as there's no wind. Better get up anchor though," and he beckoned to Janson.

The donkey-engine sent a white puff or two up into the still air, and the capstan began to complain as the chains crept through the hawse-pipes. Eccles's head appeared to announce that *one* rivet was on the collar he had fixed to the riven shaft, and he could venture on twenty turns of the screw to the minute if virtually necessary. His offer was accepted by Waller with effusion, and the screw began to churn a slow, creamy wake upon the blackness. The last of the ice swung by and whirled seaward, the clamor of its striving melting into the sluggish heat of our lame propeller as we got way upon the boat. And thus we ran landward for a length or two to find speed before we turned with the heeling tide.

Suddenly—swift as the cap of a port-fire snaps—the white glare of the moonbeams reddened, died, then leaped again to a flame glow. It wrapped the whole expanse of rock and water in a flood of crimson. The sea became blood. We spun round to face astern and see what this might be. We saw—as it seemed—a preposterous, Titanic travesty of a Crystal Palace firework exhibition. So near did the similitude run, that we listened almost with confidence for the following yawn of applause. The islands behind us were aflame with pyrotechnic devices.

They were swathed in a cloak of fiery mist, wherein great streams of falling fire darted headlong to the sea. On the summit of the central peak rose a monstrous tower of spurning, flaring, heaven-smiting flame, vomited forth as by convulsions from an inner furnace, and this roared with thunderous echoes in the very heart of the hill—echoes that sprang and smote themselves in deafening chorus from crag to crag, booming across the smooth surface of the flood that bore down upon the isles devouringly.

Hell itself was spouting forth. On the crumbling heights the flames danced in wanton, merciless hunger. They toyed in terrible mockery with their own reflection in the swift-tided sea. They shook with their fierce spasms the bursting rocks. Before them the granite dissolved into a very paste. And over all crept slowly, gently, irresistibly, a fog of rising steam, where the boiling lava met the ice-strewn ocean, wrapping the torn wounds in the cliff-side as in a soft lint upon their bleedings. Across this veil the shudders of the rending cliff played in ruddy reflections, rippling across it like searchlight rays as the hot molten matter gouted from the crags.

For a second or two no one spoke, dwelling silently upon the grim wonder of it. Then a sob of terror broke across the tension of the stillness, and Lady Delahay sank to the deck. I raised her quickly, and placed her in a deck-chair. Then I looked round me.

On my right Gerry, Denvarre, and Lessaution were clutching the rail before them in stiff, constrained attitudes. The responsive emotions worked across their faces as they watched the travail of the peak. As some gaping fissure spued up a froth of vivid flame, their lips parted in automatic unison to the sundering stone. Vi Delahay, stretching an unconscious arm, groped for something tangible to rest upon, and found Gerry's hand. One could trace the train of thought by which she buttressed her agitated soul in thus finding support for her body. Gerry remained unconscious of the honor done him. Garlicke and Janson, silhouetted against the red gleam of sea and fire, stood with mouths agape, hands on hips, and eyes that stared unwinkingly—intentness personified. Waller and Rafferty, their grasp still upon the wheel, gazed over their shoulders into the crimson distance behind them, heedless of their charge, rigid as men paralyzed. The crew, distributed each at his post where surprise had found and stiffened him, looked like so many mummies. Just in front of me, Lady Delahay, sunk upon her chair in a disordered heap, covered her face with her palms. I was beginning to peer round me uneasily for the one face I missed.

A gentle pressure upon my shoulder showed me Gwen at my side. She was facing the glare, one hand clenched upon her bosom, the other unknowingly poised upon my arm. Her little nostrils were dilated, her face was aglow, excitement was dancing in her eyes. She never turned or stirred as I edged closer, sliding my hand dishonorably under her palm. Thus stood we all, agape, waiting, staring, wondering.

Suddenly the giant column swung sideways, rushed skyward again, and then twisted itself into knots and coronals of ravening fire. As if in agony it bowed and contorted itself seaward, and the roar of its anguish sped across the ripples toward us with the shock of an Atlantic gust. It was a bellow wrung from the tortured throat of the very earth.

A sigh burst from Gwen's lips, and her grasp tightened upon my thankful fingers. She turned to face me, and I could read the new-born terror in her eyes. Her other hand she thrust with a repellent gesture towards the writhings of the crater, and rested her forehead ever so lightly upon the lapels of my coat to shut out the hideous sight. Being only a man and not a graven image my arm slipped into its appointed place. It clasped her waist of its own accord, though the wicked thrill that ran up it and settled very near my heart reminded me that I was exercising a right that was another's. But there was no getting it away by then.

Denvarre I could see still stood hypnotized into stillness with the rest of our company, who all kept to their rigid, constrained attitudes. Lessaution's lips were beginning to twitch with words for which he could find no voice, and a low moan broke from Lady Delahay. Of those who dared to look, not one could remove his concentrated gaze.

Another crash, sharp and strident as the crack of a thunder-bolt, smote across the surface of the waters. It swelled with devil-ish crescendo into a roar that threatened to burst our ear-drums. They throbbed and palpitated to the limits of tension. A blare of yellow flame filled the horizon. The island peak seemed to leap bodily heavenwards, and the lower crags toppled and reeled swayingly. Streams of lava bubbled and boiled from a thousand rifts and rendings of the rocks. The mass writhed like a tor-mented monster. A yet greater cloud of steam arose, and through it the fierce conflagration played and twined itself, till all the sea and land seemed bathed in a fog of blood and fire. As the liquid stone was vomited out in splashes, it rattled in a hissing patter round us. The eternal turmoils of the lowest pit seemed loose.

One more frightful shock and ear-splitting roar. Then a mountain seemed to grow upon the bosom of the deep. Black and awesome it rose under that flaming pall; silent, dark, and threatening it swung itself up from ocean's depths, screening from us by its awful stature the raging destruction behind. High and yet higher it mounted and swelled and rolled upon us, smooth and swart as midnight. Oily and crestless billows rippled and webbed across it in festoons. The lurid reflections gleamed upon it like the flicker of swords ashock. In a majesty of resist-less might it hung over us—a doom unavertable.

As the first slope of the hill of waters slid beneath our keel I tore myself from my trance of fascination. I dashed forward and raised Lady Delahay. With a kick I burst open the door of the companion and thrust her through, turning desperately for Gwen. With the lurch of the rising deck I staggered, slipped, and fell backward. My shoulder caught the door and slammed it to. With an oath I scrambled up to clutch her fiercely.

The whole scene was bright before me as I turned. Every soul on board stood out in a clearness like the day. Against the mast stood Gerry, one arm round it, one round Vi's waist, while before the two of them Garlicke and Lessaution had sprung, facing sternly the hill of death, jealously valiant in their pride of race. To the left Janson and Denvarre still held the rail, staring aft with wide, fascinated eyes. Waller and Rafferty at the wheel stood expectant, their shoulders squared to meet and give to the coming shock. The crew, distributed here and there in two and threes, were bracing themselves against the deck-house, mast, or funnel. In the utter quiet the last few wreaths of steam from the engine died circling into the still air.

Up, up we staggered, and little whirls and boils from the under-current shot creamy and foam-flecked to the surface. Up—still rising fast, as the billows broke suddenly from the calm, and chased each other over its heaving bosom. Up yet again, and the red glow of the volcanoes beat no longer upon the faces of the unconquered cliffs before us, but upon their very summits, and upon the wide waste of emptiness behind.

Then as the full surge of the reeling ridge of ocean swept us forward, the crown of the topmost rollers broke aboard. With a crash it roared white and foaming along our decks, and in a trice we were carried in a huddle of men and splintered spars into the deep bay of the forward bulwarks. There, bruised and speechless, breathless, with limbs entwined in limbs, and ropes and timbers woven and splayed about our bodies, we lay helpless as kittens drowning in a bucket, and the ship shot forward upon the head of the great ridge-wave straight for the cruel precipice of granite. Without a hope and stunned beyond struggling we waited for the final crash and oblivion.

As we charged along that wild race into eternity, the great crags that five minutes before had hung mockingly above our heads sank below us, and we rode high above their cringing heads.

We realized as in a moment, that the growing bulk of billows would lift us cleanly over them. A hundred yards more at speed, and the cliffs were gone, and a broad wilderness of waters swarmed over their crannies, and into the rocky void beyond. As by a miracle the skirting waves that ran before us filled the dry plain, and with half the weight of the sea-torrent still behind us we shot out on to the bosom of this sudden lake.

Like an arrow we swung across its turbid shallows, charging toward the far side, where it was bounded by a second terrace of sheer stone. The foremost waves smote the rock face full. Charging back, their defeated fury met and foamed around us, catching us before we reached the cruel reefs. The in-coming and out-flowing surges sprang together almost beneath our keel, and we tossed and reeled from one to the other in the final throb of the great convulsion. Then the fighting breakers spread abroad. Each spent its dying force upon its neighbor, and ere we could extract ourselves from the mass of wreckage that wedged us in below the bulwarks, the yacht was swinging masterless and idle upon a rippling, white-flecked lagoon, showing less turmoil than a mid-June day can raise on Windermere.

10

BEHIND THE BARRIER

Gwen was unconscious as I lifted her, and a bruise showed red and staring on her white temple. I laid her gently against the bulwark and made a dash for the saloon. Lady Delahay lay in a dead faint at the stair-foot, slipping there, I supposed, after her unceremonious bundling through the door. I snatched the whiskey from the sideboard, laid the good lady on the sofa and raced on deck again. Gerry was on his feet, and the rest gathered themselves out of the tangle one by one. Lessaution was the first to break silence.

"Behold," he said triumphantly, "that we are on the top," and he spread abroad his little arms like a glorified cock a-crow, revelling in the achievement of his hopes, and utterly ignoring the desperate result.

I shoved him impatiently on one side to get back to Gwen again. She was leaning white-faced and motionless against the bulwark, and my heart gave a queer thump when I saw how still she lay. I put my arm around her, and ever so gently tilted a few drops of spirit between her lips. A sigh and a gasp broke from her, and the color began to pass back into her cheeks. She opened her eyes, and looked at me dreamily. A satisfied little smile edged her mouth, and she settled back against my shoulder with a murmur of content, nestling into the encirclement of my arm as happily as if I was Denvarre's self.

A blow fell upon my back, and I found Gerry standing over me.

"Give it me," said he shortly, and I handed over the flask. He dashed across to Vi again and began to dose her energetically, not desisting till she coughed desperately and motioned him away with a weak gesture of her hand. The whiskey began to circulate among the others rapidly.

"What's happened?" said Gwen's low voice from my shoulder, and she opened her eyes again wearily. "Ah, I remember—the wave—and the rocks and—and all that." Her voice died away indistinctly as her eyes closed.

"It's all right," I whispered into the little ear that shone so rosy pink against the dark sodden cloth of my smoking suit, "we're all here. Nothing's amiss with anybody."

Her hand fluttered out to me, and caught and felt my arm as if to satisfy herself that one at least was there with whole body.

"Mother and Vi?" she questioned.

"Right as the mail," quoth I cheerfully, "and Denvarre too," I added circumspectly, though I don't know why she should have been shy to ask for him.

"Ah, Lord Denvarre, and Mr. Garlicke, and the Professor, and Mr. Carver, and everybody?"

"Everybody," I agreed, "though we haven't exactly called names yet. Nothing but bruises, as far as I can tell."

"I'm—I'm keeping you from doing things," she said suddenly, scrambling to her feet, "and I ought to look after mother." She tottered as she leaned against me, and I—well, of course I had to hold her up. Then I heard Denvarre's deep voice at my elbow.

"Can I be of any use?" he asked, with extraordinary politeness, and I got a look between the eyes which told me I was taking more than mere courtesy demanded.

She smiled sweetly at him, took his arm, and began to step uncertainly toward the saloon. Then she stopped suddenly and turned toward me again.

"Thank you," she said, looking over her shoulder, and went on. But I never heard the words said quite like that, I think, for I could have kissed her feet for them, as well as have cursed her for a heartless coquette.

As they disappeared I began to look up the others. Rafferty and Waller were blinking like owls, and slapping themselves, inquiringly. They had been tumbled off the bridge like shot pheasants, and had been flung down upon us as we spluttered and squirmed among the splinters. What with the fall and hitting hard wood they were pretty considerably knocked out of time. Lessaution was gesticulating wildly, asserting that he had

swallowed salt-water by the hectolitre. Forgetting to close his
astonished mouth when the wave struck us, he had engulfed it
to the full extent of his capacity, and he condemned it as the
most poisonously cold draught that had ever been forced upon
him. But even this had failed to subdue his jubilation at having
attained to the heights of his desire. Garlicke, who had been
stunned and over-dosed with neat whiskey, was coughing like a
sick sheep, and the sympathetic Janson was slapping him on
the back. Poor Eccles was being slowly extracted from below
the bowsprit with a broken collar-bone, but was bearing up
against his affliction with a Scotch impassiveness and a fat
spirit-flask. He, it appeared, was the only item in the list of casu-
alties.

He and his underlings crept back to the stoke-hole and reported
it three feet deep in water, but the fires not wholly drowned. The
shaft was still workable, and by a little stirring of the clinker
they gave us enough steam to stay our vague circlings on our
lake. We backed, as we drifted shoreward, and swung the lead.
We found twenty fathoms. So there in the centre of that new-
formed sea-pond we anchored, amidst an arid expanse of rock-
bound desolation, and left discussion of our unpleasant situation for drier circumstances. All hands slipped below to find such
changes of raiment as had been left unsoaked, and to rectify if
possible some of the more desperate confusion of saloon and
cabin. And thus ended that wondrous half-hour of terror and
upheaval.

The dawn was breaking when we reassembled on deck to look
round us. Over the cliff- top behind us we could still see the
island volcano belching smoke and steam, but it was half the
height it had stood the night before. The lake on which we
floated was about a mile long and half-a-mile broad. It was
bounded on the landward side by huge basaltic crags that shot
up ragged and desolate against a steel-blue sky.

To the right a rocky plain spread flat and unbroken for a
mile or so, terminating in uneven, boulder-strewn slopes. These
were gashed and riven in all directions by the clefts that ran
black and shadowy into the depths of the hill. To the left was a
giant mountain, and down its flanks crept river-like a stupendous

glacier, our lake lapping its blue crevasses at the nearer end. The water completely hid any moraine there might have been before the irruption of the whelming wave. Between us and the tops of the sea-cliff's was a narrow strand of rock, covered with the silt of the retreating waters. Among the litter the bodies of one or two sea-lions and seals were visible, their fur shining wet and glossy in the light of the rising sun. On the shore beneath the far cliff a whale was stranded, thwacking his huge tail resoundingly upon the boulders as he vainly tried to thrust himself back into his native element. Around us on every side great masses of sea-fowl swung and wreathed themselves in white circles, filling the air with their cries and their droppings, pouncing ever and again on the dead fish and garbage that covered the surface, fighting and howking clamorously at each other for the spoil.

It did not need a critical examination to show that we were in a trap. The wave had borne us over the cliffs a hundred feet at least above tide-level, and now they stood implacable between us and any chance of an escape seaward. Here we were in a six-hundred ton ship afloat in less than six hundred acres of water. It was not an exhilarating prospect.

Naturally I turned to Waller in this seeming *impasse*. Of all the good men who walk this uncertain earth of ours, I know none who inspire confidence to the same extent as do those who go down to the sea in ships. Their profession demands that they should briskly and at uneven intervals extract themselves—or, more often others—from the tightest of tight places. They fight the outrageous tactics of the wind and sea with happy confidence. They defeat these eternal adversaries with no sort of pride in their victories, but with painstaking completeness. And when occasionally to them comes the overthrow, they meet it with a cheer. To us of the land-lubbing profession they are, in their supreme cocksureness, as little gods.

"Well, my lord," sail the captain succinctly, "it's evident that before this southern summer's over we must send word to the Falklands. The ice will close down on us in March. We can't move the ship. We must send a boat. It is a question of finding a place to launch it. As far as one's eye goes there's nothing but a precipice for miles. We could perhaps arrange pulleys to let the cutter down, but it would be difficult. It would be easier to take her a few miles on rollers. I submit that the crying necessity at the present moment is an outlet to the sea."

"Well, then, of course we must find one," said I cheerily, "and to find one we must get ashore. Let's have the launch out as soon as possible," and I walked away to announce his views to the others.

We breakfasted before we set out, while they were setting the boat afloat and getting up steam in her tiny boiler. The ladies had not yet reappeared, so we were all able to voice our emotions and hazard our opinions without fear of making them uneasy. Lessaution as usual led the conversational *mêlée*.

His knowledge of seismic effects and huge waves produced thereby seemed intimate. He demonstrated that it was an honor to have been associated in this astounding upheaval, whence few had formerly returned alive. He cited instances from Portugal to Polynesia of similar disasters, giving gruesome categories of the demolished. He went into details that turned us from our food. It was only by the show of a universal unbelief in his theories, and a consequent rise of his sentiments to higher planes of passion, that we finally found quiet. He departed on deck furious with our want of intelligence, which he designated as of the most hog-like. We found him all agog for adventure, though still contemptuous, when we rejoined him.

The little oil dinghy was snapping and fussing away by this time, and Gerry, Denvarre, and I tumbled into her with the Frenchman, and were set ashore in five minutes. First of all we ran up the slope between us and the cliff to look seawards.

But for the steam-cloud that hung heavily over the ruined islands six miles away, and for the floating bodies of a few seals and smaller whales, there was no sign of the upheaval of the night before. The sea was lapping sleepily against the ice-smoothed rocks below, gurgling in the crannies, and the sun glittered on a still and radiant surface.

A northwest wind was just beginning to touch the glassy surface, and the floe was swinging back almost imperceptibly toward the cliffs, returning from the distance to which it had been carried by the outsuck. Terns and kittywakes were dipping backward and forward with shrill cries, hovering and quarrelling over the lumps of dead fish and other remnants of the turmoil. Here and there a sea-lion rose out of the depths to roll and play with soft splashings in the sunshine, or to stop and stare up the cliffs at us with stupid, innocent eyes.

The atmosphere was keen and clear as a winter's day in the Engadine, and we could follow the circling unbroken line of cliffs to the far horizon. There was an exhilarating nip in the air, though the sunlight that poured back from rock and sea made it quiver hazily. It was a glorious day, and would have been an uplifting one if things had not gone so perversely and entirely wrong. For instead of enjoying this heavenly sunshine on the yacht's deck in lazy contentment, we had to tramp weary miles in search of what might be unattainable.

There was no sort of doubt but that we were in a serious fix. The continuous and implacable wall of rock stretched, for all we could tell, to the world's end. There was no escape for us except by sea, and we had no proper means of launching out into the deep. We were as surely held, perched up as we were on these desolate summits, as if we had been behind the bars and bolts of a prison.

We walked about four miles along that remorseless line of crags. Never a break did we find, never a vestige of a shallow at its foot. Look where we would was green water unplumbable, and not so much as the suspicion of any shoal that could give us launching room for a boat.

We returned silent and depressed, the full significance of our plight just working into our minds. Even Lessaution, though he really concerned himself little about a departure, which he would have willingly deferred a month at least, was affected by the general dejection, and gave up attempting to instruct us further on our surroundings. Gerry and I added this new weight to our desperation phlegmatically, feeling that the cup of our misery had been full before, and might, for all we cared, run over unstayed. The four of us had much the effect of hounds slinking home out of covert, having been left therein during the run of the season.

We slouched down the shores of our little lake, and somehow the ship seemed to have come nearer since we started. How

or why Waller had considered it necessary to move her, I could
not conceive. Nor could we find the great boulder by which we
had landed, though we felt sure that we had followed the same
direction to it from the cliff-top.

We waved listlessly with our handkerchiefs for the launch
to be sent to us, waiting at the water's edge therewhile. Denvarre
was still grubbing about among the rocks farther up the stones.
Suddenly he gave a yell.

"Why, the water's sunk," he bawled. "Here's the rock we
landed on. The absurd lake's running away."

He was standing forty or fifty yards above us and we ran
and joined him. As we looked higher up the sloping shore, we
recognized what had been the water's edge when we landed.
There was no sort of doubt that the new-formed lake was leaking out again rapidly, and that our ship would very shortly be
in a regular dry-dock. We went on to consider that if the yacht
took ground on that flat, rocky bottom she would careen over,
and probably smash in her sides. We should be left homeless
amid that desolation—a pretty kettle of fish.

As soon as the dinghy had snorted across and taken us
aboard, we sought Waller and explained to him our discovery.
Occupied with other matters he had never noticed the shrink-
age, and had the lead hove at once. It gave six fathoms less than
before, but—what was more satisfactory—showed fourteen still
remaining. We knew the sea-level could not be more than fifty
feet below us, so unless the water was draining away into some
unimaginable gulf, there would remain thirty feet or more for
our good ship to float in.

This was cheering in some ways, though it detracted in no
wise from the hopelessness of our situation from the point of
view of a possible rescue.

We resolved therefore that at earliest dawn a select expedition should set forth to carry inquiry further into the land, taking
with it arms, food, and the necessary accoutrement for two days
at least, that every portion of the seaward face of the cliffs might
be examined for the greatest distance to which we could transport a boat. The party was to consist of Denvarre, Gerry, one
sailor—name of Parsons—and myself. Lessaution we judged it

best to leave, as we felt sure that his build did not fit him for prolonged exercise across the boulder-strewn confusion of this land of desolation. We felt, too, that he could amuse himself in delving around the foreshore of the lake, where antiquities were just as probable as further west; we said nothing to him of our project. Garlicke preferred to stay and "protect the ladies," as he put it, and Waller's business was on his ship. We four therefore spent the afternoon in dozing, to make up for the exertions of the night, and to prepare for the toils of the morrow. We rose for dinner, and endeavored to pass a cheerful evening, but Gerry took his cigar on deck at an early opportunity, unable to sustain the conflict with his natural passions which the sight of Garlicke's attentions to Vi provoked, and I fought down my overmastering desire to throttle Denvarre, with a stolid determination that made me extremely unsociable, and a most apathetic conversationalist. So uneasily the after-dinner period passed, and we turned in to dream of the undying fires of Erebus in collusion with the out-bursting of an uncontrolled and evergrowing Niagara.

Now behold us next morning setting forth into the unknown, with a great waving of handkerchiefs from the good folk on deck. We crossed the moat—as I christened it—scrambled ashore, and started along the incline of bare rock that led toward the clifftops. The going after the first half-mile was desperately rough. Great slab-like boulders, round and smooth-faced, lay about in gigantic masses, and the clefts between them were wide and deep. Laboriously we hopped from one to the other, getting many a bruise and thump as we slid upon their glassy surfaces. The slope that led up from the lake edge to the western hills was like a great moraine. It ran to the foot of ranged rocks that buttressed the lower shoulders of the peak. The quantities of pebbles were arranged in irregular ridge and furrow formation, growing in size and smoothness as we approached the cliff-face. We proceeded excessively slowly; half an hour's toil took us a bare mile.

As we paused and looked round, wiping our brows, a yell came sharply through the still air, and an extraordinary object staggered into our vision. Round the corner of basalt which hid the ship from us emerged a thing like a monstrous beetle. With frantic gesticulation it beckoned us to stop. It was with some difficulty we recognized the familiar form of Lessaution, for he had done his best to disguise it. His peaceful person had assumed the fantastic presentment of a mediaeval buccaneer. According to his lights, I suppose, it was the strictly correct habiliment of the explorer.

A blue cap, something like that assigned to statues of Liberty, dangled from his poll, flopping with studied *abandon* over his left ear. He wore a baggy Norfolk jacket, with pockets erupting all over it like sartorial warts; huge gray worsted stockings came over his knees and half-way up his thighs, and immense brown boots were laced over his skinny little calves. In his hand was an axe; round his waist was a belt; from this dangled a sheath-knife, flanked by an enormous Colt's revolver; above his left shoulder flaunted the muzzle of a shot-gun, the butt of which seriously incommoded the play of his right elbow. He stood forth the pirate of cheap fiction confessed.

He was scrambling over the boulders frantically. Before he had traversed twenty yards of the uncertain footing of the moraine he fell upon his face. He found the position so much to his liking that he remained on hands and knees, squirming clatteringly over the glassy pebbles. We felt that Gerry was by no means inapt in likening him to a caterpillar on eggs. We sat down to smile, take our breath, and let him overtake us. This he did in the space of about ten minutes, grunting like an overdriven cab-horse, glowing with perspiration, and begrimed with unutterable dirt. He sank with a bump of exhaustion upon a handy slab of granite and began his reproaches.

"You would leave behind your little Lessaution?" he queried accusingly. "We, who pant, do you see, to gaze upon the wonders of the land. Where had you the heart to treat him so?" and his brown eyes directed an upbraiding glance upon us that might have melted the very stones.

We explained that it was his comfort that had been our first thought, and that we had deemed the way too long and the work too arduous for him. We hinted that the ladies would experience a vivid desolation deprived of his company. We had believed that he would have found ample room and opportunity for research in the immediate vicinity of the vessel. He was not to be appeased.

"No," he replied; "when they told me that you had set forth, and unknown to me, I asked myself how I had offended you. Is it, I said, that there can be jealousy between two nations who share the responsibilities of civilization? Do they wish that France shall not have her part in this adventure? I could not believe it. I call for the boat. I accoutre myself"—and he pointed with pride to the armory that swayed about him, "and I follow with great speed. Let me offer my comradeship in this expedition. Give me my part in your perils," and he flung out his arms entreatingly.

How could one refuse a request so touchingly put forth? We welcomed him to our company with effusion, though with inward annoyance. We felt that our progress would of necessity be a great deal tardier in consequence, but in mere charity and courtesy nothing else was to be done.

He further imparted the information that he was not so young as when he was of the foremost runners of the Lycée, and that his little heart was going pit-a-pat. In effect, with this so great racing it quivered like an automobile. But of what consideration was this when he was once again amongst his dear rascals, and accompanying them in their valiant purpose of research? One minute to regain the even tenor of his pulses, and then, forward! Let us press on to victories.

We counselled him bluntly to keep his breath for pure purposes of locomotion, and after a slight rest set forward again to our monotonous stumblings among the endless reaches of heaped stone.

11

A GLACIER CAVE AND WHAT LAY THEREIN

An hour's labor saw us well over the moraine, and beginning to worm our way into the deep clefts that gaped in the flanks of the hillside. Heretofore we had kept rigidly to the neighborhood of the shore, but now we had to shift our course inland. The mountain breasted up to the water's edge sheer and inaccessible. We could see no possible chance of a break in its surface for miles.

There was nothing to do but cross the ridge before us, and take up our quest on the far side. If we found the way rough and dangerous, and deemed it impossible to carry over the sections of our cutter, we should have to return and recommence our quest along the eastern shores. But as far as we had gone there was nothing impracticable for men taking fair precautions and proceeding slowly, though at times the ground was steep and broken.

Before us a long, deep, shadowy gorge cut into the heart of the mountain. It led upward toward a narrow pass that dented into the crown of the ridge. This gave hope of a moderately easy passage to the other side. About half-a-mile in front of us the cañon narrowed, and the cliffs grew together, nearly overhanging in parts.

The going, however, was better. At times the path was as smooth as a paved street. Here and there enormous blocks of granite were ranged alongside it. They were curiously square, having almost the finished look of building material.

Gerry was the first to remark upon these things.

"There never was a better imitation of an Edinburgh street," said he wearily. "These cobbles are as hard and even as can be."

They certainly were set together in regular fashion, and we examined them inquisitively, wondering what geological freak had brought about their ordered formation. Lessaution clapped his hands and shouted.

"Aha, my friends, aha! What have you to say now? A boulevard, is it not? Who made this road, my little Iscariots? Did it make itself out of nothing? Did the stones roll themselves together? Tell me that, my braves," and he grunted triumphantly, waggling his hands at the rows of measured blocks.

"I think," said I irritably, "that any people who put them here with a set purpose must have been of a race of engineering idiots. What in the name of wonder could a road be doing here, leading to nowhere in particular out of this chaos? It's simply a geological freak. Some stratum has slipped."

"It is a road, I tell you," shrieked the *savant*, "a road, a road, a road! It has been begun to fetch stones upon—this stone that we see ready cut for moving. Is it that you are blind? Can you not see?"

I had no wish to delay the expedition further while he lectured us on this supposititious discovery. I answered him patiently.

"My dear Professor," said I, "let us agree that it is a grand staircase, or anything else you like to think it. But for goodness' sake let us get on. What we are looking for is not a highway, but a beach—unless you would like to stay and investigate the matter by yourself," I added hopefully.

He came along muttering many things. He was understood to say that some people had no more enthusiasm than a slug; that the British nation at large was utterly wanting in verve and spirituality; that in our poor company his intellect roamed desolate and companionless. But we regarded him not, striding upward till we reached the point where the cañon narrowed and darkened over us.

This defile continued for about a quarter of a mile, and along it still ran the curious effect as of a cobbled road. At the end of the neck we could see that the valley divided, one half continuing up the pass, the other striking away sharply to the right.

We reached the sharp spar of the mountain that hid the second valley from our sight. We rounded the corner, all five of us abreast. As a single man we stopped in our surprise.

Almost to our feet a mighty glacier rolled, clear, clean, and blue as the firmament, still and cold as the shadow of death. A

gasp went up simultaneously from each throat as we stepped so
swiftly and unknowingly into the presence of this mighty ice-
river, standing out in such lonely whiteness and solemnity; for
an appreciable moment no one spoke.

Then came a shrill yell from our irrepressible friend. He
pointed up the side of the new valley, his little eyes fairly blazing
in their sockets.

"There, there!" he howled, "as I told you, it is there. Name
of all the names, let us climb," and he scrabbled at the smooth
rock face that fenced the entrance of the far cañon, plucking at
it like a caged squirrel.

We followed the direction of his forefinger, and I will confess that my first feeling was one of desperate annoyance, for
on the edge of the ice, standing out yellow-gray against the blue
crevices, was something uncommonly like the wall of a ruined
or half-finished building. Nothing could explain this away, and
it seemed possible that Lessaution might have some ground for
his fancies. Any wonder or interest I might have felt in this discovery was swallowed by the irritation I felt in remembering
what scorn I had always thrown upon Gerry's and Lessaution's
imaginings, which now might well prove to be borne out by facts.
I gaped upon the phenomenon therefore distrustfully, as if it
might be, perchance, a put-up hoax.

The Frenchman was still extended upon the ice-planed rocks,
wriggling like a worm, but advancing not at all. Gerry seized
one of his outstretched legs and gave him a lusty shove. The
ungrateful little wretch never so much as offered him thanks or
a tug in return. He gathered himself up, and tore across the confusion of the ice-milled stones like a lapwing.

Parsons respectfully offered a back, as at leap-frog. We took
advantage of it to scale the tiny precipice, and follow in the
savant's tracks. The slow-blooded Mr. Parsons, after eyeing the
unaided ascent that would be his if he pursued us, sat himself
down beside the baggage, and lit his pipe with solemn content.
The rest of us joined Lessaution beside the building, or whatever it might be.

It was supposedly the rear of a house, and ended with great
abruptness where the glacier began. There was no roof, merely

three stone walls built of excessively solid blocks—not natural, but evidently quarried—and at the glacier side it broke off suddenly, as if beaten down by some sudden shock. Inside the walls was nothing but a little heap of dust.

Lessaution ran round and round it and in and out of it like a monkey exploring a new cage. He chattered and swore away to himself, paying no sort of attention to our doings. It was left to Gerry to make the next discovery. He was standing gaping down into the crevasses of the glacier edge.

"Great Heavens!" he ejaculated suddenly. "Look here, you chaps."

Ready for any further astonishment, we flocked to him greedily. He pointed to the unsullied sides of the ice-wall, and therein we saw a wonderful sight. Plain to the view, as if cased in a crystal casket, were more huge blocks of stone, the ice arching over them transparently. Most evidently they were the masonry that had formed the facade of this building, which the glacier must have in part destroyed. They had been swept down into a sort of bay or basin in the rock. In this hollow they were only covered by a shallow of the mighty river of ice, and it had rolled its slow current over them for centuries. But lying, as they did, beneath its sluggish current, they had remained flung up as in a sort of backwater, and free from injury. And here lay the wonder of the thing. For carved on these great monoliths were a hundred cabalistic figures in myriad combinations, every one, as we could clearly trace, formed of the same symbol that figured in my wonderful scroll.

When you are beaten, the grace of a neat surrender will turn tongues from your defeat. I went up to Lessaution with an outstretched hand and an ingratiating smile. He greeted me triumphantly, and with many joyous outcries, but I will say was handsome enough to forego all superior airs of patronage. He made no allusion to my previous scepticism.

I told myself that, in some ways, this discovery was a great misfortune as matters had now turned out. True enough, we had come here to investigate the possible remains of such a race as was now conclusively proved to have existed. Had matters gone as we intended we should have been gratified beyond measure at this result. But as circumstances were, the discovery of a suitable shore for launching our boat was preferable to all the antiquities south of the equator. I ventured on a modified *résumé* of these sentiments, but the Professor snapped at me like an angry parakeet.

"What!" he exploded. "Shall we leave these fine and perfect palaces? Are we to desert them to search for a beach—a muddy bank of sand? No, it is not possible. Here we can delve into a buried past, and explore the relics of a royal race. I plant myself here, and Beelzebub shall not tear me from the spot. Under correction you must see as I do. A beach now—but that is absurd," and he turned to his investigations, waving aside my suggestions superbly.

Gerry and Denvarre were a bit flushed and excited over the matter. The former opined that an hour or two's pottering round these walls might be interesting, and that discoveries worth making might be made. He suggested that the mid-day halt for food should now take place, and that if necessary Lessaution should remain afterward while we strolled forward on our way. We could pick him up on our return.

I agreed to this compromise sulkily, and marched down to where Parsons still smoked patiently among the packs. He rose to his feet, and stood at attention.

"Put up the little cooking tent," said I, "and light the little stove. We're going to camp and lunch."

He began to unfold the canvas and erect the shelter for our little oil oven. I busied myself in getting out the meat pie that Baines had provided, and extracting knives and forks from their various receptacles. Then I sat down upon a boulder and watched Parsons' further operations with a dreamy content in mere idleness and in the sunshine.

"Wonderful pretty, that, m'lord," said Parsons confidentially, as he looked up from his labors, crimson with much bending. He pointed with his finger toward the farthest side of the glacier, whence a stream rippled out patteringly.

I followed the direction of his hand and saw, what, in the general distraction of Lessaution's first find, we had overlooked.

A huge ice-grotto, blue and delicately shaded, ran deeply into the heart of the glacier. The sun sparkled on the archway that spanned the entrance, glowing through panes of clear ice in fifty azure shades and glittering prisms. The stream that purred out, born of the friction on the granite bed below the ice, looked heartsome and inviting in the sunlight. It was in contrast to the stony immobility around, and I rose and took a few steps forward to contemplate it.

The cave ran straight back from its mouth into the ice-hollows, and the reflections lit it up for some little way back into its dark recesses. It looked mysteriously fascinating, as its blue shadows melted into the impenetrable gloom. I stepped a few yards into it, admiring the delicious tints that filtered through the roof. The thought struck me that while our lunch was warming it might be amusing to investigate this sub-glacial waterway. I returned to Mr. Parsons, who had watched my motion with genuine but repressed interest.

"Have we candles?" I inquired.

"I did happen to put in a couple of dips, m'lord, thinking they might come in useful if we camped the night. Not that we have what you'd call much night here," added the sailor, as if it was an additional grievance of these outlandish realms.

He produced his greasy little parcel, and we entered the cavern, getting well dripped on by the way. The little cascades fell freely from the roof in the increasing heat of the sun.

As the gloom deepened we lit up, and I strode ahead holding my candle high in the air. Parsons followed behind, gaping. In this order we plunged into the icy mysteries before us.

The stream was a shallow one—not above four or five inches deep for the most part—and we splashed and slushed along with ease on its sandy bed. But the cold was atrocious. It struck home the deeper for our sudden withdrawal from the full sunlight. As we advanced the clear blue of the ice above the entrance deepened to a sickly green; as we went on to a lurid purple. Finally the rays ceased to percolate through the heavy masses above us. We were in thick darkness—the gloom that has never known the day.

I heard Parsons shiver behind me as he crept closer. The roof-drippings tell with a hollow splash in the pools and shallows. A fearsome stillness filled and pervaded the cave between

these patterings. Our steps and splashings seemed to roar out
with indecent echoes on the awesome quiet. A scene of imperti-
nence—of pushing forwardness—in thus invading these awful
recesses fell upon me. My steps began to slow; a shudder swept
my nerves, making me tremble creepily.

As I slowed and halted I noticed that the drip and trickle
from the roof had ceased. The cave was widening and deepening into a space that the feeble light of our candles refused to
fill. We were in the midst of a growing emptiness.

I looked above me. The roof was lost in gloom. A thick, velvety
blackness was over us, and no answering flash from ice walls
came as I waved my light. We had strayed from under the glacier,
and were overhung by some huge escarpment of the mountain-
side. On the one side of us was the wall of ice; on the other the
sullen gray cliff of granite. The floor was smooth. The stream
oozed along the foot of the ice-wall with a silent, splashless flow.

We walked half aimlessly forward, hesitating for a direction
in this uniform emptiness. Then the light passed uncertainly
upon a yellowish mass a few fathoms before us—a vague breaking of the dimness of the void. We drew toward it, and the shadows danced and played upon clean-cut blocks; there was no
mistaking their nature. They were quarried—the squared masonry
of a buried city.

Parsons crept closer again.

"'Anged if it ain't a 'ouse," he whispered, and it seemed to
me that I could hear the throb of his pulses in the stillness. "A
bloomin' 'ouse," he repeated, with the evident desire to prove
to himself that this was no delusive dream.

We both breathed hard as we continued staring at the yellow
gable, watching the waverings of the dip-light across its stones.
Emotions that varied only in degree filled our minds alike. We
were, without any doubt, horribly afraid. For half a minute we
stood unstirring. Then by a common and inquisitive impulse
we advanced shoulder to shoulder to the doorway.

There was no door. A fungus-smelling pile of sodden pulp
showed what might have been wood long centuries before. Beside
the postern lay a metal bucket, dull and dirt-colored; opposite
the doorway was an open hearth. The floor was inches deep in a

curious, strong-smelling, fungoid litter. Among it lay half-a-dozen or more utensils, all of the same dull-colored metal. In the ingle nook was a stone seat.

Another entrance gave upon an inner room. To this we strode delicately. At our entry we stayed our on-coming with a great gasp. I stepped back upon Parsons—shuffling and mowing at him unseeingly. My eyes were glued upon the far side of the room, while my feet with automatic intelligence endeavored to carry me out of it.

A stone slab filled the far side of this recess, and on it were heaped various sad-hued fabrics—bed coverings of sorts. They were discolored with age, but undecayed by reason of the undying frost. Above the tossed and furrowed ends of these rags a face appeared—a face lined with a thousand wrinkles, drawn and yellow as parchment. The features had been old and agonized or ever the breath left the body. They had been of noble outline in life, but terror had been laid like a thick mask upon the dead lineaments. It was the face of one alone with death—a death that crept to it slowly, while the soul waited in its desolation, helpless, alone, despairing.

Parsons found a cracked and reedy voice.

"Gawd pity 'im," he mumbled, closing up to me fearfully; "'e 'ad it 'eavy at the last."

The flicker of the wavering candlelight was chasing the gray shadows across and about the fear-haunted face. If was as if the agonies of centuries back had leaped to life. A drop from the roof fell upon the wick of a dip, making it hiss and sputter raggedly; the to and fro of the twittering rays made the dead lip's twitch, as it seemed. The shade that swept the rigid form, as we moved toward it, gave it the horrid appearance of shuddering, and thereat I heard Parsons' breath whistle between his teeth. The black hair fell lank and straight from the furrowed forehead, and as the thin light gleamed upon it, it seemed as if it waved in an unfelt draught.

We bent over the poor, distorted apology for a human form. The hands were crossed upon the wasted chest, each twined within the other convulsively. The eyes were half closed. The sheen of the dead pupils seemed to watch us furtively between the wrinkled lids. The lips were agape, and the teeth set stiffly upon each other. The muscles in the worn throat stood out like the kinks in the parcelling of a worn hawser. The whole face and figure gave the impression of despair personified—of death awaited lingeringly, and the bitter cup thereof drained to the last dregs.

There was a plash and gurgle from the stream behind me, and the swish of hasty stumblings through its pools. I was suddenly aware that I was alone before this gruesomeness—that down the watery pathway we had come Parsons was making for wholesome light and air at the top of his speed. He ran staggeringly, holding out his candle before him, and as I saw the outline of his body diminishingly black through the doorway, a cold dread caught me by the throat. Horror gripped my pulses clammily.

Somehow, within the next ten seconds, I found myself hunting Parsons hard down that icy waterway, with fright—pure, unadulterated funk—following desperately swift upon my footsteps. I stopped to consider nothing, save that behind me was the shadow of death centuries old in all its hoary malignancy, while in front was sunlight and nervous, warm-blooded humanity as personified by the escaping Parsons. With these considerations carven on my brain I splashed along like a hunted otter. Reeling, white-faced, shamed, but full of gratitude for the warm blessing of the sun and sea-borne air, we stumbled out into the cañon, and squatted again beside our baggage. We looked not each other in the eyes for the space of a full minute; then I gave a half-hysteric chuckle.

"It was only a mummy of sorts," I explained apologetically to James Parsons, seaman and coward.

"That's as mebbe, m'lord," quoth Mr. Parsons with dogged deliberation, "but it 'appens to be the first I've seen of whatever it 'appens to be, an' please the Lord I'll never see another." He capped this slightly involved indication of his views with a mighty spit into the clearness of the stream, the while he shifted his quid thankfully.

"Nonsense," said I, with a great show of spirit and discipline, "you must come back with me at once. I dare say there are discoveries to be made of lots of things. Gold, very likely, and other valuables," and I rolled my eyes at him. He only sniffled doubtfully.

"With all due respeck, m'lord," answered the seaman firmly, "I would not go back if you dammed the brook with di'monds."

"You're a coward, Parsons," said I disgustedly. "What's there to be afraid of? It's simply the body of a man who was caught by the glacier when it overwhelmed this valley, as it evidently has done. It's the cold that's kept him fresh."

"Yes, m'lord," answered Parsons, without conviction.

"So of course we ought to look into the matter further. Who knows what there may be besides what we've seen? I shall call the others."

"Yes, m'lord," quoth Mr. Parsons, with steadfast respect. "I should certainly call the others."

I turned away, disgusted with his cowardice, scrambled up the side of the ravine again, and strolled back to where they were still delving away among the rubbish. They took no notice of me, and I lit a cigarette with deliberation before I inquired if they had found anything.

"Ouf! but you annoy me with your questions," snapped Lessaution. "Is it that you expect us to examine the whole of this affair in ten minutes? This is the discovery of the century—the most magnificent one that has been made about peoples of which we know nothing. And you say have you found anything? We have found a house, and have been here the littlest half-hour."

"Ah," said I superciliously; "I think you're wasting your time."

He boiled over at me, his face the color of beetroot.

"Can you not search for your beach without disturbing the important investigations of *savants*? What is your beach to me? Go you on and look for it, and leave us to dig at our leisure." He snorted with indignation as he turned away.

"Well," said I apathetically, "of course you know best. If this roofless hovel is enough for you, well and good. But when a few hundred yards away a whole city awaits your inspection, I should have thought—"

"What!" they all bawled, leaping up. "Where? Which?" and they stared round them as if they expected to see it perched on the adjoining precipices.

"Anywhere but where you're looking," I returned dryly. "*There*, if you're so anxious to know," and I pointed into the depths of the glacier.

"But how—" began Gerry.

"By the front door," said I, interrupting. "There's a passage right into the heart of it, and here have you all been idling about this one outlying bothie, while Parsons and I with some show of energy have been finding out—" It was no use continuing, for they had all forsaken me and raced down the slope toward the baggage, bawling aloud to Parsons for the candles. I followed at a more leisurely pace, and before I had time to overtake them, they had disappeared into the cavern with the only two lights. As I did not feel inclined to follow in the dark, I sat myself down to inspect the meat pie, and await their return.

They came staggering out in about half-an-hour, bearing something between the three of them. What sense of decency or of the fitness of things they possessed I don't know, but it was the mummy they'd got, arranged on a sort of hammock of their coats, which they carried by the sleeves. The unfortunate corpse rolled and crumbled hideously as it came thus immodestly out into the sunlight after its centuries of seclusion. I could not restrain my indignation. Even Parsons was moved.

"It ain't 'ardly decent," he observed, looking across at me.

"I think you're the most disreputable scoundrels I ever came across," said I warmly, advancing upon the party. "You're worse than Burke or Hare. Why couldn't you let the wretched carcass sleep in peace?"

"Humbug!" quoth Gerry discourteously. "D'you think we're going to let the only Mayan extant rot away in the bowels of a glacier for want of a little embalming? The Professor's going to stuff it."

"Oh, he is, is he?" said I, and smiled into my mustache. I had a good idea of what would occur when this worn carrion had been out in the sunlight for an hour or two. "I wish him joy," I added politely.

They set it down upon a smooth lump of granite, and the Professor tripped round it ecstatically. Denvarre and Gerry listened to his chatterings with the solemn attention of profound ignorance, and Parsons eyed the whole proceeding with melancholy and distrust. The sun was exceedingly powerful, and I lit another cigarette. After about ten minutes I sniffed suspiciously.

"Your beastly mummy's waking up," I hazarded. "There's a confounded smell of musk."

Lessaution opened his mouth to answer me. His eyes were agleam with native fire, and his podgy little nostrils and upper lip were curled into a sneer. I perceived that he proposed to wither me with a torrent of sarcasm.

As he stood opposite me his gaze took in the whole of the upper valley over my shoulder. Instead of the volley of winged words that I expected, the only sound that escaped between his teeth was a raucous croak. His mouth stayed, gaping widely. The fire died from his eyes, and I saw terror settle in them like a gray mist. His cap rose distinctly an inch upon his head, and he splayed out his hands before him, thrusting away from his white face as if to keep off a horror unimaginable.

We four wheeled in our tracks. Then my throat dried up within me; my lips twitched; my knees were stricken with sudden palsy. For if ever nightmare walked abroad embodied on God's earth, it was there confessed before my eyes.

12

THE GREAT GOD CAY

High up the slope of the mountain-side, lurching slowly across the bare, bleak slabs of granite, was a Beast, and he was like unto nothing known outside the frenzy of delirium. Swartly green was his huge lizard-like body, and covered with filthy excrescences of a livid hue. His neck was the lithe neck of a boa-constrictor, but glossy as with a sweat of oil. A coarse, heavy, serrated tail dragged and lolluped along the rocks behind him, leaving in its wake a glutinous, snail-like smear. Four great feet or flippers paddled and shushed beside—rather than under—this mass of living horror, urging it lingeringly and remorselessly toward us. The great neck swayed and hovered before it, poising the little malignant head. The horny eyelids winked languidly over the deep-set wicked eyes. The lean, red tongue, slavering over the thin, hide-like lips, wagged out at us as if in mockery. The teeth, and the nails in the webbed, puddy feet, were yellow and tusk-like, and a skinny dewlap rustled as it crawled across the stones.

Three hundred yards away the Thing stopped and shook and swung its horrid neck at us almost derisively. The luminous eyes shone iridescent beneath the slow winking lids. The poised head swayed uncertainly.

Suddenly the long neck stiffened. It set stiff as a rope that warps a ship from harbor. The eyes settled into a glassy stare. The swallowings that had pulsed at the junctions of the neck and dewlap ceased. The muscles became rigid. A hideous paralysis seemed to fall upon it as if by magic.

A sigh—almost a sob—shivered up into the stillness, and I looked at my companions. All of them were staring, staring, staring—three of them with eager, human, living faces, the fourth with the carven visage of the dead.

124

Parsons might have been graven from the rock. His hands were caught upon the lapels of his jacket; his lips and teeth were slightly parted; his eyes burnt their steadfast gaze upon the Beast unblinkingly. But for the measured rise and fall of his chest, he was as unstirring as one of the cañon boulders.

Then I saw that the ghastly Thing was staring with concentration at Parsons. As I watched, it gaped upon him. Parsons opened his jaws with measured, automatic motion, and gaped back. The sinuous neck swayed. Parsons stretched his throat with horrifying imitation. The thing advanced three ponderous steps. Parsons lurched forward a like space draggingly. The long serrated tail lashed to and fro once and again. Parson waggled his body monstrously.

I glanced at the glacier cave which opened invitingly fifty yards away. Then I turned to measure the Horror intently with my eye. Beyond a doubt his gigantic limbs could never pass it. I rushed at Parsons, and seized his coat-collar. He struck at me furiously and unseeingly, his eyes gluing themselves to the fascination before him. I yelled to the others, and then simultaneously we made a rush to the cleft in the glacier face, bearing with us the struggling sailor. He hit out madly, his frozen death-like eyes still rapt upon the Beast. Shrieking, fighting, but still staring, we shoved him through the icy waterway, and heaved him with great splashings round the corner that screened the entrance.

As we lugged him back into the blue dimness of the cavern I pressed my palms upon his eyelids, and bawled reassuringly into his ear. As if a garment fell from him his body lost its rigidity; as I removed my hand his eyes looked back into mine with the natural light soft within them. The tense glare of a moment before was gone. He began to sob and cling to me.

"Oh Lord, oh Lord, oh Lord," he yammered, gripping my arm till I could have yelled with the pain; "the eyes of him—the blisterin' eyes. They dragged me like a puppy on a string. I 'ad to go an' be thankful for goin'. 'E'll 'ave me yet, 'e'll 'ave me yet. 'E'll nip me up an' break my back as if I was a bilge rat, an' no more. Oh, for the Lord's sake 'old on to me, or I'll be cracked like a nut in 'is 'orrid jaws, an' I didn't sign for no dragons, m'lord, but only as deck 'and an' not for no wanderin's in devils' lands." And so on and so forth did he incoherently complain, covering his face from the sight of the approaching monster, grovelling at my feet on the damp sandy floor, as we others watched the gaunt Fearsomeness approach.

As it waddled clumsily up to the entrance we shrank further back into the gloom of the cavern. It stopped as it straddled across the out-gushing stream, damming the waters with its ungainly hulk, and forming a turbid pool. It lifted its pink, pointed snout curiously, and sniffed the air with parted lips. Then the little triangular head swung the full length of the neck into the cave, and the smell of noxious breath and musk clouded down upon us, making us cough with its disgusting effluvia.

The teeth snapped asunder as the lithe tongue licked across them, and as they closed again the breath hissed between them. The green light from its eyes shone luminous in the twilight of the overhanging ice. There was a swish and rush of released waters as it moved forward, and closed in upon the cave mouth. The dimness grew to utter night save for the faintest glow that filtered in from above, and the two pitiless eyes shone poised in the darkness like living coals.

I fumbled for the match-box, and tried to strike a vesta, but my trembling fingers spilled the half of them. The few seconds of horror, while I picked and fiddled at them in the darkness, and those two orbs of searching horror swayed above me, is an experience I am not likely to forget if I live to be a hundred.

As the dips took flame, and we saw the nearness of the Thing, we gasped with the freezing fear of it and backed still further into the recesses of the glacier. The ice began to melt where the heat of the horny excrescences pressed upon it, and for one unreasoning moment I seriously considered if he meant to break in upon us by this slow means. But the sight of the thick, curtain-like glacier, dark above us with its hundreds of feet of virgin ice, reassured me. Little by little, as the first shock of terror began to dull, I pulled myself together.

The others too, I noticed, were beginning to bear themselves more like men and less like whipped puppies. Lessaution actually donned a triumphant expression, and his lips moved. For a moment or so, though, his voice failed to respond to the call of his intelligence. Finally he burst into words.

"Well, my friends, well! What have you to say? Here you have the god Cay—the great Beast of the document, the great absurdity that could not possibly exist. Do we see him? Is he here, or is it possibly a dream, and we shall all awake together?" and the little wretch laughed, actually laughed exultingly, as he grinned round upon us.

As for me, when I heard his words my heart gave a great leap. I had utterly forgotten the horrible old story of the document. Looking on this atrocity, I could but wonder if there was any truth in it, and in the fearful tale of the devouring of Alfa, the sacrificial virgin. And as I speculated on Hardal's wild frenzy if he saw her set in the path of this filthy monstrosity, I did not marvel that he had been hot to avenge his love or to die with her, even if unavailingly.

And then, as you may imagine, my thoughts wandered off swiftly to Gwen, and my gorge rose and my pulses leaped outrageously at the bare idea of seeing her or any other human being in the bestial Thing's maw. The remembrance that she and two-score other souls were swinging on that open pool, the easiest possible prey to this crawling Horror, made me curse deeply below my breath, while behind the imprecation followed earnestly a prayer.

Parsons still babbled and chattered in the background with his face to earth. Denvarre and Gerry stood silent, their faces as white as the ice-splits beside them, but Lessaution's color was returning, and his show of bravado increased. He strode a pace or two nearer the swinging head, and began to look up at it inquisitively, waving his hand and strutting as if he stood before a class.

"You see, my friends, you see," he expatiated with a platform manner, "this is of the supposedly extinct race of the Dinosauria. Of this animal and others like him we have examples in the Secondary period and the Jurassic formation. Of this class, but not of this order, is the great Sea Serpent, at which imbeciles pretend to laugh, but it has been seen—ah, yes, even as we see this monster before us. Since the days before history he has been here—this great and wonderful beast, and to us—to us who have toiled, comes the honor—the supreme honor to discover him. He was old when the race of Maya came; he is older now. And yet we stand familiarly before him. We look up at him, and there you see he wags his head. So we say *belle chance de faire votre connaissance, monsieur*, and we bow to introduce ourselves," and the little man smirked and bobbed to the hideous head as, shuttle-like, it weaved restlessly from side to side of the cavern before his eyes.

It was the most absurdly ghastly combination of the horrible and the ridiculous that ever presented itself to a sane brain, to see that self-important little ass parade himself and point before that loathsome presence. His round little stomach was silhouetted black against the glistening ice, his arms were spread abroad, his toes out-turned, and swagger perspired from his every pore; while above him swung that living climax of horror, arrant in its filthy gruesomeness, indecently manifest in the face of nature. One might well be forgiven if one barely gave credence to one's own eyesight.

As the Frenchman made obeisance forward, spreading his palms outward, and shrugging his shoulders with this outrageous buffoonery and travesty of courage, like a flash the gaping mouth dropped down upon him, and the red, sinuous tongue lapped out at him.

Uttering a shrill cry he stepped backward. His footsteps were hasty and uncertain, and his feet slipped upon the smoothness of the roof drip that swamped the rocky floor. His feet fled from under him, and he rolled over, falling within reach of the eager, straining lips.

The tip of the curling tongue fell upon his shoulder. The roughnesses of it clung to his jacket, fastening themselves to the coarse texture. He struck out at it wildly, and his palm brushed the red, rasping surface. His hand fell back bleeding and flayed, torn by the ragged point as it scored across it. He shrieked aloud, squirming and dragging desperately at the hold upon his arm, wriggling frantically. Above him the green eyes flamed scornfully, gloating upon him as a stoat might on a struggling rabbit. Out of the open jaws the saliva poured upon him, drenching him with noisomeness.

For one stupefying second we were paralyzed, fascinated by abounding horror. Then Denvarre's rifle sprang to his shoulder, and as we leaped forward a shot re-echoed clatteringly down the dark aisles of the icy passages. A deep, livid gap showed angrily and red in the lapping, sinuous tongue. With the swiftness of light it swept its hold upon the jacket, rending the stout cloth in the suddenness of the release. Before the crack of the rifle had died into the silences we seized the little man's outstretched arms, and shot him back into safety. We heaved him to his feet, gasping, panting, his teeth chattering with the black terror of his escape.

The light and the untainted air began to rush back into the cave, as with a heavy lurch the beast withdrew its blocking body from the entrance. The dark blood was dripping in gouts from its wounded tongue, mixing with its saliva in pools upon the rocks, and sinking swearingly into the sand. Even in that moment of horror I couldn't help noticing how the red stains shone upon the yellow nails in each webby foot, and how the pulses in its wrinkled dewlap increased their throbbings with the sudden pain of the wound.

As it waddled sulkily away from the cave mouth, Denvarre slipped in another cartridge, and aiming carefully for its head, fired again. The merest shred of horny skin flicked away from above its eyelid as the bullet thudded home, and not a vestige of blood showed upon the green hide. Evidently those scales were bullet-proof.

It turned with a puzzled air as it felt the rap of the ball, looking back at us in an almost meditative manner, as if wondering if we had anything to do with this thing. Then its eye caught and dwelt upon the Mayan mummy, which still lay half divested of its coverings upon the slab of stone beside the stream. It ambled forward a pace or two, nosing at the carrion uncertainly. Then it swung its head toward the ice-stream, and laved and slobbered its tongue in the water till the bleeding had well-nigh ceased. There was a snap of his bony jaws and a twist of the hard lips as the head shot back again. A single gulp sufficed, and both coats and body were gone. Nothing remained but the slowly-sinking swelling of the long thick throat, and a ragged shred or two of cloth upon the gray stones at its feet.

With heavy strides it moved off ponderously in the direction whence it came, clambering up the rubble of the volcanic slope. For a quarter of an hour we saw it dwindle into the distance of the mountain-side, till finally it rounded a spur of the cañon and disappeared from our view.

Then we left our staring, to which we had kept with an intentness which only those who have experienced a like nerve-sapping fear can understand. First we examined poor Lessaution's palm and shoulder. They were in a sorry case indeed.

The surface of his flesh where the rasping tongue had swept it was scored as if by some huge nutmeg-grater. The skin was hanging from it in thin strips and filaments. Where the utmost tip had touched his cheek in the swift withdrawal was a deep, livid scar like the brand of a hot iron. His left palm was raw, not a vestige of skin remained upon it.

We set the unfortunate little chap upon a boulder outside the cave, and I tore a rag or two from my shirt, wrung them out in the stream, and washed and cleansed the wound to the best of my ability. With the remaining lint I bound up the quivering hand and shoulder, and improvised a sling from a handkerchief. Then we set ourselves to consider what should be done.

"We ought to follow the brute and not rest till we've finally polished him off," said Denvarre emphatically. "Supposing he descended upon the ship when we were away?"

"I am supposing it," said I, "and it makes me sick when I think of it, and that's why I say return to the ship at once to warn them in case he pays them a visit. How are we to track him among all these rifts and gorges of the mountain-side? and meanwhile he may be rolling down upon that undefended ship in that open pool. No. Home first, hunting him down afterward— if you like. As for me, I fail to see how we are going to do it without losing our own lives over the job."

They all seemed to have a good deal to say upon this point. Lessaution, in spite of the pain of his wounds, had not lost his voice, and offered plan after plan of the most strategic order, being frantic for further interviews with the monster, the discovery of which he regarded as the culminating honor of the expedition. But by degrees Gerry and I managed to instill a little sense into him.

We pointed out that we were not prepared to cope with this bullet-resisting abomination, our only chance of destroying him being apparently to decoy him within range of our little six-pounder signal gun, and see if that would have any influence with him. We did not know the recesses of the gorge as he did, and should be at a great disadvantage, for he was liable at any moment, if disturbed, to suddenly emerge from round a corner, and, as Mr. Parsons described it, "nip us like bilge rats." That while we were wasting time discovering a lair which might well be empty, he might recover himself of his wound, and bear down upon the unprepared ship's company. That for the present he had fed, his wound was smarting, and he was unlikely to follow and overtake us in the open as the Frenchman suggested. And thus after much talk our decision was taken for return.

So down the cañon we retreated hastily, with many backward looks, as you may well imagine, our hearts quaking at the thought of what might happen if we were tracked to the shallowing lake and there trapped in our helplessness. I must own that little Lessaution came out a trump. The agony of his half-dressed wounds must have been great, but he made light of them as veriest pin-pricks, actually laughing over his adventure as the best of jokes against himself. For the pride of our achievement, in finding not only a buried race but an extinct animal also, had lifted him above all considerations of common sense. He revelled in a sort of scientific ecstasy which obliterated all remembrance of the narrowest squeak ever man had from a fate of unimaginable horror. And so he ceased not his happy chatterings for so much as a single instant.

Parsons moaned and groaned respectfully all along the way, referring in dismal undertones to the land of his birth, and the extremely slender probability of his ever seeing the same again, regretting fervently his past treatment of his maternal progenitor, with many fanciful pictures of her emotions could she see the hapless case of the son of her constant sorrow. And he spent so much of his time looking jerkily over his shoulder, as sudden spasms of fear convinced him that we were being pursued, that his falls averaged not less than twenty per mile. Gerry was silent, brooding, as I could understand, over the perils that might be menacing the ship in our absence, and it was a phase of thought which commanded my full sympathy and respect. Denvarre, who is a keen sportsman, whenever Lessaution gave him a chance, discoursed learnedly on rifles, displaying much technical knowledge of initial velocities and expanding bullets, as bearing on the chance of penetrating the monster's hide. But I fear he lacked an audience. And as the hours slipped by we reached the far end of the gorge, and stumbled out on to the roughnesses of the farther moraine. Here we had to give all the assistance we could to Lessaution, whose useless arm was a terrible handicap to him on such going, and it was with great thankfulness we saw a few hundred yards before us the point at which the boulders ceased, and the smooth going stretched to the shores of our little lake. We reached the corner that screened the ship and the pool from us, and turned it, rounding the jutting rock with eager eyes. As one man we stopped to gape upon the empty foreground. Both ship and lake were gone.

13

A CLOJED DOOR

In the morning we had left a pool of clear, shining blue, still as a Thames backwater, and the tall ship resting motionless on its pliant bosom. Every spar and rope had been distinctly out-lined and reflected on the gleaming surface, which mirrored the very lines of the cutwater. Now, instead of the soft glitter of the lake laving the foot of the climbing glacier, an empty round of bleak and ice-worn rock confronted us, standing out hard and barren in the red glow of the sunset.

With a yell we raced over the flats of smooth stone to gaze into the hollow shadows where the morning shine of the pool had been. With wide-eyed wonder we gazed down the sloping bank. An extraordinary sight was there displayed.

A huge crack ran across the empty basin of the lake, seam-ing the granite at its deepest part for a space of about fifty yards. Wedged in the grip of it was the old *Raccoon*, half supported by the nip of the rock, half leaning on the little launch which lay beside her, buttressing her with its funnel and bulwarks. Higher up the slope from us one of her great anchors was caught in a crevice of the rocks, and a hawser was rove from a pulley on the shank of it to the bows of the ship. A group of the crew was hauling at this with chorused shoutings, while astern a like arrange-ment had been tautened out.

The ship was trembling and wobbling as the thrills of the hawser shook her bows, and the granite edges scored and frayed her timbers as she wrestled in the mouth of the cleft. In another group farther off, the ladies stood upon the still dripping stones to watch the operations, keeping cautiously their distance, in case the ship should lurch over before the ropes had her fast. The bellowings of Waller and the boatswain echoed thunderously

across the amphitheatre of stone as they urged the men to re-
newed efforts.

The unexpected wonder of this sight held us silent for a score
of seconds; then Gerry gave expression to the sentiments of the
company at large.

"Well, I *am* damned," quoth he emphatically.

"I wish the lake had been," I answered ruefully. "There goes
the last of the *Raccoon*. If she topples over we're done for."

"But look here," went on Gerry, gazing at the empty basin
with an air of stupefied surprise, "the pool's fallen below the level
of the sea outside. How in the name of wonder do you account
for that?"

Lessaution found his voice. "It is one of the many wonders
of the volcanic actions which we discover so plentifully in this
country. The water withdraws itself—is sucked, if you will—into
the bowels of the earth. Perhaps it will rise again. Who knows?"

"In that case," said I, "we shall live in perpetual dread of
sudden drowning, if she's roped down to the bed of the lake
like that. We shall have to buttress her up some other fashion.
We must build supports of stone beneath her; then if she should
suddenly be floated again she won't be swamped. But we'd better
get down and hear the news."

The slope below us was short and steep. Lessaution looked
down it cautiously. He removed the shot-gun which swung from
his back, seated himself upon his cartridge-bag, and splayed out
his legs before him. Having thus ingeniously converted himself
into a human sledge, he pushed off, and in a moment was flying
down the damp, smooth rocks, arriving within a hundred yards
of the ship with safety and despatch, and greeted by the ladies
with a shrill cheer.

It was undignified, no doubt, but an eminently practical device.
We were by no means slow to follow his example, and straddling upon the shining slope, fled down after him with much
the effect of luggage being transferred to the Dover boat, and
reached the bottom with swiftness and without mishap.

The ladies met us with effusion. Since our departure, they
seemed by their own account to have lived on the edge of eternity, expecting fearful disaster at any moment. We learned that

the ship had continued to sink all morning, to their great disquietude, though Waller confidently assured them that there must certainly be fathoms of good sea-water between them and the bottom when the fall ceased, as they could not possibly drop lower than the tide-line. Resting on these assurances, they had betaken themselves to lunch, and only discovered the depths of his mistake when the keel took ground, and the ship began to subside crabwise on to the launch, upsetting the table, and wrecking the saloon for the second time in eight-and-forty hours. In great affright they had then scrambled hastily on deck, and camping meanwhile on the slope where we had found them, within half an hour had seen the last of the water gurgle gently into the great fissure below.

Waller's presence of mind had not failed him under this inglorious defeat of his prophetic powers, and he had immediately summoned the crew to stay the reeling ship with windlass and hawser, before she broke down the precarious support of the launch. We found this work being carried to a successful conclusion when we arrived.

After Lessaution's warning, and as all immediate danger of the ship's toppling was overcome, I summoned Waller and Janson to me, and explained to them my plan for more accurately bringing about the stability of the ship, and at the same time avoiding the danger of her being swamped if the waters rose again. They agreed as to the soundness of these proposals, called to them the crew, and set forth immediately to the cliff-top to collect boulders.

We of the expedition, meanwhile, having gone without lunch, attacked the meat pie which we had brought back unbroken in our haste, dining heartily, with the bare rocks for table. The ladies waited upon us most assiduously, hearing at the same time an edited account of the day's perils, for we judged it best to keep from Lady Delahay's ears, at any rate, the story of the great beast that roamed abroad so near her resting-place. Then we joined the crew who had ascended by devious ways the steep escarpment of the basin, and helped them collect the boulders of the moraine upon the cliff-top in quantities. Here we cast them down headlong till sufficient for my purpose were heaped beside the ship.

As night came down upon us—or rather dusk, for in those latitudes darkness was never complete—we descended in the manner first patented and approved by Lessaution, a system of travel received with great good-will and jocund outcry by the common sailor men, and then and there resolved by them into a race meeting on first principles. In which sporting event the heaviest weights in collusion with the smoothest breeches were favorites.

This combination appeared in its most perfected form in the person and habit of Mr. Rafferty, boatswain, who out-distanced all competitors. But unfortunately the rapidity of his descent was in inverse ratio to the stoutness of his nether garments, and when he rose from his too facile progress, the company turned from him with feigned unconsciousness and ill-concealed smiles. Poor Mr. Rafferty, his victory thus shamefully dulled, had to seek the shelter of the ship and his Sunday trousers, re-appearing after some few minutes clad in the latter, and with a chastened air. Daring with fiery glances the titters of the crew, he thereupon joined us in our work of rolling the great stones below the ship's timbers.

A couple of hours' hard work saw buttresses raised sufficiently strong to avert all danger of the ship's upsetting. From stem to stern we wedged the great boulders firmly beneath her, and alongside the edges of the cleft that gaped below her keel, and were enabled to release the hawsers from the sustaining anchors without causing her so much as a tremble. Then, thoroughly tired out, we sought supper and, finally, bed, too weary to so much as dream of the wonders of this truly astounding day.

It was a lovely calm morning when I got on deck nine or ten hours later; and the sun was pouring down into the rocky hollow, flooding us with uplifting warmth and wholesomeness. Nor did the day lose its brightness when I found Gwen pacing the deck forward, enjoying a bath of sunshine before breakfast.

"Good-morning," said she brightly, as I stepped up. "Any the worse for your striving with beasts yesterday?"

"I suppose Gerry has let the cat out, then?" I returned. "Too bad of him. There is no good in alarming you unnecessarily."

"But, my dear Lord Heatherslie, one doesn't stumble over a Dinosaurus, or a Plesiosaurus, or whatever egregious monster it was, every day of one's life. I should have been desperately annoyed if he hadn't told me. I think it's most delightfully exciting."

"Do you?" said I dryly. "I think if you'd seen Lessaution squealing in his jaws yesterday, like a rabbit in a snare, you would have agreed that the pleasant excitement was rather discounted by the very unpleasant terror of it. I sincerely hope your mother has heard nothing about it."

She smiled. "Of course not. Mother has no imagination, and a very practical dislike of the out-of-place. Not that a Plesiosaurus, or for the matter of that a unicorn, would be out of place in this astounding land. After what we've gone through I'm by no means surprised."

"Please God he doesn't come straggling down here," said I devoutly. "What should you have done if he had turned up yesterday when you were all unprepared? I was nearly frantic at the thought."

"Done? Why, gone to ground like a badger," she answered, pointing to the cleft in the rent rock-bed. "If he's half the size Mr. Carver makes out, we could sit in there and make faces at him. He wouldn't have a chance to reach us."

"What a very practical imagination you have," I declared admiringly, as I peered over the bulwarks into the fissure. It sloped gently down from our stern into the darkness, in width about five feet—infinitely too small a space for the great brute to pass, as I could see. "That makes me feel much more comfortable. Now if by any chance he does appear, I shall know you have a refuge at hand. But we hope to kill him," I added reassuringly.

"Kill the only Dinosaur extant!" she expostulated, "I'm convinced Monsieur Lessaution will never allow it."

"I think after his experience of yesterday he is resigned to the sacrifice. He'll enjoy cutting him up dead quite as much as admiring him from a distance living. Besides, according to him your sanctuary may at any moment fail you. The water, he says, may rise again as suddenly as it has disappeared."

"My goodness! that would be humiliating, wouldn't it? Fancy if we were safely ensconced in there, and the waters that are under the earth vomited us out into his jaws. What an ignoble end to a yachting cruise."

"I'm afraid in any case you'll have a rough time of it before we can get away," said I, a little sadly. "We are going to do our best to send word to the Falklands, but it is bound to be a long business. I hope you won't mind—much."

She looked at me with a smile that I can only describe as distracting. "My dear Lord Heatherslie," she said quite earnestly, "I'm looking forward to it as one of the most delightful periods of my life. I have all I want to make me happy. If it wasn't for mother I should be quite prepared to stay here months."

"I shouldn't," said I, quite gruffly, as the sound of the breakfast gong turned us toward the companion. "But then, you see, I haven't all I want to make me happy," and my voice shook the tiniest bit as I said it.

She half stopped at the head of the stairs, and looked at me half inquiringly. She parted her lips as if she was going to speak, but thought better of it, and ran lightly down into the cabin, where she took her seat without a word, and it struck me that she was more silent than usual during breakfast. As for me, I had no strength to waste on mere conversation, my time being fully occupied in assimilating my victuals, and in fighting down the black temper which had me in its grip.

For, truth to tell, my battle with my jealous self was wearing me sadly. I still went on loving Gwen for all I was worth, and the hopeless weeks that stretched before me wherein I must be in her constant company loomed dark and desperate. Every time she spoke to me was a pang; her very innocent friendliness an agony. No doubt physical weakness and the stress of the last few days had something to do with it, but I could have ended my existence at that time with much satisfaction to myself, and I think it was only a sneaking sense of the utter cowardliness of the thing that stayed me. You can understand that I did not linger over breakfast. I took my cigar on deck at the earliest opportunity, and wrestled there alone with the devils of despair that had me in their grip, till I felt calmer and fit again for the toils of the coming day.

I called Waller to me before the others came on deck, and we held consultation on our future movements. Our observations of the previous day had pretty well determined us that no means of launching a boat along the shores of the western cliff was to be found. The terrible toil that would be involved in getting the sections of the launch across the rocky crevices of the moraine had decided us that we must look eastward if we wanted to find a beach to launch from before the winter closed down upon us and shut the surrounding waters with closest harriers of ice. Eastward we therefore would make our day's quest.

Before we left I made time to investigate the cavern that opened down beneath our keel. I got a rope and fastened it to the bowsprit, and taking a turn of it round my elbow, lit a dip and crawled carefully down the sloping sides of the pit. The slant was steep, but there were numerous ledges and footholds, and about six feet below the surface a recess was hollowed out in the sides of the split, evidently caused by some lump of granite shivering off during the upheaval, and dropping further down into the fissure.

In this the damp of the receding waters still glistened, and lay in pools upon the floor. There was a bright, new riven appearance about the walls, showing that the strata-slip was recent. Bits of mica and other minerals, as yet undulled by exposure to the atmosphere, made this very plain. The huge cleft continued down in a thin well from the larger rent at the surface, losing itself in a darkness which might well be unplumbable. I could see one or two lumps of stone still sticking in the jaws of the gap—evidently remains of what had slipped down from the cavern in which I stood. Beyond these was emptiness. Though my eyes found nothing in this void, my nose was assailed by a smell of sulphur as strong as the after-blow of a blasting fuse.

I crept out again into the air, my throat very sore from the fumes that kept rising from below. I called the carpenter and one or two of the men, and set them to hack steps in the rock as far as the recess below, and directed them to cover the continuance of the fissure with planks. We unearthed a spare rudder-chain, and trailed it from a stanchion driven into the rocks. Thus we had a moderately easy passage into the chamber below, which could be used by the company at large if the Horror of the cañon attempted to attack them. So, with minds comparatively at ease, Garlicke, Gerry and I set forth to carry our exploration eastward across the glacier, leaving poor little Lessaution behind us, a melancholy object indeed, because his wounded shoulder prevented his joining us in our researches.

The eastern shore ran along the glacier edge for about a mile, gradually narrowing and mounting upward with an easy gradient. Finally the rock disappeared under the encroaching ice, and the glacier fronted on the cliff head. The chance of a landing-place between us and this point was plainly out of the question. Our plan was to surmount the glacier itself and explore the country beyond. Provided the going was not too rough or too broken by crevasses, it might be quite possible to convey the sections of our launch across it to any landing-place we might discover on the far side.

So, armed with ice-axes, we three set out as a small advance party, meaning only to go a day's journey and then return with our report. For if no chance of a beach was likely within a reasonable distance, we should waste no more time in expeditions, but set ourselves to lower the boat down the cliffs as best we could.

All three of us have knocked about the Alps a bit. Therefore we managed our crawlings about the blue crevasses with a certain amount of ease, nor did the occasional dropping-in of an ice bridge occasion us great excitement. We were roped of course, and moved with steadiness, but after a bit found that our mountaineering muscles were not in the best of condition. Nor had we reckoned on the heat of the midday sun or its effect when reflected back from these glassy surfaces.

After about two hours of heavy going and copious perspiration our skins began to fray most painfully, and our faces were the hue of rosy-fingered dawn. Gerry's expressive features were literally hanging in rags, and Garlicke and I, tougher-hided animals though we were, saw the rocks that bordered the far side of the ice-field with no small gratitude.

We left the ice and stepped out on to the narrow margin of rock that flanked it. A few paces forward we found that the crags sunk sheer from our feet. Below us, some twenty fathoms or more, a still, black pool laved their base, rippleless as a Lethean lake. At the seaward end it was broken by rocks, piled and tumbled as if tossed there by some great convulsion. It was not hard to understand how this inland sea-pool had come into being.

Originally it had been a bay or inlet with a narrow, land-locked entrance. Some upheaval—volcanic, no doubt—had shut down the guarding cliffs upon the opening as a curtain falls across a stage. The huge splinters, piled as they were across the narrows of this fiord, could scarcely be distinguished from the cliffs off which they had been rent.

At the foot of the barrier an eddy rose now and again, creaming white among the reefs that broke the sheen of the pool. This was where some subterranean entrance must keep the waters to tide-level. Now and again the shining poll of a sea-lion gleamed upon the surface, another proof that a sea-cave communicated with the outside. Opposite, on the eastward side of the bay, were cliffs as steep as those among whose pinnacles we stood, and the lake swept away inland and was lost behind a spur of the mountain-side.

This was an unexpected obstruction to our travel, and put a final stop to any idea of getting our launch to the sea from a beach. We turned to the left along the glacier edge to see what was hid from us by the flank of the hill, scrambling alternately from rock to ice. In about twenty minutes we reached the corner and rounded it. Then we saw the far end of the inlet.

Half-a-mile further on, shining and yellow below us, was a beach of sand wet with the receding tide. Streaked across it were many little rivulets, draining either from the glacier, or from sea-pools that filtered slowly through the ooze of the shore. Scarcely a ripple broke the calm. It sank down the beach, drooping imperceptibly without any of the roll that usually marks the defiant outgoing of the ebb. An oily stillness lay upon the waters.

Dotted on the strand were various black objects, some larger, some smaller, but too far distant to be distinguishable. The smooth silt ran upward between narrowing cliffs, merging into the rock rubble that climbed the mountainside. It lost itself among the crags of the summit.

Clouds of terns and kittywakes were wheeling in the air, or strutting and scratching on the beach; the larger birds—gulls, cormorants, and such-like—were pecking and fighting over the black objects, while in solemn battalions the penguins marched and countermarched along the water's edge.

Under the circumstances the view took the nature of an ironical jest at the hand of fate. Here at last was the very object of our search, but mocking us in the very act of discovery. A beauteous, slow-sloping shallow of lovely sand, and no outlet to the sea. The ideal place to launch our cutter, and the barrier of the cliffs lay between us and the outer ocean impenetrable.

I swore softly to myself as I realized these things, cursing the luck that dogged me maddeningly. Fate had evidently willed that I should not escape from my jealous torments yet awhile.

Gerry broke the silence.

"This place means to keep us now it's got us, you may depend upon it," said he. "That's what I call a pretty strict blockade of their only port," and he pointed down the fiord to the barrier at the far end where the rocks were piled across the entrance.

"The earthquake may have done that," said I.

"An earthquake may have done it," said Garlicke, "but not the one of three nights back. I can see great patches of lichen on the rocks. It's centuries old—that great shutting of the door. Look at the banks of seaweed across it."

Gerry had turned to stare up the ravine that rose from high-water mark to the mountainside. Suddenly he stretched across to Garlicke for the glass, and began examining the far crags. Nothing that moved was visible to the naked eye, but as he put down the telescope he whistled softly.

"It's either an extraordinary coincidence or a blessed funny thing," he ejaculated.

"What?" we demanded.

"The black line that runs across the cliff up there," he went on. "We shall find that that's coal, when we get nearer, I don't mind betting. Through the glass I can distinctly see the shine and gloss of it, and it's perished and crumbled away as coal would—in square lumps."

"Well," said I irritably, "what if it is? Why shouldn't there be coal? Nothing would surprise me less than to find that those black things upon the beach are patent stoves. Nothing would be too outrageous for this land of sudden upheavals."

He looked at me with much contempt.

"Lessaution's estimate of your intelligence was not far out," he remarked. "Do you mean to say you have forgotten the coal the Mayans found—the 'stone with fern marks upon it' that burnt—the stone, that is, not the fern marks? Well, there's your seam of stone or coal or whatever you like to call it, and here's the very spot on which the Mayans landed three hundred years ago. That's the place where the Beast munched up poor Alfa and Hardal. The penguins which they knocked aver and roasted—or rather their descendants—are there, and this is the intricate passage by which they found harbor, only the rocks have barred the entrance. There isn't a doubt about it."

I looked around me, and there seemed every possibility that he was right. All these circumstances dovetailed into one another most remarkably—the coal, the sandy shore, the penguins, and what not. The only thing wanting to complete the picture was the "Great god Cay with mouth agape," and though for the time being he was not on view, we knew only too well that he was a very unpleasant reality. So down the red-hot cliffs we scrambled for a nearer examination of these possibilities, and after half-an-hour's toil by ways devious and hard to find dropped upon the shining sands at the bottom.

14

IN THE NINTH CIRCLE

As we arrived our noses were greeted with a most stupendous and enwrapping stench. It took me just about the twentieth part of a second to realize that the black objects that lay above the tide mark were the half-dismembered bodies of sea-lions, the intestines protruding black and decayed upon the smeared and oily sand. Round about them were tramplings and churnings of the mud, and spreading away across the landward rubble to the entrance of the ravine were great sloppy paddings—the slow trudge of some ponderous and long-nailed quadruped.

It was almost with gratified expectation that I recognized the trail of the Horror of the cañon. Here doubtless was his feeding-ground, his private *abattoir*, where he came down to prey upon the sleeping sea-lion, even as centuries before he had lumbered down upon Alfa, Hardal, and probably many another of those hapless immigrants besides. Here as in a trap he found his prey. Often one could suppose the sea-lions passed through the sea entrance at the far end of the bay, failed to find exit, and, tired with wearily threshing round their prison walls, lauded to take their siesta in the sun. Here asleep they fell unawares into his maw, or, surprised in the rock-ringed pool, gave him many a jovial hunt in the clear depths between the cliffs.*

At the far side of the beach were other lumps, embedded in the sand. To them we strode and began to dig at them with our

---

*Lord Heatherslie makes a mistake here. Professor Lessaution's subsequent researches proved "the god Cay" to be without doubt *Brontosaurus excelsus*, remains of which have been found in the Jurassic formation of Colorado. It was purely a land animal.—F.S.

axes. It scarcely came as a surprise when the powdery silt fell aside to disclose timbers sticking up gauntly from below—the worn joists and ribs of some stranded vessel.

One or two of the great timbers—carven and decorated by hands long dead—were now wind-planed and worn by the sand drift, and slanted deep into the pebbles. We shovelled and scraped to trace them further. Below the soil they rounded almost at right angles, and we uncovered one of them at full length. It measured a good forty paces—the keel, as we could but suppose, of some Mayan bark, sole remnant of what had been a gallant ship in the squadron of that lost and hapless race.

We scratched and delved, but nothing further than dried wood splinters did we discover. Finally we decided to explore the ravine for traces of the Mayans, or for the track of the great Beast. This latter was plain as a cart trail on the softer ground, but soon faded and was lost among the rubble.

We felt no fear of consequences should we suddenly unlair the monster, for though the walls of the cañon were steep, they were broken by ledges. Up these we could skip swiftly enough, while he, with his ungainly body, would be unable to follow. So up the loose, rattling pebbles we toiled to draw near by degrees to the top, where the ravine passed into a scar of the mountain ridge, and then sinking rapidly, clove its way deep among the spurs and gullies of the far side.

At this point the immensity of the glacier we had crossed that morning was apparent. It stretched away westward in broad, horizon-touching acres of snowfield. Through another cleft a branch of it sank into the valley below us. Far down we could see a streamlet issue from its foot. From the heights above, the tumble of crevasses converged in the narrows like the handle of some huge fan. It smote into the gorge at its straitest, the brook pools glinting away between the rocks. On the spur between the valleys was broken rubble dotted with great boulders. Above all, in sunlit, cloudlike purity the snow crest hung majestic. Out in the distance, seen through the tunnel-like formation of the cliffs, the sea glanced and gleamed, flecked with white bergs to the far horizon.

It was the sight of this last that brought us up all standing. It seemed a trifle astounding to be confronted with the sea again when we had thus turned inland, and for some few moments we debated on the problem unavailingly. Then as I gazed round me various things seemed familiar.

In an instant the explanation came. We were standing in the very cañon up which we had marched the previous day, only we were entering the other end. No wonder that I had thought I had seen before that blue glacier foot and that chain of broken pools down the stream. I had—not twenty-four hours before, too—but from the other side. Our ship and the sunk lake basin were on a great promontory. We had followed the circle of the eastern shore and turned inland. Thus we had cut across the cape as the great fissure did—almost at right angles. If we had followed the cañon the previous day we should have attained to the very spot on which we stood.

It was evident that the glacier, into the recesses of which we had penetrated, and on the edge of which the ruined temple hung, was a branch of the one we had crossed an hour or two back. Amidst this identical chaos of boulders we had watched the wounded beast disappear, and from some unseen cave or cranny he might now be spying us with gloating eyes. I stared round me apprehensively, but nothing moved to break the long waste of gray rock and virgin ice. I turned to explain my discovery to my companions.

It did not take them long to recognize the familiar landmarks when I pointed them out, and they at once agreed with me that it was useless to carry further our quest for a beach. It was borne upon us with great conviction that the cliff barrier here stood just as remorselessly between us and the sea as it did on the western side of our lake. We might, therefore, as well give up at once all thought of launching our boat in the ordinary manner. With the endless line of crags stretching for miles in either direction, it but remained to essay the lowering of it by davits or windlasses down the precipice, to chance its escaping uncrushed by the floating floe. For the present we set gloomily back across the glacier to carry news of our discovery to our friends.

We roped up as we left the cliffs, proceeding gingerly upon our way. The crevasses honeycombed the ice at every step; some we bridged with our poles; some we jumped unhandily; some,

too broad for either leaping or bridging, we rounded by circui-
tous ways which took us far out of our dead point for home. At
this height upon the glacier slopes we found the passage far
more difficult and broken than upon the lower levels we had
crossed in the earlier morning.

It was after a couple of hours of hard work, that, with red
and glistening faces, we found ourselves within a few score feet
of the further side. We stopped to mop our streaming brows
and to congratulate ourselves on the conclusion of the hardest
part of our labors. I produced my flask, at which the others
smiled approvingly.

I took an inspiriting pull, handing it on to Garlicke, who was
roped between Gerry and myself. He took it with unfeigned
gratitude, and sucked at it sensuously, bestowing a wink at Gerry
over the rim. The latter observed him earnestly as the flask
tipped gradually higher, and then, dropping his axe upon the
ice, strode towards his friend with a very unbenignant air and
an outstretched hand. The axe fell with its point buried in the
rough surface at Garlicke's feet; the blade on the opposite side
of the handle was uppermost.

"Kindly leave a saltspoonful," said Gerry irritably. "I happen
to be just about as thirsty as you."

Garlicke turned slowly, the bottle still glued to his lips. He
winked again with an indescribably annoying slyness. Gerry—
with a touch of temper, it must be owned—snatched at his hand.
Garlicke, with mock ferocity, warded him off.

There was a crackling sound as Gerry's foot burst in an ice-
bubble, and he stumbled. He rocked forward to fall prone beside a
crevasse edge. The tense cord fell dead upon the keen blade of
the axe set so rigidly uppermost.

There was a hum and a flick as the rope parted, the two released ends springing apart like rent elastic. Gerry gave a wild
scrabble at the glass-like, elusive surface, and shot like a flash into
the yawning gap. There was a yell and a fierce rush from Garlicke,
and I instinctively dug my heels into a crevice, bracing myself
starkly to meet his sudden pull. I thrust my own axe-point into the
ice, buttressing myself upon it. But for this three bodies would have
been racing into the womb of the ice-hill instead of one.

A dull thud came echoing up from the dark shadows beneath us; a few glassy splinters crackled and pattered downward; then came a silence broken only by the throb of our pulses as they sang dull and muffled in our ears.

Garlicke was as one possessed. "My God, my God," he shrieked, "I've murdered him—murdered him. What am I to do? What am I to do? Speak, you fool," he yammered, "tell me what I'm to do—to do," and his voice rose to a scream, while he shook at my coat tempestuously. "Don't tell me that we can't reach him. My God, I shall go mad," and he flung himself down upon the ice, tearing at it with bruised and bleeding fingers as he chattered hysterically. "For God's sake, Heatherslie, say there's hope—that we can get him up. We must—we must. Lord, have mercy upon me; what am I to do?" and he leaned desperately over the crumbling edge, peering hopelessly into the depths.

Do you know the horrible, leaden, choking pain that leaps up and takes you by the throat, strangling you in a very fog of horror, when, suddenly, swiftly, in the midst of light and laughter, the Great Shadow falls between you and one at your very side? When your heart swells with quivering pulses that shake your flesh? When your eyes burn and the deafness of despair is in your ears; when your knees rock, and the guides and thews within you string themselves like cords against your tense nerves?

Those of you who have been in like case to mine can realize what I felt, when I saw the friend who had been to me as a brother, snatched into the darkness of that cold pit. You of the majority, who have stood in no such brain-wrenching mist of terror—to you no words can describe it. Those two seconds stand out redly scarred against the map of my life. They seemed ages untold of cruel anguish.

The strain of Garlicke's weight had nearly knocked all the breath out of my body, but I managed to swing him to his feet.

"Oh, you fool, you—you, what are you?" I gasped. "Pull yourself into the semblance of a man. Race to the ship for help. Get ropes. Run, you fool, run," and I thrust him from me roughly as I sat down panting.

He tottered across the few yards of ice between us and the rocks, and began to reel unsteadily down the slopes toward the great basin and the ship. As he disappeared, and the breath began to slide back into my cramped lungs, I seized my axe and hewed myself a standing-place beside the crevasse. Then I lay down upon my face, my head and shoulders outstretching far above the blue gulf, and set myself to listen with hopeless ears.

The hard damp silence of a vault was over all. No vestige of a sound was there, but the chill drip of the inciting ice, and far away out of the distance the half-heard break of waves upon the sea-cliffs. Now and again the wail of a tern or the call of a gull broke jarringly across the stillness, but from the grave below came nothing—no smallest sound to poise a hope upon; only the hush of death and the ceaseless drip.

Yet—was it the self-mesmerism of a hope that would not be denied?—so faint that it left the merest echo of a tremor in my ears, a tiny sound seemed to float up from the depths. I called aloud. I shrieked to a fierce unnatural falsetto in my excitement. I struggled desperately to pierce the dulling thicknesses of ice. I strained hazardously across the gulf in my agony to listen, listen, listen for the ghost of a reply. Still no answer came; only the pitiless drip pattered on monotonously. I pictured it falling on Gerry's cold, upturned face.

I struck savagely at the opposite wall of the crevasse. I cut a cranny and thrust the point of my axe-handle in it. Then leaning on the head I hung out over the depths, my shoulders almost half-way across the cleft.

There was a jerk as the sharp point snapped through the brittle support. My head plunged forward, hitting with tremendous force the smooth, blue surface beyond me. A thousand stars and planets flashed before my eyes, spreading from a core of foaming light. Then swart and sudden as the night closes over a tropical lightning flash followed darkness and insensibility.

I blinked curiously, groping with owl-like eyes in the gray-green light that swathed me. Before me rose a slope of ice—a gleaming hill blue with the cold azure of undying frost. The smooth surface shone duskily; the twilight fell upon it from above in uncertain patches. Behind and above me was a curtain-like overshadowment of rock.

To my right rose the columns and porticoes of a building, shaded and deepening into blackness where the cloistered frontage retreated into the background. Close to my head, rising with gentle gradient from the pebbly floor, was a paved ascent to the main door of the building. To the left was a dark emptiness, and bell-like out of the hollow distance came the tinkle of running water.

A few yards away lay a man's form—face to earth and still. The forehead leaned upon the fore-arm; the other hand was stretched abroad, as if grasping an unseen hold. The whole body had the pose of death as we find it when met with suddenness. In the tired apathy that follows a great shock I stared upon it wearily—unthinking, unreasoning, seeing something of familiarity, but with listless inability to follow the crude remembrancing of my brain.

As intelligence grew slowly back to me I struggled weakly and sat up. It was as in a long-forgotten and half-remembered vision that I knew Gerry's brown shooting-jacket and his greasy field-boots. With further recognition memory began to ooze back.

Gerry had been upon the glacier with me. And Garlicke. And my flask. Gerry had wanted the flask. Well, he couldn't have it now. I'd lost it. I tried wretchedly to remember how or where. Why, of course! that was what Garlicke had taken. That ice-hill, now, over there—just like the toboggan slide at Toronto two winters ago. I wondered if old Jim Paleriste was still *aide*. No; seen him in town since. Then there was that sweet little—Oh, my God! Gerry had fallen in—fallen in—and I listened—and the tern had shrieked just as I thought I heard something. Well, that was Gerry—must be—snoozing away over there on his face. And that building? Well—Why, of course, this was a dream. There was that absurd beast. That was part of a dream. Why on earth couldn't I wake myself? Baines would bring my hot water directly. Beastly unpleasant; just as well to know it was a dream. I'd have another wink or two. Confounded wet and cold—and, by Jove, cord breeches on. In bed. And blood upon them. Ouf! how my shoulder hurt. And what a scratch upon my palm!

A huge drop splashed from the roof upon my forehead.

At the touch of the cold water, suddenly as the sunbeams rend the sea-mist, my senses leaped back to me, and dread—sickening dread—took possession of my heart.

I stared across intently at Gerry's rigid limbs. So we had fallen together into the depths—into the cold that kills. He was dead, no doubt; a little struggle against the numbing cold, and I too should pass into the land beyond forgetfulness. We had found the ninth circle of the lost.

I rose and touched and stretched myself warily. How my back and shoulders ached, and what a sharp pang ran through my ankle as I dragged myself across the floor. I knelt beside Gerry and turned his face to the light. It was white and hollow-checked; his eyes were closed. I ran my hand beneath his coat and laid it above his heart. Was it still?—or was it my own anxious pulse that beat beneath my palm?

No, there was a stirring—a fluttering, faint and scarce discernible, but the life-light still burned. I placed my eyeball before his parted lips. The out-draught of his breathing struck against it, though ever so lightly. I moved his arms. They were limp, but with no unnatural droop. Very, very gently, but perceptibly, his chest rose and fell again, and something like a sigh fluttered out from between his lips. There was a faint flicker of an eyelid, and his fingers twitched automatically at the pebbles.

The worst of the overpowering weight of dread slid away from me hesitatingly. Perhaps after all Gerry was no more than knocked out of time—not injured fatally at all. I shouted into his ear; a tiny movement of the eyelid answered me. I raised his head, scraping the loose sand into a pillow beneath it. I took his hand and began to rub it briskly, clapping it against its fellow. A faint shade of color rose into his cheek; he sighed perceptibly. Again his eyelids fluttered, half closed again, and then opened wonderingly to their widest. He stared about him, his gaze wandering with a drowsy air of astonishment from point to point. His hand swept the floor, picking at the little stones, and his breathing grew louder and more regular.

I called aloud his name, smiting him on the shoulder. He jerked a look at me from his drowsy eyes, frowned, made as if he would turn his head, and then a sudden faint consciousness seemed to return to him.

"W'as'r matter?" he whispered indistinctly.

"Good man," I bawled joyously. "Wake up, wake up, old chap. Are you hurt? Feel yourself," and I dragged him to a sitting posture.

"W'as'r time?" he gurgled again sleepily.

"Time! Hang the time. You're not in bed. We're in the glacier. Get up and feel yourself."

He scrabbled weakly at the ground, caught at my sleeve, and leaned against me. He stared at his surroundings, regarding the temple portico with desperate astonishment. Then the ice-hill, sinking down to our very feet, caught his eye. He turned to me with wild amazement in every feature.

"It's a nightmare," he declared.

"No such luck," quoth I, sadly. "We're here right enough. The question is how to get out before we're frozen stiff. Can you stand?"

He staggered to his feet, still lurching against me, and began gingerly to press his limbs and ribs. He moaned eloquently as his fingers roamed about his battered bones, making fearful grimaces.

"Ribs nearly bashed in," he remarked, "but no other damage that I can discover, bar bruises."

"That's all right. Now let's hustle round and see if there's any sort of way out. That stream over there must go somewhere, if there's room to follow it. I can hear it tinkling away down some sort of channel."

In the direction in which I pointed the sides of overhanging rock and glacier converged till they almost met, forming a low tunnel which struck further into the blackness. It was from this burrow that the sound of running water came.

Gerry looked at the dark entrance with much distaste.

"Ugh," said he, "filthy and cold it'll be. Don't you think—"

Click, click, click, and he stopped his argument to stare up to where something clattered above our heads. Gently, invitingly, a flask pattered into view, sliding down the slopes of the ice-hill at the end of a string. It hopped and jigged away most suggestively. We both gave a tumultuous yell of welcome, and dashed at it. I seized it, opened it, and poured half its contents down Gerry's throat before he could make any demur. Then I took a good pull at it myself, smacking my lips with intense enjoyment. We clutched the string and tugged at it lustily, and those above tugged gladsomely and heartily back. Then I found an old envelope and began to scribble on it, using a rifle-bullet for pencil.

"All right. Get a rope!" was the terse message I attached to the string, and we saw it flit upward when our pressure relaxed, watching it disappear into the blue shadows of the ice-roof with indescribable sensations of relief.

In a few seconds the yell of voices was borne down to us, faint as the chirp of a bird, but delightfully distinct, and we knew that our bulletin was received. Within a minute the flask dropped down for the second time—full too—and on it another bit of paper showed white and welcome. The inscription was—

"Have no rope long as this string. Parsons has gone down for another to splice. Hope all well."—S.G.

We knew that this meant a wait of half-an-hour at the least, and we took another pull at the spirit to fortify ourselves against the cold, which was wrapping us creepily in its embrace. Then we stamped and tramped violently round the cavern once or twice to enliven our circulations, and this brought us face to face with the stone portico at the back of the cave. We halted before it to stare at each other inquiringly.

I nodded; then together we sauntered up the steps and stood in the entrance.

The temple was square fronted, with an oval doorway; along the *facade* ran pillared cloisters. It was built of carefully cut and morticed stones, hewn—as we could plainly see by the gaps—from the cliff behind us. Upon the twelve great pillars of the portico were decorated pilasters, chiselled with a clean nicety in the hard stone. They gave evidence of a patient skill and an artistic conception beyond the average. Within their shadow was a pavement, whereon a mosaic of graceful lines and figures entwined themselves. Centrally opened the portal.

The light filtered dimly through the entrance, and as we stood upon the threshold the interior was black and mysterious before us. As our eyes grew more accustomed to the gloom, and the shapes of things defined themselves in the twilight, we discerned the grandeur and the horror of the place.

The interior was round—in shape something like the Roman Pantheon—and along the circling walls ran long inscriptions in the Mayan symbol, twisted in varying folds and weavings of devices. The floor was wide and thick with dust. The disturbance of our footsteps made gaps in this, showing the smooth, hard-blocked granite that paved it. It rang hollow beneath our feet, when the nails of our shooting-boots reached it through the carpet of powdery refuse.

At the far end was a towering erection, dominating the empti-ness, dimly shadowing through the dusk. It was not till we ap-proached within a yard or two of it that we knew it for a graven similitude of the great Beast. It stood in a sort of chancel of the building, looming high upon a rough majestic mass of granite. This pedestal—a boulder without any mark of hammer or chisel apparent upon it—filled one side of the sanctuary, and the image—carved from virgin rock—reached to the domed roof.

Every loathsome detail of the Thing was reproduced with a skill most marvellous. The horrid foot-webs with claws aspread were there; the long, lowering neck; the malignant head fiend-ishly erect; the saw-like, serrated tail; the horrible dewlap; the filthy bloatings of the carcass; the thick legs, with bunches of muscle staring harshly out of the stone fore-arms. Below were inscriptions in the familiar symbol.

Far up in the fiercely poised head were eyes that glinted evilly—eyes that licked up into themselves all the poor light of the dim vault and concentrated it into two glistening points of wickedness. They seemed to follow us with such poignancy that we shuddered.

But the greater wonder and the heavier horror lay not in this foul image, terrible though it was in its life-like imitation.

Circling round the throned idol—symbol of the loathliest worship, as I suppose, and the cruellest that the world has ever seen—was a ring of brown and shrivelled objects. They were cloaked with rotting garments, and lean with the waste of cen-turies. They were mummified by time, but, in the undying cold, undecayed. It was the last worship of the priests of Cay, over-whelmed in the sanctuary, defying the long-drawn death of numbing famine in the presence of their god.

We two drew very near together, and I laid my hand upon Gerry's shoulder for mere support of a warm and sentient body. The fog of our startled breathings went up steamingly in the air. It smoked like incense before a yet sacred shrine of evil. We gasped as those who seek fresh air in a stuffy atmosphere, and at the same time huddled to one another far warmth. Never in any other condition of heat or cold do I remember to have experienced a freezingly hot oppression.

There were thirty of these poor hapless souls; all were face to earth, with garments hanging about them by mere stillness of pose. Their hands were yellow and claw-like, and were spread abroad upon the pavement. Their faces were swathed in brown hoods that covered their features utterly. Their bony, shrunken outlines showed haggard through the musty rags that clothed them.

We looked questioningly in each other's eyes before we laid hands upon the rigid kneeling form nearest us. We raised the low-laid face from the floor and turned it towards the scanty light.

The wrinkled features were drawn and crisp with the dryness of a hundred frozen years; the deep-sunk eyes were blurred—the smoothness of the pupils dulled to roughness by the shrinking of the temporal muscles and nerves. As we moved the head, a tooth or two clattered on the floor from the dried, fleshless gums, and gleamed white against the dust. The arms, set stiffly in their parchmenty skin, flopped helplessly abroad as we raised the body from its crouching position. The joints were tense as the bones. The whole body moved as one solid piece, as if it had been run into an invisible mould. Across the drawn forehead was a white band, and on it was broadly sealed the similitude of the great Beast. On the floor in patches remained a few rags of the texture of the rotten clothing.

Silently we gazed on this luckless remnant of a long-forgotten religion and race; then the ghastliness of the thing crowded upon our nerves fearsomely. Reverently we placed the poor gaunt body in its original position, and turned hastily to the door. We shivered as we gained the portico, and I passed the flask to Gerry. At the moment he gulped at the spirit the rope came flapping and uncoiling down the ice-hill opposite, and slipped up almost to our feet.

I sprang forward to catch it up, and began briskly to knot a running loop at the end of it. Gerry eyed me with approval.

"That's right, old chap," he remarked. "Up you go."

I wasted no time or words in argument, being well aware that he would defend for half-an-hour if necessary his proposition that I should have the first chance of ascent. I merely smiled upon him compassionately, reeving a deft hangman's knot. This done I flung myself suddenly upon my companion, threw the loop over his shoulders and drew it tight beneath his arm-pits. Then I yelled lustily, dragging at the rope with hearty tugs.

Amid the faint echo of an answering shout from above, I had the pleasure of seeing my friend fly swiftly toward the roof of the cavern, using language which might well have melted the adjoining ice. In a very halo of cursing his legs disappeared into the intricacies of the ice-dome, his feet kicking extravagantly at space and dislodging an occasional icicle upon me like a malediction. There was silence, and I was left alone with the ceaseless drip and the dreamy tinkle of the underground waterway.

I will own that for the few moments I was left companionless in the near presence of that musty ring of shrivelled corpses I felt as uncomfortable as I remember to have felt in my life.

You must not forget that I was physically weak from the shock of my fall, and that my nerves had been wrung past tension point by my anxiety for Gerry. Then you will understand that the drip, the purr of the stream ripple, the gray-green light from above in the uncertainty of its shadowing, the knowledge of the gruesomeness behind me, and the vault-like atmosphere, combined to make me almost hysterical. I could have screamed aloud, but didn't for reasons only known to my English birthright of prejudice and pride.

I wrestled through these æon-long instants of mental breakdown, and then there came the heartsome sound of a crack from above. I opened my eyes to see the rope fall anew upon the pebbly floor. With eager fingers I looped it over my shoulders, and with a mighty jerk gave the signal to haul away. So I fled cherubim-like up out of the glassy solitudes into the untainted air and the blessedness of the sun, and never have I rejoiced with more whole-souled gratitude in the same.

15

THE MOUNTAIN WAKES

As I shot beamingly out into the wholesome light of day a cheer rang out, waking the cold echoes delightfully. More than half the ship's company was ringing the crevasse mouth, Mr. Rafferty and half-a-dozen sailors hauling at the rope with a vigor that bespoke their entire satisfaction in the job. It was with a mighty tug that they finally yanked me on to the glacier, and I unwound myself and crawled on to the flat ice most thankfully.

Gwen was there with Denvarre, and Vi was standing talking to Gerry, who leaned back luxuriously on a rug, enjoying the sunlight and the smiles of the ladies. Waller, his usual apathetic calm broken by an obvious air of relief, was the first to take my hand, and Lessaution, bandages and all, was ready to weep with a joy that I really believe was unaffected.

He had already gleaned from Gerry a slight inkling of the wonders that lay beneath his feet, was demanding to be immediately lowered into their presence. His gratitude at our marvellous escape had a strong rival for the possession of his soul in the jealousy he felt that this notable discovery should have fallen to any one but himself.

I think Gwen, happy as she may have been in her new-found love for Denvarre, could not altogether have forgotten that she and I, though we had never acknowledged it definitely, had once been more than friends. Her face—I could but note it as I sped up from the mouth of the pit—had been white and anxious, and as I rolled unharmed from the edge to her feet, had flushed rosy red with what I could but hope was joy. She smiled at me as I rose to my feet, and shyly put her hand in mine, her eyes humid and wistful as she felt my answering grasp. But her words were few. "Thank God" was all she whispered, as she drew back to let

157

Lessaution fling himself upon me with a flood of gratulation and inquiry.

We reasoned fluently with the Professor as he escorted us back to the ship, disclaiming any desire to compete with him in the realms of research, and explaining to what simple and unsought chance our discovery was due. No argument, however, would move him from his set purpose. He demanded that he should be lowered without delay into the Mayan hamlet, vociferating his determination with a volubility that drowned all reason in mere noise. Finally we compromised. We put it before him that the launching of the boat was the supreme need of the whole party, and would take all the power and ropes at our disposal. No one could be spared to attend to his gropings in the glacier. If he agreed to postpone his desires till the launch was accomplished, we on our parts solemnly promised that he, first of any, should descend into the mystic solitudes below, solitudes, which we represented, were still practically unexplored. He gave a grudging assent, and thereafter quiet reigned.

Gwen walked between Denvarre and me, and somehow a sense of discomfort seemed to hang about my companions. Despite my thumped understanding I thought that I was bearing myself not ingloriously in the conversational *mêlée*, but the interest they manifested in my recital seemed to lag. Denvarre was distinctly gloomy, and Gwen was so desperately vivacious that I easily understood that she was not listening, but was occupied with other and unpleasant thoughts. I caught my breath as I wondered if by any possible chance they could have quarrelled, trying with all my might not to dwell on the possibilities that such a matter might have for myself.

They seemed all right again at dinner, both of them, and Baines served a special effort to signalize our great deliverance. A bottle or two of Heidsieck made every one of a cheerful countenance, whatever feelings their hearts may have held, and we speedily forgot the gray shadow of borderland that had hung so heavily over two of us.

After dinner we sat upon the deck in the starlight, and discussed coffee, cigarettes, and the chances of getting away. That these depended utterly on ourselves seemed entirely conclusive.

A passing whaler was the tiniest of probabilities, nor would she be likely to sight any signal of ours on these desolate shores. True enough old Crum had a fair idea of our destination, but it would be many months before he would think it his duty to send to look for us. Nothing obviously remained but to attempt the launch of the boat, and decide who should go in it.

It was quite certain that the ladies could not face fifteen or twenty days in an open boat. If they could not go, Garlicke and Denvarre wouldn't. Gerry was in no fit condition to face hardships after his knocking about, no more was I. The man to take charge then was Waller or Janson.

Waller we felt was the man for the job, but on the other hand we had also a strong feeling that bereft of his society and counsel we should be like children without their nurse. We decided to put the case before him, leaving the decision to his own good sense and knowledge.

I did not think the men would refuse a chance to go if it was offered them. I felt confident that a sufficiency of them would prefer a cruise on open water, even in an open boat, to sitting longshore and hauling at hawsers for the entirely unprofessional object (from a seaman's point of view) of bracing up what had become a land domicile. This especially would be so if the former procedure brought about a hope of eventually coming to a land of civilization, hard food, and good liquor—we had put them on an allowance of both—and away from horrifying fears of unknown and uncouth dragons. For Mr. Parsons had not been idle in his conversational moments, and the details of our adventure in the cañon had been painted by him with an unsparing wealth of imaginative incident.

Waller picked his men, reporting to me that any one of the ship's company would have jumped at the chance to go. This matter being settled, it remained to arrange the practicalities of the launch. Not only had we to drop our boat handsomely down a hundred feet of sheer cliff, but we had first to transport her bodily up the steep slopes of the basin before us. Looking at the job made it seem no more likeable; but the next morning we rose betimes and flung ourselves upon the business.

First of all we cut down the yacht's topmasts and sawed them into rollers. We did this with a light heart, well knowing that we could never want to test our ship's sailing qualities again. Then with levers we inserted them under the cutter's keel. This done we began to roll her proudly across the smooth rock floor—a transit we performed with consummate ease—and pointed her bows up the steep slope cliffward.

Over the unavailing wretchedness of the next two days I must draw a veil. Shortly, we gave the business a very ample trial, and were thoroughly beaten at the start. Tug as we would the task was entirely beyond us—vanquished us hip and thigh. The angle, which at first was moderate enough, increased to about forty-five degrees. The weight was about ten tons. If you would like to try the experiment we did, and test our physical inferiority, take to yourself a dozen other fools and try to drag a wheelless railway truck up Arthur's Seat, for instance, on rollers. Then let me have a written statement of your experiences. If it doesn't give points to many of the foremost writers of the impressionist school I shall be strenuously surprised.

By the evening of the second day we had progressed about two hundred and fifty yards, and the worst was still to come. We had expended enough perspiration to float the boat, and had just paused to shove in the wedges behind the rollers while we rested. We did this carelessly. They slithered on the smooth stone, the rollers revolved smartly, and before we could arrest her progress with levers, the wretched cutter was half-way back to the bottom again, bumping and straining her timbers viciously.

Gerry sat down and voiced the sentiments of the whole company at this point. He explained that to him it was obvious that no less period of time than a century would suffice to see our labor approach completion. As the span of human life was now ordered, we were unlikely, any of us, to attain to this age. Why then waste time that might just as profitably be spent in twiddling our thumbs? He added comprehensive anathemas on any who should attempt to combat this opinion, and then relapsed into surly silence, while the panting crew waited apathetically for further developments.

Then Waller suggested that our present attempt being a failure, the plan for reducing the launch to sections should be tried. This we had resolved to leave as a last resource, from haunting

fears that once dismembered, we might well fail to put her together again, the book of explanations supplied by her makers
having been lost. I lifted my head wearily to meet his proposal,
when my words were checked in the very utterance.

A dull boom, sullen and muffled at first, but swelling with
grating intensity to a thunderous crash, rolled and re-echoed
down and around the gray rock basin that surrounded us. The
cutter swayed and danced, hammering and splintering the rollers under her. We ourselves fell in unstudied helplessness on
the hard stone slabs. The earth quivered in our sight as the heat
haze quivers in the June sunlight. A current of hot air swept
over us, seeming to swamp us in murkiness. The little loose
pebbles sang and clattered as they rolled down the slope, running together and leaping upon one another in little swirls and
piles. A giant crag fell from the glacier foot. The roar of it
slammed across the hollow ponderously, the splinters scatter-
ing on the hard flooring of the lake bed, shooting out and across
the smooth granite in a thousand chips of glancing, flashing
crystal. The sun glistened upon them gloriously in many-hued,
rainbow rays. Behind us a great pinnacle of basalt was flung
from the peak, falling on the glacier with the crash of an artillery salute. A moan trembled out from the vitals of the riven
glacier, as if from a prisoned soul within. The impulse of the
crushed ice billowed out a dark spate of water at its foot.

Awe-inspiring as were these manifestations, they did not
affect us as did one slighter, but close at hand. A grate and crack
from below made us turn swiftly. The fissure across which our
ship was buttressed with walls of boulder gaped widely. Into
this sudden cleft the *Raccoon* slipped to the level of her bulwarks; the hawsers strained, tightened, thrummed tensely, and
then snapped apart like the flick of returning thongs. The masts
whipped to and fro quivering, and the stays shook uneasily. Then
with a grinding of copper the ship sagged over and lay still,
propped by the ragged edge of the rock.

As we raced back across the lake bed towards her, a round,
middle-aged shriek broke the stillness of the after-quiet. Lady
Delahay was vomited up from the saloon as Baines and the cook
erupted from the galley. She stumbled across the deck, and, with

the aid of the valet's deferential hand, mounted upon the bulwarks. The rocks were now level with the stanchions, and she stepped upon them to sink down thereon in desolate helplessness, Baines hanging over her with well-bred but astonished sympathy.

Gwen and Vi had been upon the heights above us, trying to sketch the line of needle-like pinnacles that crowned the ridge. Gwen, it appeared, had been engaged upon the very one that had fallen upon the glacier, and had been utterly stupefied, as it bowed toward her and then precipitated itself into the depths below. Both of them were dismayed beyond measure by the upheaval and the partial disappearance of the ship, and came flying down the slope, frightened to death by the roar and thrilling of the solid earth, confidently expecting further shocks and total engulfment. We met around Lady Delahay's prostrate form amid much excitement.

Nothing further occurred, but an oppressive silence seemed to have fallen over the land. The cries of the sea-birds melted out seaward, and not one of them showed far or near. The glacier stream had swept all its volume into that one great spout of a few minutes back, and not a single splash came from the empty opening in the ice. No sound was to be heard from the cliffs, though a minute or two before the fall and return of the surges had risen to us mellow and distinct.

We climbed the slope to look abroad upon the sea. It was oily and glass smooth as quicksilver, and far west the glow of the sunset was beginning to show upon its bosom, but not clear and gleaming. It was lurid and suffused as with vapor mist. The floe was clustered in strange herdings, and ringed beside the larger bergs were floating splinters from their summits. The dark lanes of water between the walls of ice were strangely regular—almost like the parallel lines of irrigation works. The usual motion of the unending swell had ceased utterly.

Suddenly Rafferty gave a shout.

"Saints in glory!" he exclaimed excitedly, "'tis the mountain that's afire."

We wheeled round to face the peak behind us. The torn scar left by the unseated pinnacle showed hard and raw in the evening light. From the dip between the snow caps a thin column of smoke was rising into the still windless air, commencing straight as a lance, but mushrooming out over our heads a few hundred feet up as if in weariness of its own weight.

It poured out of some new-hewn chimney in the rock relentlessly slow indeed, and lazily, but with a very business-like steadfastness. A few smuts were wafted to us, falling upon our clothes and faces.

From that moment a very large lump of despair began to settle upon my heart and stayed there. I began to fully realize the nature of the trap we were in. It must take days, work as we would, to get the boat up the slopes, put it together again on the top—even provided we didn't break it in the process—and drop it in safety down the cliffs. Waller might with very great luck get to the Falklands in three weeks. There might possibly be a ship there which would come to our rescue; very probably there might not. Giving everything the very best possible chance of succeeding, we couldn't get away from this horrible place under six or eight weeks. On the other hand, Waller might never reach the Falklands at all. Every hazard of sea and ice would be against him. If he got there he might never get back, for the berg might close. Our provisions might fail; the birds and the sea-lions would depart. The ship might sink further into the cleft and take our home and stores with her, for it was of course no more than likely that another earthquake shock would ensue. And above all this, there was the Horror of the cañon prowling around, ready to interrupt our proceedings at any moment. So beneath my breath I cursed the race of Maya, my besotted old ancestor, Crum, Gerry, Lessaution, and many other animate and inanimate influences that had brought about this disastrous expedition, and had landed us in this unspeakable plight. When I had thus softly vented my feelings upon the smut-filled air, forbearing open complaint as a bad ensample for the men, I turned to see what the others were thinking in the matter.

There was a grim look on Gerry's face. He too, I gathered, was beginning to understand what was meant by that black cloud which now rolled between us and the sun like some monstrous umbrella. Denvarre was looking at Gwen, and she, I gathered from the sudden motion of her face as I turned toward her, had but lately been staring at me, trying, I suppose, to understand what I thought of it. Garlicke eyed the phenomenon through his eye-glass, viewing it as if it was some second-rate performance which had to be endured, but equally to be depreciated. Lessaution gaped up at it open-mouthed; he nodded like a mandarin, showing by his expression his complete satisfaction with these arrangements for further volcanic demonstrations. Vi looked on with placid astonishment, being by now used to vagaries in this strange land of topsy-turvydom, and not wishing to appear unnecessarily surprised. The members of the crew made unanimous use of the common adjective to opine that the smoke was sanguinarily droll, and at that they left it. Waller's lips were compressed, though moving now and again in what I took to be *sotto voce* swearings. He shared no doubt with me a silent uneasiness that he preferred not to express.

An earthquake is no joke. One has absolute belief in the stability of the ground beneath one's feet—a belief which it takes much to destroy. When therefore you see the land shake like an ill-made jelly, when it grins and grimaces at you like a third-rate comedian, the traditions of a lifetime are undermined. That upon which you have planked the whole of your confidence deceives you. Faith is no longer a rock. Belief of every kind is vain. Stability in leaving the earth leaves all else unstable, and your spirit dies within you. Nothing is impregnable or unassailable thereafter. You are, to put it tersely, most horribly afraid.

At any rate I was. For at least six weeks and possibly for a year we were to live under this shadow of death. The cave, that we had chosen as a refuge should the Beast crawl down upon us, had now become a possible death-trap more horrible than his maw itself. The mountain was obviously volcanic, and as obviously was the cleft the result of volcanic action. Suppose it to close when we were in it. Like worms beneath a cart-wheel we should be crushed. Suppose it to suddenly widen. Like worms again should we be dropped into the very bowels of earth to be hopelessly cast away.

So again I cursed my fate and those who had been its arbiters, and assumed a cheerful countenance.

"I think that's all for the present," I remarked courteously to the company at large, "so if you have seen all you require perhaps you'll return to business."

They turned from their starings at the mountain, and Gerry chucked down the lever he still held with a surly air.

"So we're to start all over again?" said he. "Have you anything else to suggest?"

He found no answer but a grunt, and I explained that Captain Waller's proposition seemed the only feasible one. We must reduce the launch to sections, and carry them one by one to the cliff-top. I invited amendments, but none were forthcoming, and collecting spanners, we turned wearily to work again.

By good luck the lost plan of construction turned up. It was ingenious, but fiendishly intricate, and it was hours before we properly mastered it. Then with wrenches and screwdrivers we flung ourselves upon the boat, covering ourselves with dirt and wretchedness. This, however, only after stupendous wranglings over the writing and the interpretation thereof; in which wordy *mêlée* Gerry and Lessaution nearly came to blows, sneering over every mortice, and displaying directly opposite views concerning every nut and screw.

Yet within the course of the next day, by superhuman exertions, we managed to dismember the boat, and transport it in sections to the cliff-top. Here we found that the undoing of her was but child's-play to the putting of her together again. During the next three days language, temper, and filthiness of person bore hideous rule, and discomfort enveloped us like a fog.

Across these things I draw a discreet veil. Suffice it to say that on the evening of the third day, somehow or other, we had got the boat patched together and ready for lowering. Then we transported one of the ship's wind-lasses up the rocks, and fixed it firmly with stanchions at the edge of the crags. We made a sort of cradle of hawsers. With immense care, with ropes thickly parcelled to avoid the frayings of the ledges, and with fenders firmly fastened to her sides, we were enabled to lower the cutter by slow degrees to the water, and to see her sit thereon unharmed.

Rafferty slid down to her, and there were lowered to him tow, chisels, and a pot of pitch. With these he contrived to give her an inside calk where her seams leaked worst from her unhandy rebuilding. We left her floating for the night, with two men aboard to keep watch and watch lest the sea rising should dash her against the cliffs, or the floe bear down to nip her against the rocks. Upon the cliff-top two more camped to be within rope's reach of the boatmen if need arose.

No misfortune happily occurred, and the next day found us toiling up the cliff with stores for her provisioning, and water to fill her breakers. All these we passed down the swinging rope to Rafferty, who bestowed them in her lockers with nautical precision and neatness. Finally by eventide Waller and his six chosen associates descended, and amid the cheers of the assembled company took their places at the oars.

Then with one last encouraging shout, and amid great wavings of handkerchiefs and caps, they pulled away steadily up the channels between the pack-ice.

We watched them as they gradually faded to a black speck among the lanes in the floe and berg, and then disappeared to come into view again on the open water. There we saw their sail rise against the rays of the setting sun, and slant away slowly toward the horizon. At last even this vague dot upon the emptiness of ocean was not, and we turned away to seek the ship in the growing darkness.

There was sadness and an irresistible presentiment of coming evil in my heart; undefined it was; but none the easier borne. It was a silent and joyless meal we took before turning in, and I think every man of us sent up a prayer that night for our comrades on the open main; whose lives bore double burden, in that, if evil befell them, we should all likewise perish.

16

THE TEMPLE AND THE LAIR OF CAY

Though during the days of hard work, while the boat was being launched, we continued to live in the ship, we did so by compulsion of necessity alone, not having the time to seek another dwelling-place. Now the strain was over, we felt that it behoved us to seek shelter elsewhere, since another shock of earthquake might easily destroy the *Raccoon* and leave us utterly without abode in this land of desolation. Therefore we cast about for a refuge which should be stable enough to withstand earthquakes, and also form a protection in case the Beast came down upon us.

Several moderate-sized peaks rose from the glacier foot. They were precipitous in parts, but broken with ledges and crevices, making their ascent arduous, but by no means difficult. One of these, a mass of granite shaped something like a pyramid with a flattened top, seemed to meet the case admirably. The breadth of its base made it unlikely that it would topple however much it might be shaken, and its summit was scarred with deep clefts. Any of these might he roofed over with a few planks to make a famous shelter.

Janson and I made the ascent with some of the crew and made examination of the spot. We got up some timbers and a tarpaulin or two and soon arranged an excellent series of little cabins, sufficient to house the whole party if the need arose. We transported up to this eyrie a certain proportion of our provisions and stores, arranged hammocks for ourselves and cots for the ladies, and then felt that we had a satisfactory alternative abode if the ship should fail us.

This being accomplished, we had time and opportunity to turn to less pressing matters. We set forth on the following morning therefore to investigate the matter of the Mayan temple beneath the glacier, anent which Lessaution had muttered many jealous words during the last six or seven days. For he openly declared that Gerry and I wished to keep the glory of this discovery intact, and were delaying his entrance into its mysteries of malice prepense.

We took our ropes, poles, and a ladder to the cliff-top, found the crevasse, which we had marked with a cross hewn in the ice, and according to promise lowered the Frenchman first therein. I followed him, and in due order came Gerry, Denvarre, and Garlicke.

I found the little Professor trotting round the temple, exclamations of wonder and delight hurtling from between his teeth. His little arms waved, his little lean face beamed with scientific glee. His self-made dictionary and his grammar of the Mayan symbols was in his hands.

In the pauses of his ecstasy he was trying to divine the inscriptions. Now and again he stopped to examine the prone figures of the shrivelled priests, turning them about and picking at them with a minuteness that struck me as both hard-hearted and indelicate. Finally he dragged himself out of this haphazard *abandon* of discovery, and settling down before the base of the great pedestal, began to decipher the inscriptions with serious attention.

For some few minutes he sat silently between Gerry and myself, who held candles by him. He conned the twisted devices, turning from them to his note-book, and tracing out each symbol carefully. Suddenly signs of the greatest excitement manifested themselves. He jumped up with an exclamation, nearly upsetting both of us, and rushed round to the back of the image. Here he began to butt at the solid stone in a manner that seemed little short of imbecile.

In the midst of these scrabblings a panel—as it seemed—gave beneath his hand; we stared wonderingly as a door slid open at his very feet.

Two steps were revealed, dropping down into a chamber in the stone. Into the blackness of this vault our friend flung himself, chattering furiously in French, without waiting to be offered a light. We only stayed for an additional candle to be lit and then followed him smartly.

It was a small dark room, and without exit to the air save by the way we had entered. Round the sides of rock-hewn wall ran a slab. Upon it were arranged various basons, salvers, spits, and other sacrificial instruments to which we could give neither names nor use. But what made our eyes sparkle and our breath come short and ecstatically, was the fact that each and all of these outlandish vessels shone yellow and lustrous in the candle-light. They were in no degree discolored by age or by damp. At the which we knew that here indeed we had fallen upon the Mayan booty of which my uncle had spoken— "the ancestral treasures of that hapless race."

We stared with greedy eyes upon this hidden hoard. With awesome fingers we touched and handled the beakers, the basons, and the curious two-pronged forks and skewers. All bore traces of use, but we were at a loss to account for the jagged notches in the handles of some of the sword-like spits. They leaned against the rocky ledge, arranged in exact order along the floor. At the upper part of each were wavering scars in solid metal; we might have imagined them to be decorative patterns, but for their scratchiness and irregularity. I took one in my hands and examined it carefully.

It had a hilt about half-a-foot long at the thickest end. It was just below this that the dents eat into the metal. I caught hold of Lessaution by the arm to demand his explanations of this matter.

At first he contemned my curiosity, explaining that matters of much greater interest demanded his attention. He ran his fingers over the criss-cross work, and suddenly shuddered, handing the thing back to me with a repellent gesture.

"It is explained there," he said, pointing to the device that ran above the ledge. "Those are the rituals of sacrifice. It is necessary to slay the victim according to the religion of Cay. So they stab the sword through the shoulder and pierce the lung, and the victim dies slowly—very slowly, and he calls for long. So they think the god is well pleased. Then the poor people who die, they are in agonies—ah, so great a pain, and they bite and snap at the handle with their teeth. So here we see the marks. It is not nice—that, no it is of the most horrible. But what would you? They were brutes, this people, but oh, so ancient," and he shrugged his shoulders as if much might be forgiven to a people who had conducted their devilries from time immemorial.

I dropped the thing with a shiver and a tingling of my fingers. Brutes they were, indeed, these fearsome Mayans of the centuries of long ago. I could only give fervent thanks that they were not alive to welcome us to these savage shores. I could well imagine the delight that would be theirs in spitting us on their horrible prongs, and leaving us to slow agony, tickling, as they would doubtless believe, their god's ears with our delightful tortures. And if they had not left us to pant out our lives before this bestial image, we should have been offered up alive to the monster himself, to meet a swifter doom, perhaps, but one as fearful.

I asked him how he was so sure of the matter. He explained that the whole of the devices that ran round the walls were the detailed dogma and rubric of the worship of Cay. Not only did these give full directions for sacrificial orgies, and prescribe particularly the transfixing of the victims in the manner spoken of, but also alluded to the keeping alive of these tormented wretches—I am only quoting from what he translated—with various drugs, the names of which he was unable to understand. The inscription laid stress on the fact that the cries of these unfortunates were beloved of the god, and that, therefore, they were to be prolonged as far as possible.

It was only to be considered natural that the worship of such a filthy monstrosity should breed degraded cruelties, but I puzzled my head to think how Mayans in Central America could have possibly divined the existence of anything resembling this antediluvian Horror in the Antarctic Circle. I questioned Lessaution on this point also.

He said that his researches had led him to think that the last home of the Mastodon had been in Central America, and that before he became extinct he might have become the holy beast of the Mayan religion, much as the bull is to the Hindoos. He went on to explain his theory that as by lapse of time the huge beast became a memory and a myth, he rose from being a symbol of the godhead to being confounded with the god himself. His proportions had probably been exaggerated by half-forgotten rumor, and with his size had grown his sacredness. To make themselves strong the priesthood had invented the human sacrifices, by which, doubtless, they could remove their special antipathies or heretics.

It was not surprising, he added, that the Mayans, born and nurtured in the service of this superstitious horror, should conceive the Dinosaur, when he thus descended upon them, to be their god in very deed. We must also reckon the effect their miraculous bringing to this desolate coast would have upon them. There was no doubt that they had frequently striven to do their divinity honor by human sacrifices, and that one of their first acts must have been the building of this temple under the shadow of the overhanging rock.

It was to be supposed that the glacier had been diverted from its former channel by some earthquake shock, and had poured upon the building from above, bringing to utter destruction the town that had stood round it, the only exceptions being the house we had found upon the mountain-side, and the one Parsons and I had discovered in the glacier. This last had been saved by the shielding cliff above it, though walled in by impenetrable thicknesses of ice.

The priests of Cay, evidently fanatic to the last, had seen no chance of escape. They had stored away their golden vessels, swept and garnished their sanctuary, and then lain down in grim hopelessness to die at the feet of their god. Swiftly numbed by the overpowering cold, without provision or proper clothing, they had passed away in silent submission to the decrees of fate, and probably without much feeling or pain. Lessaution surmised that the lone corpse Parsons and I had stumbled upon in the other dwelling was the remains of some unfortunate wretch who had been longer fortified by food and raiment, and who had fought the cold with full knowledge of the ultimate issue. So in solitude and great fear he had met his death.

I pondered these ideas of the Professor's while we collected together the vessels of the sanctuary. We roped them up in

heaps, and transported them to the foot of the ice-hill. Then we
signalled to Rafferty, whom we had left above in charge of half-
a-dozen of the sailors, and had the pleasure of seeing our trove
whizz up into the sunshine, to be bestowed finally in the lockers of the ship, there to await the possibilities of our ultimate
rescue.

As the last sheaf of spits disappeared into the gloom of the
roof, we turned for further explorations. Lessaution held—and
we felt that there might be something in it—that by following
the course of the ice-stream that tinkled into the channel at the
extreme end of the cave, we might chance upon other remains
of the Mayan village, or at any rate find more relics of their com-
munity. Not wishing to leave any chance untried of discovering
all we could of this strange people's habitation, we lit dips, took
one apiece, and crawled into the mouth of the waterway.

It was low-roofed and narrow, and we groped and splashed
along it like rats in a sewer. The light played and spangled on
the ice walls, and the gurgle of the ripples and our splashings
re-echoed hollow and gloomily. A draught sang back into our
faces, making the candles sputter noisily. We thought that we must
be approaching an outer entrance, though no light came through
the ice. We wondered if by any chance we were in any communi-
cating by-way of the cavern that Parsons and I had first explored.

Suddenly the ice faded from about us, and with the falling
splash of a small cascade the rivulet ran into an opening in a
rock wall which faced us.

This we took to be without doubt the overhanging side of
the mountain which backed the basin in which lay our ship. We
peered down the tunnel, and seeing the fall to be but a foot or
two ventured in. For the first fifty yards the way was straight
enough, but then began to turn and twist deviously, narrowing,
though it grew higher. We easily understood that the water had
worn a way through the granite by eating out a lode of softer
mineral. We were enabled to walk erect, though I heard Lessaution grunt complainingly behind me as he squeezed through the
narrows, where the sides reached out to one another sharply.

A couple of hundred yards more, and a turn—sharper than
any we had yet passed—whipped us round almost in our tracks.

Before I could realize it we were striding out into a great hall in the granite, and the stream was almost lost in the sandy floor.

With the disappearance of the reflecting walls the darkness seemed to swallow the thin light of our candles utterly. A heavy effluvia-like smell hung in the air. In the act of wheeling round to speak to my companions I tripped. I plunged forward, grasping the elusive sand, and ploughing a groove in it with my chin.

My candle went out as I struck the ground, but before its light snapped into nothingness I saw beside my face five long yellow objects spreading out ghastlily distinct upon the dark floor. Looking back I saw the obstruction over which I had stumbled begin to roll slowly from between me and the lights of my companions. It was silhouetted in irregular dents and jaggednesses against the dim illumination. I also saw the long yellow gleams move lingeringly from beside me in the twilight.

A yell went up from the others, and an odor still more pungent assailed my nostrils. I heard the slow, lurching sound of a heavy body churning the silt of the floor. But it needed not that to tell me in what plight I was. We had penetrated to the very lair of the Monster. I had fallen headlong across his tail as it stretched in my path. Beside me was his webbed foot; my face nearly touched his clammy nails.

He was turning—turning—turning; in another second his huge neck would swing round upon me; I should be a mere swelling in that monstrous throat.

My knees were palsied by a terror that scarcely allowed me to rise. My joints were as water within me. If ever man realized the terrors of nightmare in the flesh, I did so during those two fearful seconds when I scrambled to my feet, and raced across the ten yards that separated me from the mouth of the tunnel in the rock. I leaped into it like a rabbit before the greedy jaws of a terrier.

The others were already jammed in its narrow recesses. As I joined them the last light fell into the stream with a hiss. Kicking, reeling, panting, snatching at each other and at the rocks, we fought along that pipe-like passage, every nerve in our bodies tingling with expectant terror. My hair bristled on my head as I heard the snap of those grim jaws behind me, and for one awful moment I felt the horrible breath sing past my cheek. I ducked to very earth, and at the same moment felt the rasp of the eager tongue upon my heel. Calling aloud in abject terror I plunged forward, bearing down Gerry and Lessaution with me. We struggled together in the darkness, splashing up a little stream, and wallowing in the turbid mud, while above our very heads, it seemed, we could hear the hiss and pant of the straining lips. On hands and knees we jostled and crawled in the darkness.

As we drew away from the sounds behind us, I managed after a nervous effort or two to strike a vesta. The match sputtered, flared, and then burnt up steadily. Lessaution was still grasping his extinguished dip, and thrust the wick into the flame. As it took fire he held it up, and in its steady light we saw the nearness of our escape.

Not ten yards away the long neck strained and weaved desperately, bowing towards us with frantic efforts. The wicked green eyes flamed, and the teeth snapped and chattered greedily. The murky breath from between them flooded the cavern noisomely. The whole horrible scene stood out in frightful distinctness against the background of dark rock.

Then the dip-flame reached Lessaution's fingers, and with a curse he dropped it. The fall of the darkness upon that brief but all too vivid glimpse of horror unmanned us all. With a gasp we turned and fled recklessly into the darkness of the waterway without waiting for a light, paddling and splashing through the pools, tripping each other up, reeling, wrestling, smiting and bruising our limbs against the rocks. Finally with bleeding fingers, and wet with perspiration and roof-drip we stumbled out into the dimness of the temple cave, panting, dishevelled, like whipped curs, coughing still with the vile stench of that fearful kennel, shivering yet with the narrowness of our escape.

With broken sentences and half-coherent words we arranged the order of our ascent, and were hauled up one by one. With grateful lungs and dazzled eyes we greeted the freshness of the glacier slopes, though it was with dejected mien we slunk back to the ship. We sought victual, and later, tobacco, discussing the same on deck for appreciable minutes before any one ventured to refer to our adventure, even Lessaution's fund of conversation being dried up by his sense of defeat.

It was Garlicke who opened the conversation, and from a sporting point of view. He is a sort of *sans appel* on the subject of weapons of the chase, being a noted man at the running deer and such-like competitions, as well as a keen game shot. He demonstrated that the sporting Mannlicher rifle was the instrument marked out for the destruction of the Monster, giving his reasons for supposing that its bullet would penetrate any hide, provided that the missile had a hollow point. He regretted intensely that he had not had one of these useful implements at hand during the late *rencontre*.

Then the babble joined upon this issue and others flowing from it, and we felt our nerves grow back to us with our words, each of us expressing the opinion that to the determined man, armed with modern weapons, Dinosaurs were not necessarily invulnerable, and each asking, on reflection, no better than to beard the Beast again in his lair with suitable arms.

In which wordy tournament Lessaution, as was to be expected, rode triumphant down the lists, being willing, so he assured us, to compete with the Great Atrocity, equipped with no more than his native intelligence and a squirt.

This latter he proposed to fill with diluted prussic acid—of the commodity in question we possessed not a molecule, which he regarded as beside the question—and therewith advance down the passage up which two hours before he had so ingloriously fled. Arriving within range of the gaping mouth, he would fill it with the fatal fluid. But one frightful writhe and M. le Dinosaure would lie dead at his feet. *V'là tout.*

This versatile proposal was met with abounding laughter, the which daunted him in no degree, but cheered us all immensely. For with laughter returned self-respect, which had dropped from us in its entirety during the disgraceful rout of the morning, and we shook our fear from us as dogs shake their dripping coats. To each came great resolves to personally seek out and destroy the Monster, and complacent with the future renown thus inwardly promised, each turned patronizing attention to the talk of his fellows, using their banal conversation to cloak the deep and secret devices that seethed within his own brain. So content grew beneath the cloud of tobacco smoke, and pleasant

talk expanded itself, and finally the ladies, under the persua-
sive tinkling of Gerry's banjo, consented to enliven the rocky
solitudes with a song.

17

A LITTLE DOG'S STUMBLE

It was as Gwen began to lift her voice sweetly in the opening notes of "Just a little bit of string," that with harassing appropriateness the hawser, which had that morning again been tightened between the anchor and the ship, snapped with a ringing crack. The deck quivered villainously, and I, who had just risen to reach for more tobacco, fell upon my chair and smashed it to matchwood. The doors of the companion flapped to and fro, and the rigging quivered and thrummed. We could hear the jar of the rattled machinery in the engine-room.

At the same moment we were aware that the rocks were grinding upon the ship with a scissor-like movement, though happily they did not close. Had they done so we should have been nipped in their jaws with a very remote chance of escape. We also realized that the smoke-cloud, which had risen and grown thinner during the day, was expanding and thickening, making the twilight of the short Antarctic night a very business-like gloom.

We slipped across the gangways hurriedly, and grouped ourselves upon the rocks. A low rumble came creeping across the empty silences of the glacier. It rolled up to us like the muffled groaning of a buried army. We could fancy that the tombed city of long ago was sending out its desperate call for succor. The rocks shook beneath us. The gravel danced and pattered about our feet. We staggered, catching at one another aimlessly. Gwen, who was next me, tripped comfortably into my arms, where I held her with much content, both of us swaying absurdly.

The dull roar became abruptly a sharp crash. The ground rippled and worked horribly, and we were flung to earth, grasping at the rolling boulders. The cleft beneath the ship yawned like some Titanic mouth. As the remaining hawser parted, the keel sank further into the opening with a thud, and the stones we had built up beneath it went clattering down into the abyss. Not ten yards from where Gwen and I fell abroad, and not two feet from where Lessaution grovelled, a fissure opened and shut with a snap as of teeth. The Professor in fact declared that for one hair-raising moment he looked into the very deepest fastnesses of death.

As the gap closed, a puff of sulphurous steam was shot into the air. It clouded over us, making us cough. A clatter of ice and falling water came from the glacier; a splinter or two fell from the peak. Then, suddenly as came the upheaval, quiet returned and fell upon the scene.

From that moment, though, the darkness was riven. The mushroom-like pall of smoke now hung over us rosy-red from fires that burnt beneath it in the lap of the hill. The crimson light flared down into the empty lake-basin, reflected back luridly from the rocks. A small, fine rain of soot, gray and woolly, began to fall; it got into our eyes and nostrils, and set us sneezing and winking prodigiously. Then in trembling and with hopelessness in our hearts we climbed the slopes to the cliff-tops, filled with desolation in that the earth having turned traitor, we had but the sea to look to. How vainly we might look and how long we knew but too well.

The red glow wavered upon crestless surges that moved slowly upon the crags. Far out to sea the islands of the first eruption showed black and shattered, dim outlines in the cinder rain. This fell mercilessly on floe and berg, blackening them to filthy patches upon the rosy sea. Far away we could still see the gleam of moonlight upon the outer ocean, peaceful and silvered against the blood-like hue of the landward waters. From above us came the boom of irregular explosions, and gray tufts of smoke shot up into the darkness. Here and there crimson splashes of flame cut the smoke tower. They were spouts of molten stone, the slag of that mighty furnace. The snap and hiss as these fell upon the glacier was like the over-boiling of some stupendous kettle.

My eyes were seared with unrest in this hopelessness of sea and land. I turned them upon Gwen, who stood beside me, to give them comfort. She had a lace shawl about her head and arched over her face, shading it from the steady drizzle of cinders. These lay upon the few unprotected curls that flecked her forehead, giving her a *poudré* effect that in that deep twilight radiance was simply ravishing. The same scarlet duskiness beat upon her complexion, giving it the tint of a moss-rose. Her eyes shone anxiously, but like stars.

I gnawed restlessly at my mustache. I was but human and desperately in love. The desire to take her in my arms and swear that nothing on earth should hurt her was just on the borders of being irresistible.

"Magnificent sight, isn't it?" I questioned, looking down at her pleasantly.

"Gorgeous," she answered briefly, coming a step nearer. It was with a curious catch in her voice she added: "But what if it overflows?"

"Oh, it won't," I answered confidently. "Besides, the glacier's between us and it."

"Another earthquake might split the glacier."

"We'll wait till it does," said I cheerfully. "We shall be well away before anything of that kind happens."

She stood silent for a minute or two, tapping her fingers idly on the boulder beside her. Then she looked up at me with a quick smile.

"After all, it would be very soon over, wouldn't it?"

"Quite soon," said I, with assurance. "And—and we should be all together."

She glanced up at me again with a queer little smile that tried to cover the catch of her voice.

"I don't know that I was thinking of—all," she said, and turned away to join the others as they began to wander back towards the ship, and I strode beside her, fighting my passionate impulses in silence. For no doubt she had meant it for a reminder. Denvarre was the thought of her heart now that possible disaster hung over us, and I, in my blundering way, wanted to shove myself into an equality with him. I chewed the cud of this reflection as we all strolled down the slope, and the bitter hope that the end might come as she had pictured it almost crept into my heart, so far outside the bounds of common sense does the fever of jealousy carry one. But I'm thankful to say that my English birthright of self-possession came back to me within a score of strides, leaving me rational again.

I explained—and the others found it remarkably easy to understand—that it would be folly to think of sleeping aboard again that night. We must take up our residence on the cliff where we had prepared our shelter. So up the ledges of the rock pyramid we scrambled, and lodged ourselves in the tarpaulined crevices at the top. We mostly slept, I believe, but I was restless. For I had realized only too well that the great smoke pall that overhung us and made long the night was Death's Shadow indeed.

As the dawn began to filter in under the fog of dust, I woke and strode out to see how fared the world of fire and ice. A great hush had fallen with the livid morning light. The thunderous boom of the crater had ceased, and from above came only the distant purr and simmer of undying fires. The boil and roar of active eruption had died down. The great smoke curtain stretched away in a long wreath inland, carried before the cool sea breeze. The heavy sulphur mist had lightened with the same fresh draught, and the gulls had returned and were clamoring overhead in their hundreds. The sea lay in purple splendor, save where it was broken by the soot-begrimed floe. The swish of ripples on the cliff-foot was peaceful as the drip of a well-bucket.

I glanced down to where our ship lay. She seemed to have slipped over yet further in the night. A soft mist clung about her, and I puzzled myself to think how vapor could rise from barren and solid stone. It was dissolving upward as I watched, but ever forming anew. Then I understood that it was coming out of the fissure—the steam, no doubt, of some underground geyser. The carcass of the great whale that had been stranded by the volcanic wave had slidden down the incline of smooth rock almost into the centre of the basin. I reflected with dissatisfaction that the stench of this offal so close to our headquarters would be by no means pleasant.

My eyes wandered to the cliff-top where we had stood the night before, dwelling upon it with half-painful, half-pleasurable reminiscence. How sweet Gwen had looked, and how unattainable.

I began the everlasting fight with my inner self that was new and old every morning, thrusting forward to my soul's attention every possible argument why I should think of her no more, and doing so naturally with the same pain and the same enjoyment as much as ever.

Into the midst of my musings came a sudden jar of unfamiliarity as I stared at the edge of the crags. I blinked unbelievingly. A black breadth of shadow intersected the rocks as if a knife had carved them rigidly to the line. I rubbed my eyes. There was no doubt about it. A clean-cut cleft was in the rocks, some twenty feet broad. How deep I could not tell.

I clambered down the ledges softly from hold to hold, avoiding noise that the others might have their fill of healthful sleep. I crossed the bare flat between me and the new-made fissure, and stood upon the edge. I peered in.

The gash was driven deep into the bosom of the cliff, reaching to within twenty feet of the tide-line. A lump or two of granite had fallen from the parting edges and lay in the nip of the angle below. As I looked, one of them slipped in the vice-like hold, and settled nearer the bottom. A few seconds later another did the same. Then I understood that the gap was widening before me as clay cracks in the June sunshine.

I hung over the pit, gazing into it with hopeful eyes. Would the cliff be riven to its base, and the sea be let in upon us? Then, by Jove, we'd have the old *Raccoon* afloat again. We should escape from this land of desolation like rats from an opened trap. Into a slow opening like this the sea would pour gently. It would not overwhelm the ship with a sudden cascade. Such luck would be too stupendous—I assured myself of it most determinedly. Yet—yet—what a joyous awakening it would be for my companions if so outrageous a thing could come about. How melodramatically we should sweep out into the free spread of waters beyond!

My chain of cheerful prophecy here got a sudden set back. As I looked at the largest stone in the crack, it split across. In spider-like ramifications cracks multiplied upon it. It fell apart into rubble. Finally only dust filled the crevice. The rocks were closing even as they had opened. A stratum cleavage was here. It worked uneasily in the travail of the mountain behind—yawning in weariness of the constant convulsions. Now in the rest following the upheaval it was settling together again.

As I stood and pondered these things another eruption roared in the crater mouth. The ground rocked uneasily beneath my feet; I stumbled to my knees. With a snap the jaws of the cliff closed, nothing remaining but the ragged dent where the edges had been riven. As I scrambled to my feet a shrill yell re-echoed above the closing roar of the earthquake. I turned hastily to see a funny sight.

Down the lower slopes of the crag we had camped upon rolled a round object; it emitted screams of the most piercing description, and advanced with gathering speed. I recognized the gorgeous sleeping-suit affected by Lessaution, and the eye-searing yellow tassel of his nightcap. They made a vivid flash of meteoric color down the sombre rocks.

The little *savant* was scrabbling at the stone stairway as he fled along, tearing unavailingly at clumps of lichen, and snatching at the loose boulders. These last he had managed to set moving in some quantity, and they enveloped him in a clattering halo of pebbles that grew in velocity and in volume. The clamor of his onset was prodigious. He revolved like a catherine-wheel. His expressive countenance glared witheringly out into space during the curt moments it was uppermost, returning with a baffled air to face the earth as he flew swiftly round. His little legs threshed desperately into emptiness. Finally with a preposterous bounce he dropped over a ledge some four feet high, and swept out from the crag foot amid his escort of boulders, squirming fearfully.

Choking back my laughter I ran to him with an expression of deepest solicitude. Before I reached him he had risen, and groaning pathetically, began to slap himself about the more outlying portions of his person, slipping his hand from limb to limb delicately, and cursing with fluency as bruise after bruise became manifest. Fortunately his injured shoulder had been well swathed in lint, and showed no signs of having broken out again.

He explained that he was murdered in effect—yes, he had no whole bone in his body. The horrible boulders had mangled him into a fricassee. He would be tender eating for M. le

Dinosaure, to whom his remains would be welcome. He, Emil Saiger Lessaution, had for them no further use—no, in their present unbelievable state they would be of no slightest good. He was one large weal. I might figure to myself that, seeing me below, he had started down to join me. After the disgusting sulphurous stenches of the night before, he had had the intention to smell the freshness of the sea. Thus, when he was half-way down, behold the earthquake had swept him from his feet. Engulfed in tumultuous rubble he had been borne down the cliff as in a torrent. His skin was obtused to the baring of the flesh, and his joints—yes, his joints, let it be observed—strained as by a rack. A thousand thunders! These tremblings of the earth were afrighting. For him—he did not care when he left so unsafe a region.

I armed him gently up the ascent to where the rest of our party—also aroused by the eruption—were watching us. I surrendered him into the hands of Rafferty, who, on the strength of the possession of a case of sticking-plaster, had constituted himself surgeon to the ship's company. From his hands the Professor emerged a few minutes later, with an intricate pattern decking his features, to receive the full sympathy of us all.

After this we proceeded to breakfast, with certain apprehensions of what might happen in the way of further earthquakes, but still with moderate appetite. There was one slight rocking of the ground, but it did not so much as upset a tumbler, and we concluded that the worst was, for the present, over.

As the morning drew on we descended to the ship to examine her plight. She was leaning over at an angle of forty-five degrees, propped by the edge of the crevasse. Her keel was straining at the splinters jammed in the narrows of the opening. She lay so that her bulge almost covered the chamber in the rock. The hot fumes were still rising from below, smelling, for all the world, like the baths at Aix.

We got aboard and went down into the saloon. Everything was in the wildest disorder. The table, being screwed to the floor, was still unmoved, but everything else was piled in heaps between the floor and the lockers. Hardly a bit of crockery but had its crack or two, and many of the plates and glasses were broken outright. In the hold the bilge was leaking through her strained sides, dripping down the rocks against which she leaned. Not a rat squeaked or scampered in this—their usual stronghold—and their damp footprints were visible leading away from the ship.

Evidently this dry clock was not to their liking.

We set to work to get up some coal from the bunkers and some provisions from the storeroom. All of us—even the ladies—carried a larger or a smaller package, and in about an hour the procession set back to the cliff abode.

Gerry and Vi were alone on deck as I emerged last from the companion. Gerry's face was a study in scarlet and surprise. Something had most certainly occurred within the last few minutes to move him greatly, and as I appeared he strode toward me with an air of joyful importance. At the same moment, Vi, who had turned away as I stepped out of the doorway, swung quickly round again toward him.

"Hush!" she ejaculated, frowning with a meaning look toward the accommodation ladder, and Denvarre's head rose into view as he ascended.

Gerry stopped with a look of indecision. Then with a beneficent grin he wheeled round and offered her his hand to step down off the deck. I saw that below, the others were grouped upon the rocks, waiting for us to begin the ascent again. I was at a loss to account for Gerry's extraordinary behavior, especially the fact that he was walking happily enough with Vi, after avoiding her like the plague ever since he'd learned of her engagement.

I stepped down to join the party as Denvarre plunged hastily down the companion to fetch, as he explained, another pipe. I began to saunter along with Gwen and Lessaution, still watching with amazement Gerry's enthusiastic escort of Vi. In two or three minutes Denvarre overtook us. I noticed that Gwen shot a look at him as he reached us, which I found difficult to explain. He was wearing a stony expression, and avoided meeting her gaze. He began to talk to Lessaution with great vivacity, and the two gradually drew ahead of us, swinging between them the sack of coal that the little Frenchman had been staggering under alone. We were all more or less weighed down with stores, even the girls carrying their share. Gwen bore in one hand a pound of candles, and in the other a tin of mustard.

As the other two drew out of earshot, the silence deepened uncomfortably between Gwen and myself. I cannot explain it, but there seemed to be a sense of strain between us. I looked up once to find her regarding me with a fixed expression, and she reddened deeply as I caught the glance. She turned her head away hurriedly. Then as if by an effort she faced me again. I could see by the catch in her pretty throat that she was gathering herself together to say something—something that she found it difficult to express. There came a sudden interruption.

Fidget, the fox-terrier, had been gambolling and ambling aimlessly about. Suddenly, raising her nose, she sniffed the air curiously. She barked sharply, pattering back toward the ship. She leaped the narrowest end of the fissure, and trotted up the further slopes of the basin still yapping angrily. Her nose was in the air defiantly; the bristles of her withers stood up.

She stopped with a quick jerk as she neared the top. Planting her fore-legs stiffly before her, she began a series of shrill yelpings, dancing in her excitement.

Her bark leaped a couple of octaves into a shriek of fear, and out from behind a boulder loomed the hideous triangular head we knew too well. The Monster of the cañon lumbered into view, and the little dog turned and flew for us frantically, not the merest indication of her tail in evidence, so tightly was it tucked between her legs.

In her unseeing terror she fled straight toward us, not avoiding the cleft. Consequently she came slap upon it, and unable to stop, charged straight into it. With a thump and a squeak she fell into the angle of the bottom. Being so far above her, we could plainly see how she was caught in the nip of the crevice, where she remained struggling desperately upon her back, howling piercingly as she twisted and wriggled between the cruel stones.

We had commenced to run for our rock, which was fortunately only about two hundred yards distant. The Beast was still about a quarter of a mile from the ship and the fissure, out of which still came poor Fidget's heart-rending veils.

"Poor little wretch," I remarked to Gwen, as I turned back to face the ascent. "But I expect it'll be mercifully quick and soon over."

No answer came, and I was aware—and the blood within me seemed to freeze with the knowledge—that Gwen was flying down the slope to where the little dog lay howling, her eyes ablaze, her curls streaming in the wind. She was calling Fidget desperately by name, while toward her with steadfast, leisured tread rolled that great Horror, as three centuries before he had swung down upon the hapless Mayan maiden.

"Stop," I screamed, "for God's sake stop," and I flung away my burden and raced madly down the slope. She gave no heed, still calling loudly to Fidget, whose whinings increased as we drew nearer. I ran as I have never run before or since; I saw the eyes of the Beast glint emerald-sheened in the sun; I saw his ungainly waddle break into a cumbersome trot, and the desperation of my speed brought me to Gwen's side in a couple of seconds.

"Stop! Are you mad?" I yelled. "What's a dog's life to yours?" and I snatched at her shoulder to drag her back.

A pebble shot from under my feet, glancing upon the water-smooth granite; I feel heavily, while a thousand stars danced before my eyes. As I scrambled dazedly to my feet, I saw Gwen thirty yards away lifting Fidget from the cleft, and rushed to meet her as she turned to run toward me. The Beast was a short furlong distant.

I looked up the quarter-of-mile of steep rock escarpment that lay between us and safety, and knew that I, at least, dizzy as I was, could never mount it before he would be upon us. And Gwen might fall. Anything might happen. No, the cavern beneath the ship was the only chance. I staggered forward and caught her elbow as she ran.

"It's no good," I said. "We're done. The cave beneath the ship's the only possible place."

"Can't we run for it?" she gasped.

"I can't, at any rate," I answered sadly, "and I don't think you'd better try."

"Oh, you're hurt—you're hurt," she whispered pantingly as we raced toward the ship. "And it's my fault. But I couldn't stand

the screams of the poor little wretch—I couldn't have seen her
torn and mangled. Hadn't we better get into it?" and she pointed
up the ship's side above us.

"No," I answered, as I handed her swiftly on to the ledge,
and helped her down into the cave beyond, "he might manage
to break in upon us. Here we're safe for the present, at any rate.
He may try to starve us out, but it isn't likely. After a bit, when
he finds he can't get at us, he'll shuffle away as he came."

Fidget was barking furiously, and bristling up her hair, but
at the farthest end of the cavern. A sludgy, dragging movement
became audible, and the murky odor of the Horror clouded down
to us. Looking out from under the overhanging roof I saw a
single shining claw project over the edge of the cleft. Then the
half of the pad came into view, the rock dinting its podginess.

The brute swung his head over me, and parted his thin, inquisitive lips almost to a sneer. For one halting second the head was
poised motionless. Then, swift as a dropping stone, it smote
down at me, and I flung myself back, the evil eyes flashing past
not five yards away. There they hung and balanced, glinting
evilly at us, while the long pendant neck strained into the cleft
from above. The huge body made twilight in the cavern, swelling eagerly into the space between the rock and the ship. The
muscular fore-arms kneaded and crumbled the edges of the fissure. So were we desperately prisoned, and such was our jailer.

18

A DESPERATE BETROTHAL

At the farthest limit of the cave we leaned upon the rock, and looked at that wicked, weaving head. Twice before had I seen it, but never in such circumstances as this. On both occasions we had been men alone. The peril had been distributed, so to speak, amongst us all. But with a girl, and a beautiful girl moreover, with whom I happened to be desperately in love—to have that outrageous atrocity mouthing upon her and me alone, and to feel that any accident might send her into its bestial maw—Good God! it might turn any brain. I stood between Gwen and the entrance and tried to smile into her face.

"I wouldn't look that way, if I were you," said I persuasively. "He'll take himself off directly, I hope."

Her lips were very white and they trembled unrestrainedly, but she smiled back into my eyes—a ghostly, uncertain sort of smile, though, I must confess.

"I don't mind. Not much at least." Then with a strained attempt to look at the humorous side of it she added, "What an opportunity for M. Lessaution and his squirt."

I loved to see the pluck of her, and answered cheerfully.

"Garlicke will be distracting the brute's attention directly with that Mannlicher rifle," said I. "I happen to know he took it up with him when we moved camp, for use in just such a possibility as this. He'll be trying the effect of the bullet with the top bitten off," I added to keep the light side of the question uppermost, though it was a watery sort of sprightliness at the best.

From the edge above, where the weight of the great body was pressing, a lump of granite fell, and splashed into splinters in the narrows of the gulf. It widened the mouth of the fissure by a foot or more. The horrible trunk surged forward a yard or two, and one of the huge legs, dropping from between the belly and the rock, slid into the opening. The five white claws waggled and gripped at empty space, and the gloom in the cave increased. Fidget was beyond barking now, and backed against the uttermost crevices with a sort of bleating gasp. I think that never have I seen unadulterated terror more plainly expressed on an animal's features.

With the increased room for the body, the long sinuous neck came forward a like space. The thin snout was now fairly in the cavern. The nauseous breath hissed at us in gusts—sickening as a plague wind.

Suddenly the lithe neck stiffened. The evil eyes concentrated their gaze upon Gwen. Their stare seemed to go past my cheek with the searing directness of a flash-light. In an instant the memory of the power that lay in that wicked glare came back to me.

I dashed forward and clapped my palms upon Gwen's face, calling to her wildly to close her eyes. I gathered her to my bosom—and oh, the ecstasy of it, even in that desperate stress— and stammered incoherently of the fatal trap that lay in that unwinking gaze. She was content enough to bury her face in the folds of my loose jacket, and thus for a moment we stood shuddering. Fidget crept and fawned shiveringly about Gwen's skirts.

I kicked my foot against an object on the floor. It was the tin of mustard Gwen had been carrying when she started on that mad race down the boulders. It was new and shining, just out of store. I held it before my face to look at the reflection therein.

Finding his efforts unavailing, the Monster was drawing his head back into the outer part of the cave, relaxing his tense glare. We turned to face him. He curved his neck into a half-circle, his great throat muscles working with swallowings. Then with a sudden dart he flung it out upon us, gaping wide his mouth.

With a rasp and a roar his breath burst upon us, and upon the wall of rock at our back, hissing stridently like a gale through taut rigging. It beat us back almost irresistibly in the return draught, thrusting us out from the back of the cave toward his waiting lips. For one desperate moment we swayed in that noisome gust, and my free arm—for one still encircled Gwen's waist—whirled in the air frantically as I braced myself to meet it. But as its first strength died down I flung myself with Gwen upon the ground, and grasping at a ledge hung on with despair's own grip.

In the case of Fidget the Monster's wile defeated his object. The back-swirl of his breath whisked the little dog like a leaf past the lowering head and on into the outer cleft. With a sound half bark, half squeal, she leaped upon the unwieldy body before the neck could coil itself out of the inner cave. We heard her yapping pass swiftly out among the boulders, and die away up the empty lake-side.

There was the thud of a bullet on the thick hide, and the crack of a rifle followed smartly on the shot. A flake or scale of parchmenty skin floated past the cave mouth, and rustled slowly into the depths below; not by so much as the flicker of an eyelid did the brute show that he had felt anything. Another shot followed, with the same result. They clattered on—above a score of them—but they worried him no more than the buzzings of mosquitoes. Finally one must have hit a wart-like excrescence on his shoulder. A lump about the size of my fist fell with a flop upon the stones, glanced ruddily for a second, and bounced on into the depths below. But it left a tell-tale smear upon the granite, and scarlet drops trickled down the hanging neck, dripping in a small pool at the threshold of the cave. Yet the Monster lay unheeding, and we began to gasp with the unutterable murkiness of his breathing, which filled the air.

At Gwen's request I passed her the tin of mustard, and she held it like a smelling-bottle to her nostrils, to get relief from the disgusting fog. We began to pass it backward and forward to one another, and it was then that an inspiration—I think I may justly call it that—flashed into my brain.

With the tin in my hand I turned to face the great head again, waiting till the thin lips parted in one of their deep-drawn breaths. Then I tossed my missile accurately toward the open jaws, and like a flash of crimson the gums gaped wide and the yellow teeth closed upon it. For a single instant we saw it gleam brightly between them.

There was a scrunch and a grinding sound among the great fangs, and then the yellow powder sank bitingly into the saliva.

The brute opened his mouth, and a bellow pealed out of the strained throat, enveloping us in a volume of merciless sound and hot, putrid air. The long pink tongue slavered and twisted between the burning gums, showing ruddy streaks where the metal had gashed it. In one such ragged wound a remnant of the bright tin was still sticking; the flaming paste of powder and saliva was filling the torn veins with agony.

He dashed his head desperately from side to side, slamming it on the hard rock sides of the cavern. His unearthly screams threatened to burst our ear-drums. He beat the air with his great clumsy foot, and we could hear the thunderous boom of his great tail against the timbers of the ship.

Finally with the swiftness of an escaping bird the tortured head fled out of the cave mouth, and we heard his great carcass drag and rustle from the cleft. The blessed sunlight began to flow down to us again, and the filthy stench began to fade.

I let go my grip upon the rock, and, more unwillingly, my encirclement of Gwen's waist. I looked inquiringly into her eyes as I helped her up. She staggered as she rose, and for one delightful moment clung to me. I felt that mere courtesy bade me tender again my support, and so for two or three delicious seconds we stood. Then she found her voice and the ghost of a smile.

"I think you're quite the cleverest person I ever met," she said gratefully. "How on earth did you come to think of the mustard?"

"I really haven't the least idea," said I honestly. "His mouth was there and I had the tin in my hand. It seemed the most natural thing in the world to throw it in. The effect was more than I dared to hope for."

She drew herself unostentatiously away from my arm as she spoke, and leaned against the rocks behind her.

"Well," she remarked, "we've saved poor little Fidget, at any rate. Even if we're doomed to be devoured we shall have the satisfaction of knowing that."

"We!" said I rebukingly. "Should *I* ever have been such a sentimentalist as to risk a horrible death for a dog?"

"I rank above Fidget in your opinion then, as you have chosen to accompany me into this trap. You do me too much honor," and she bowed to me charmingly.

I couldn't quite command myself to answer this in any ordered phrase, but I suppose the expression on my face must have spoken. At any rate Gwen blushed delightfully, and continued rather hurriedly, "Don't you think we might make a run for it now?"

"I'll reconnoitre," said I, "and see if he's really taken himself off or not."

I climbed gingerly out of the cleft, and very cautiously raised my head above the edge. No, by no manner of means was he gone. He was lying about fifty yards away, banging his head upon the ground and lashing the boulders with his tail; some of them were smitten to splinters as I watched. His mouth still dripped yellow saliva, and his teeth were meeting with resounding cracks. His tongue still lapped itself about his tortured lips, and in his agony he rolled over, writhing upon his back and beating his four great limbs convulsively toward the sky. Lumps of his scaly skin were scattered about on the granite as feathers scatter from a shot bird. His nails clattered as they swept an overhanging mass of granite in one of their aimless gyrations. Finally there was one last angry flurry of legs and tail, and he rolled back upon his belly; his horny eyelids closed; his head sank wearily upon his fore-arms.

As I turned to tell Gwen I kicked a stone beside me. It fell with a metallic clang, and in a moment the green eyes were open and staring at me. He lifted his head, and his huge limbs began to shove his carcass back toward me. There was a revengeful glare in those baleful eyes, and I popped back into the cleft like a rabbit into his burrow.

I heard him come dragging along above. Then, looking up, I saw the thin snout just overlap the edge and lie still. Evidently he was settling down to his sentinelship. Afraid of another dose of the biting pain we had inflicted, he did not dare to venture his head again into our cave. He meant to starve us out.

Gwen looked up hopefully as I returned, but I had to shake my head at her glance of inquiry.

"No good just at present, I'm afraid. He's like the hosts of Midian, prowling and prowling around."

"Well, I suppose it can't be helped. But I do wish we'd had something a little more nutritious than mustard, useful as it's been. I'm simply starving. It's more than lunch-time by half an hour."

"That can be arranged," said I airily. "I'll nip up the other side of the ship and get aboard. I can get hold of plenty of stuff in the pantry."

"As if I should allow it for a moment. I forbid it absolutely," and she brought her little foot with a stamp upon the rock floor.

I still edged toward the cave mouth, explaining that the danger was practically nil, though well did I know the contrary. Still a man can't sit still to watch a particularly sweet woman starve, even if he has to risk a bit to bring her victual.

"I cannot stand the ignominy of starvation," I assured her, "not to mention the discomfort."

She came toward me with her eyes so sweetly appealing that I fell sick with temptation. "If you go," she said almost tearfully—there really was a humid look in her blue eyes— "I shall simply die of fright. I won't be left alone."

I hesitated and was lost. She put her hand upon my sleeve, and looked up searchingly into my face. "Please, please, please, don't go. I really am very frightened."

Goodness knows what I should have done next. Probably taken her in my arms and sworn neither to leave her then nor ever again, regardless of Denvarre or any question of mere Honor. But fate took matters out of my hand.

The brute above us gave a hiccough; I believe he meant it for a sneeze, but as a minor explosion of sorts it might have held up its head with cordite cartridges or an oil motorcar. Gwen, whose nerves were, as you may imagine, a trifle beyond control by now, gave a cry and fled into my arms, which opened of themselves to receive her. And so for a minute we stood silent and listening, while my pulses rioted within me.

After a moment or two we were aware that the foetid odor of the great Beast was being overpowered by a resistless smell of sulphur. This was doubtless giving our friend a sore throat, and titillating his nostrils. I hoped devoutly that the unpleasantness of it would be too much for him. He snorted once or twice again, and then a faint steam began to rise from the depths, as I had seen it do in the morning. Far below us I could hear the faint lap of water upon the stones.

Then a horrible fear took possession of me. The water was rising, hot from some volcanic spring. Shortly it would gurgle out at our feet and flood our refuge. Then we should have the necessity before us of deciding whether we would drown—or perchance be parboiled—or step resignedly into the jaws of the Monster outside.

I looked fixedly at Gwen as these terrors hunted each other through my brain, and I suppose my thoughts shadowed out upon my face.

She turned her eyes to mine as I held her, looking questioningly at me, as if she would read my very soul. A sob and gurgle from the rising water sounded out bell-like and clear, moaning distinctly across the silence. I knew by the shudder that ran through her that she was realizing what must happen when it lapped up to us. Her face fell upon my breast; her hands rose tremblingly to my shoulders; so for a few moments we stood, and silence hung between us.

The white clouds of steam began to weave and whirl fantastically across the mouth of the cave. The warm, damp air played about us. The suck and splash of the waters sounded ever nearer and clearer from below. Above we could hear the wheeze and the occasional gasp of the watching Monster, and his feet moved restlessly, sending down showers of little stones into the abyss, where they no longer clattered into emptiness, but fell with splashings into the growing flood. Then a thrill pulsed through the rocks, and we could feel the sickening heave and roll of the earth as a new eruption shook the crater. In a second or two the roar of it came dully down to us, drowning the sound of the rifle shots which still pattered at intervals on the rocks, or thudded on that sensationless hide.

Finally the water rose to view, creeping with slow, silent tide up the rocks, gaining inch by inch upon the sides of the cleft. A wreath of steam hung mistily upon its surface. I bent and touched it with my finger. It was warm—about eighty degrees I should imagine—but not unbearable.

I stepped again to the cave mouth and peered up. The cruel snout still projected over the edge above, waiting, waiting remorselessly. As I watched the triangular head moved forward a space, and, turning sideways, looked down at me with hot, revengeful eyes. I stepped back into the shadow of the cave, and down flashed the head, hanging in eager, swaying motion before us, gloating for the moment when we should be thrust out to it by the rising flood.

I slushed back to the end of the cave—the water was now at our knees—and took Gwen in my arms, shielding the gruesome sight from her with my breast. She drooped into my embrace again, trembling, but with a little thankful sigh for companionship in this last desperate pang.

"It'll soon be over," I said as steadily as I could, while my hand brushed her hair smoothingly. "Just a little struggle, and then a dream that carries you right across the border, and—and I shall be there to meet you. Do you see, dear?"

I had no right to call her dear, I know, she being Denvarre's and not mine, but it was the last time, and, poor little soul, she wanted comfort for the last wrench. She looked up at me, and I could see that her lips were parched and dry, though there was a curious light shining in her eyes.

"Is there no chance at all?—are you sure?" she whispered, and for all the horror that was closing down upon us, a smile shone in her eyes.

"None, I fear," said I; "but—but I don't think it'll be bad—people who have been nearly drowned say that—"

"Ah, I don't mean that. Only I wanted to tell you before the end—I meant to tell you in any case, but it's easier now. Vi only found out this morning that mother had led you to think that we had accepted those two—but—but it isn't so. Lord Denvarre asked me, but I told him I didn't think I possibly could—only—he wanted me to wait six months and see—and then we met again, and—I knew—then—" But my lips upon hers stayed her, and my arms went fiercely about her again.

"My darling, my darling," I cried, "and I thought you'd forgotten me utterly, and taken Denvarre for all he could bring you. And now, sweetheart, now—oh, my God," I groaned, "what can I do, what can I do?"

Her voice was quite steady, and she leaned forward to put her face up to mine. "Then you still want me, dear," she whispered.

"Well, I'm yours till—till the end," and a tiny sob shook her voice for a moment. "But I want a gift from you before we part, my darling," and she touched my cheek with a little soft caress.

"A gift?" I stared back into her eyes, devouring with hungry gaze the sweet face that was mine, only to be lost to me again.

"Yes, dear. You have your revolver."

I thrust her back from me wildly. My God, how could she ask it? I, to send the bullet into that dear heart that beat for me. I, to give her death, who longed with every passionate impulse of my being to give her life, who would have perilled not only my unworthy body but my very soul to save her pain. The thought of it was more than could be borne; the doing of it—Merciful God! it was impossible.

"*Please*, my darling. I should only struggle when the last moment came, and fight out into his jaws." She pressed back close to me again, looking up at me with a pleading that was terrible. "Just one embrace, my own, and then—" and her hands rose round my neck, and for one delicious instant her dear lips pressed passionately against mine. Then, with a little triumphant smile she drew back, and repeated quietly, "Now, dear."

The water was at my shoulders, and it was only by holding Gwen tightly to me that I kept her face above the surface. There was but a bare three inches between my pistol hand and the roof. I looked at the cartridges with some faint hope that they might be wetted, and that this last terrible duty might be yet taken from me. But the brass cases had held only too well. I raised my revolver, pointing it downward, and looked into those dear eyes. Her eyelids drooped as the steel barrel shone, and I felt her fingers tighten upon my arm. The water was at my lips, but with one supreme effort I raised her to me. One last look into the dearest face in all the world—one last kiss—one touch of that golden hair—then—

Crash—crash—crash—outside was a grating roar, and caught by the rising tide the ship surged forward. The bulge of it swung against the cave mouth, and in an instant caught and gripped the pendant neck, sawing and grinding its flesh against the jagged edges. The prisoned head in its agony beat frantically against the surface, and the water shot right and left in angry ripples as the breath of the Monster's scream burst upon it.

The revolver dropped from my hand. I snatched Gwen to me, and dived into the hot, turbid flood—down beneath the struggling head, down beneath the ship's keel, out into the warm stillness of the cleft beyond.

Gasping and choking from our sudden immersion I dragged my darling over the edge, and half-led, half-carried her up the rocky slope, leaving a long wet drip upon the granite. The enraged and baffled yelling of the captured Beast rang out piercingly among the cliff echoes; the lashings of his great tail smote upon the empty hold of the ship as upon a drum. In his vain attempts to draw his neck from the trap he drove and spurred at the boulders frantically, and the clatter of his long nails upon the pebbles sounded like the scratchings of some monstrous cat.

Our clothes were sodden and heavy, and our nerves unstrung from terror and excitement. We were in no condition for a swift escape.

My own state of mind I can in nowise describe, such a confusion of fright and ecstasy raged therein. Firstly, the horrors of a hideous death still hung over us, though for the moment passed by. My pulses still tingled with the sick despair of that last terrible moment. Death had been my betrothal gift to my love—death to save her from agony. Another second, and she would have received it at my hand. Thank God that there are few who can realize the æons of torture that swelled into those few instants of good-bye. Death was still at our backs, and might follow hard upon our footsteps, but I was so uplifted in the knowledge of my darling's love, and in learning that no point of honor stood between us, that I scarce gave a thought to remembering that we might yet stand together in the Valley of the Shadow.

Up the slope we toiled, and very like one of those terrible hills that we climb in dreams did it appear. Gwen clung to me desperately, her dear eyes hunted and shining with affright. Her knees trembled—she strove to run, but her dripping skirts caught her limbs and made her stumble.

Still up we reeled, the pebbles spinning from our unsteady feet, the smooth rock silt churning to mud upon our shoes. From above came cries of encouragement, and from the heights I

seemed to see dark forms speed down toward us. Another crash
echoed from behind. I threw a quick glance across my shoulder. The *Raccoon* was slanting back from the cave mouth, and
the Monster was free. I saw him turn and crawl slowly from the
pool in which the ship was beginning to right herself and sit
swan-like.

He lifted his head, and I saw the blood flow in streams from
his gashed throat. It steamed as it made puddles upon the cold
rocks. He sniffed the breeze. Then his evil eyes settled their stare
in our direction. The huge body began to waddle and slide toward us.

I caught Gwen up in my arms and fled upward, terror thrusting me on. She gave one gasp of protest; then she settled into
my embrace with a little sigh of relief as she nestled to me. So
the race for life began.

I ran almost unseeingly, the great pulses throbbing and
thrumming in my bosom. Now and again I stumbled; once I
nearly fell. Gwen's arm came with a jolt against a boulder top. I
cursed my awkwardness, hurrying on and trying to pick my way
amongst the great, loose lumps more carefully. Some rubble gave
beneath my feet. I rolled over sideways; somehow—though how
I can't say myself—I managed to fall upon my elbows and save
my burden from harm. I rocked up to my feet, and saw as in a
dream the cliff-foot two hundred yards away, and upon it the
forms of men who ran toward me.

I turned my face over my shoulder again. The Brute was a
short half-furlong away—his tongue lolling from his wide expectant jaws.

He strained his neck toward us, his eyes aglint; he seemed
almost to trot rather than waddle in his greedy haste. Determination and despair drove me forward as with a goad; I panted
with the horror of his oncoming.

Above me sat Garlicke, rifle in hand, breaking the clean outline of the ridge against the sky. The rifle was silhouetted thin
and delicate as a needle against the brightness. A spurt of blue
smoke burst from the muzzle, and the crack of it rang across the
hollow. I heard a thud as the bullet struck the mass of hungry
desire behind me, and glanced again quickly, hoping for effect.

A red weal shone upon one of the horny eyelids. He stopped, blinking stupidly, and half-stunned by the shock. But the ball had not penetrated, and with a puzzled swinging of the wounded neck he resumed his scrambling, ungainly gait.

Still a hundred yards, and my eyes grew dizzy. A red mist seemed to close upon them, which, lifting now and again, showed me surrounding objects defined as on the slides of a magic lantern. My breath rasped with such a wheezing whistle that I looked wonderingly to see whence the sound could come. My arms were like wire ropes, strained to the breaking. My legs shuffled painfully under me. I felt the strength going out from me as water leaks from an unbunged cask. The sound of Garlicke's shots struck fainter and fainter upon my ears. I stumbled again, and only saved myself from plunging forward by an instinctive straightening of my shoulders. The sunlight was shadowing to a night—a black darkness that could be felt.

Then, dimly, a familiar voice broke upon my ears; I was conscious of a hand seizing my arm; of some one struggling with me for Gwen. Yet, thought I, we will die together. Then the friendly hand, leaving this useless striving, dragged me forward; behind me some unseen power was thrusting me with mad shoves up the Titan steps of the cliff face. Suddenly came clearness of vision, and I knew Denvarre and Gerry, who were hauling and jerking me up the crevices of our rock of defence. Gwen was still in my arms, and below, the great monster scrabbled at the cliff-foot, reaching up his neck in raging, ravenous disappointment.

So, Denvarre dragging and Gerry butting like some benevolent goat, from niche to niche I stumbled with my burden, the little stones rattling down in their thousands upon the Beast below. Upon the top I staggered forward into the shelter of the tarpaulin, and laid Gwen down upon the rocky floor. Then, in the sudden impulse of her love, and in her revulsion from that great dread, she flung her arms about me as I stooped over her, and before them all kissed me on the lips. And who was I that I should not kiss back once and again?

So my love and I came to an understanding, and sealed our betrothal as the shadow of death passed from us—passing as a cloud when the breeze is strong and out leaps the sun: while above us the mountain still belched fire and molten stone, and below the Beast prowled, and sought hungrily for our blood. And I take it that never have man and maid plighted troth in stranger circumstance.

19

A WONDROUS BREACHING OF THE WALL

A good man all through is Denvarre, as I said before, and like a good man he took the failure of his hopes. And they had never been anything more. For as he explained to me, when we had changed our dripping clothes and joined the others on the cliff-top, he had no knowledge of Lady Delahay's very distorted rendering of the situation. And he shook my hand and looked me straight in the eyes, and then, like the gentleman he was, went away to leave my sweetheart and me to say all we had to say to each other behind a ledge of rock that screened us from the others. And he took with him my unstinted admiration and esteem.

My future mother-in-law was in no condition for the exchanging of ideas or reproaches. The horrors of the situation crowded her understanding, leaving no room for such trivialities as the arrangement of her daughter's welfare. Apathetically she took the plain statement I thought it only my duty to render to her, making no remark thereon save that "Nothing mattered when we should all be dead before the day was out." And to this pessimistic view of the situation we had perforce to leave her, while we all waited for what should betide us at the hand of fate.

In the corner apart Gwen and I held each the other's hand, and sought each other's eyes. And in the bliss that was mine I thanked God, nearly sparing a blessing for the great Beast who still prowled below, for how but for him should I have come into my kingdom of delight? So in happiness that even the great smoke pall could not overshadow we sat to watch the day die, and the blood-red glow of the mountain wax scarlet on the dark cloud above us, while the pulse of the undying fires vibrated across the heavens after each succeeding roar and shudder of the melting rocks.

As we watched the travail of the hills, across the edge of the
crater where it was lowest in the lap of the peak, a thin line
showed. Faint it was at first, then thickening to a broad scarlet,
where the range of ringing rocks dipped lowest. For seconds it
hung there, a red bar of palpitating, blood-like flame. Then with
a roar it broke over the barrier and swept on headlong down
the spur of the hill, engulfing the smaller rocks, and laving the
bases of the larger ones that stemmed its current island-like.

After the first mad burst the roaring spate of fire slowed on
a slighter slope; then rolled massively, grimly down upon the
glacier head through the vale of granite. As the lava drained to the
bottom level of the rent in the crater the flow lessened. Finally
it ceased. Ere half a mile of the distance between the orifice and
the glacier had been covered the crimson glow began to fade.
The surface of the flood dulled to a dark crimson, then to a living
blackness as of velvet. The crest of the advancing flood sank
down sluggishly and stayed, its bosom curving menacingly, the
advance guard of an army irresistible.

A flaring pillar of flame-dyed, guttering stone shot skyward
again, the splashes of it thudding about us heavily. One molten
lump, stiffening as it fell, smote on our tarpaulin roof, slashing
through it to the stone floor. A shriek went up from Lady
Delahay as she shrank back from its still living glow, and the
tarpaulin burst into sudden flame. A dozen willing hands tore it
down and wrapped it together, smothering the fire in the folds.
Poor little Fidget—utterly cowed by terror fast following on terror—came slinking toward me, and nestling in between Gwen
and myself, hid her little nose deferentially in my sleeve. My
darling gave her a little friendly pat, and I cuddled the little
dog gratefully myself. But a shudder followed fast on the caress
as I thought of what might have been when she had been kicking and screaming in that death-trap in the cleft.

We peered down at the Beast. He was still rambling restlessly about, snuffling now and again at the cliff-foot, aimlessly
pawing and snatching at the boulders that banked the rock face.
Once just below us, where the sheer crag melted into a more
slanting angle, he rose clumsily upon his hind limbs, leant forward, and stretched his head toward us, pricking out his long

tongue. As it licked across his lips the jag of broken tin flashed redly in the glow, and we could hear it grate as his teeth closed.

His head reached up to within forty yards of us as he swarmed against the cliff, and Garlicke aimed carefully for his eye. The bullet only grazed the unscarred eyebrow, giving it a curious uniformity with the other one. The brute merely blinked impatiently as the ball thudded on the shell-like lid, but did not twitch a muscle. As it splayed out its feet on the bank of loose stones, seeking purchase to strain higher, the rubble gave way, and it rolled back with a thump upon its side. Its green belly shone a loathsome pink in the glare from above, and for a moment it lay prone, its great legs kicking convulsively. Then with an effort it righted itself, and crawled sulkily away to resume its sentinelship at the cliff-foot. It continued to ramble to and fro unceasingly, casting ever greedy eyes at us, the hideous snout lifted to the breeze, the long tongue lolling from between the yellow teeth.

Down in the hollow a growing sheet of water spread. On it the ship floated lopsided and aimlessly. Long widening ripples welled from where the cleft was submerged, and a steam cloud was hazy upon the surface. The hull was all untrue upon its keel with the shifting of the ballast, and as the ripples swung her, drifted in slow circles. With her lost topmast she looked like nothing so much as a wounded wild duck. The fire glow gave the increasing water the effect of blood issuing from a wound in the bosom of earth. On it were reflected crimson throbs from the arch of ruddy fog; they were as pulses across an opened vein.

Another quiver rocked our pyramid of granite, and the glacier was riven across. The following roar gushed down to us deafeningly. The lane showed dark and mysterious across the ice-field, clean cut as by an axe blow, and this new-made cañon ran with scarce an obstacle nearly to the foot of our refuge. We seemed to get a vision, swift and fleeting as a lightning flash, of the hidden mysteries of the ice. I could have declared I saw the yellow *facade* of the buried temple show up against a black background of rock. Then as the flying lava sank back again into the bath of fire, darkness closed over this half-seen apparition.

Once again the red bar glowed across the dip in the crater brim. For one tense moment it hovered, and then crashed down upon its dying forerunner, covering it anew with living fire. Along this smoothed path it rushed headlong, leaped down from the lava crest upon the stones, and rolled with measured grandeur down the groove the earthquake had riven. Blocks of ice, fallen from the glacier sides, lay in its course and were swallowed in a moment. Like the roar of a bursting shell the steam bubbles smashed to the surface, and floated up in white circling clouds to lose themselves in the fog above. Unhalting the torrent ran, engulfing all before it; stones, ice, and the rock itself disappeared. Then in slow-growing blackness it stayed, sank and died, even as its predecessor. But this time the wave reached to the end of the fissure, and the heat of it beat up to us, lapping us in a bath of sultry, stifling air.

The Beast shifted his sentry walk uneasily, stretching out his neck toward the lava wall, and snouting at the warm draught suspiciously. For a moment he seemed to waver. His nostrils dilated curiously. Then he glanced toward the rising lake, and we thought he would give over his seeking for our lives. As he hesitated, now looking lakeward, now peering up to us, another crash resounded from the mountain. Like the tearing of a sheet of paper the glacier cañon split further shoreward, and opened beneath his very feet. Half his bulk rolled into the cleft thus riven; his tail and one hind limb disappeared. Slipping and spurring frantically he managed to support himself on his huge elbows, but lost ground with every rock of the shuddering earth. The cleft yawned, then half closed again. Thus as in a vice he was held, his leg and tail mangled in the nip of the fissure. He looked like some stupendous stoat caught in a gigantic gin.

The bellow of his agony pierced even above the thunderous roll of the mountain. The blood spurted from his sides, bathing them in a darker tinge than the flame glow. His fore-feet beat and thudded on the stones, sweeping them into ridges with the convulsions of his agony. He swung his neck across his shoulders, tearing rabidly at his wounds.

The sight was almost too much for human eyes. Gwen had already buried hers against my coat. The breathing of the sailors behind me grew stertorous, as their chests rose and fell in unconscious sympathy. Speech was taken from us by a very paralysis of horror. But worse was to come.

The fiery matter that fevered the volcano burst forth again. Again the mountain shuddered, belching forth its flames. Down the dead waves another living torrent rushed, roared in the deep channel through the glacier, and foamed—yes, foamed—into the widening split. A scream, anguish-born and like the crowded wails of ten thousand souls in torment, rose from the prisoned Beast. A pungent, choking smell of roasting flesh rose up to us. Then the red tide flowed on over the charred carrion, and burst asunder again; a gout of steaming gas shot up, sole remnant of the tissues of that enormous carcass. The stream touched and laved lightly at our refuge. Then slowly it dimmed, and the velvet surface grew up on it again. The current halted and grew still. Its force was spent.

The heat beat up to us scorchingly. We felt, but saw it not. Our faces were averted, and nausea had us by the throat. As the great Beast had died, so might we come to die, and that right soon. The realization of the matter was more than we could see and not blench. For some half-minute no one spoke, and dread hung over us thick as the cloud of cinder dust that filled the sky.

As I raised my eyes again to look on the things of earth, a broad line showed across the seaward cliffs that hedged us in. It increased visibly as I stared at it, and I knew that again the cliffs were rending between the sea and the growing pool. I leaned across and touched Janson on the shoulder, pointing silently. As he too caught sight of the rift the light of hope grew across his haggard face.

"If it cuts down to the sea—" he muttered, glancing to where our ship and the little launch wandered masterlessly about among the steam wreaths. He turned to me and pointed to them.

"Let's get aboard, my lord. It's only a hundred to one chance, but it might widen and give channel. Here's only quick roasting, at any rate."

"How about the propeller-shaft?" I queried sadly. "We shan't be able to get steam on her."

"That's no matter," he said, shaking his head impatiently. "We can get steam in the launch for a tow, or if that takes too long, ten oars in one of the boats would shift her, lopsided as she is."

"Who's to board her, Mr. Janson? It means swimming."

"I can if nobody else will, but I'll give Rafferty the job. He's a fine swimmer," and he beckoned to the boatswain.

"Board the launch," quoth Janson to him curtly, "and bring her ashore."

Rafferty made no remark on this terse order, but slipped quickly down the ledges that led to the rocks below. He kicked off his boots, dropped his jacket upon the stones, and poising his hands above his head, sprang like a dart into the still pool. There was scarcely a splash as he struck the surface, but he rose almost instantly in a circle of foam, while a shrill yell of agony burst from his lips. He threshed desperately back to the shore, still screaming horribly.

Howling and cursing, he flung himself upon the stones, and, oblivious of all considerations of modesty, tore off his clothes. He apostrophized every saint in the Catholic calendar. He squirmed, he bellowed, and believing him struck with sudden madness we raced toward him, utterly at fault to find explanation of this sudden explosion. But as we drew near our eyes soon found a cause.

The unfortunate seaman was red as any lobster. His skin was blistered and parboiled. It hung, as he himself explained in no uncertain voice, "in tathers and shtrips." The waters of the rising lake had scalded him horribly.

We caught the unfortunate seaman as he wriggled upon the cool stones, and wrapped him in our coats. One of the men ran back for our blankets, nothing, as I well knew, being so dangerous for him as exposure to the air. What he needed most was thick coverings and oil. But, unfortunately, the whole stock of the latter was aboard the ship.

In this extremity the long black bulk of the stranded whale beneath the cliff caught my eye. It was no time for discussion. Gerry and I snatched up the kicking mariner, and bore him loudly complaining toward the carcass. We hacked great greasy lumps from its reeking sides, and then, as the blankets arrived, packed the victim tightly in this carrion, twisting the folds of blanket round the layers of blubber. So, muttering condemnation on all and sundry, and sniffing most melancholiously as the stench of the putrid wrapping filled his nostrils, we set him down, while we devised other means of reaching the ship across the steaming lake.

The launch was now only about sixty yards away, turning slowly as the ripples rose from the centre of the pool. One of the sailors produced a ball of string. To one end of this we tied a sizable pebble, and Gerry, who is a noted man at throwing the cricket ball, managed after some half-dozen attempts to land the stone in the bottom of the boat. Careful tugs brought her ashore, and in less than a minute we were aboard the ship.

I ran forward and knotted a loose rope to the foremast. Then, taking the slack, we jumped back into the boat, and bent our backs to the oars. Ever so slowly the ship got way and followed us, till the grating of the keel against the shallows told us she could come no further. We looked at the cleavage of the rocks. We saw with gladness that it had widened yet more, for the blue horizon line of ocean shone distinct across it, and the peaks of the nearer bergs jutted up into the vista. The others who had watched us from the heights now began to descend the granite stairway.

In straggling procession, the sailors weighed down with our surplus stores, they joined us as we strained upon the rope. The ladies were quickly ferried across the few yards between the rocks and the ship, and some of us tossed the various impedimenta aboard, while half a dozen ran back up the rocks to collect all leavings. Then, dumping everything anyhow upon the deck, we got a strong crew of six in one of the boats, hoisted the launch aboard, and gradually got the bows turned cliffward.

The waters were still gushing up and widening upon the basin, the circling eddies helping our towers as they dragged us tediously toward the cleft. The shocks from the mountain came with greater frequency, making the pool shiver into tiny surges that fled across it, to break in ripples on the further shore. Another of the peaks toppled and fell with a resounding crash.

The fissure began to disappear amid the cloud of low-hung steam, and it was with difficulty we steered our course for it. A sudden outcry from the boat that strained ahead made us aware that we were forging with all the powers of six stout oars straight at an opening that was yet a dozen feet above tide-level. It was only by the smartness of the boat's crew, who doubled sharply in their tracks and snatched a rope flung to them from our stern, that we escaped inglorious shipwreck. They tugged lustily in the contrary direction and managed to stop the ship's way. Then, having us more or less motionless, they rested on their oars, and we floated aimlessly, waiting further developments, for the fissure still widened.

We were silent, for the awe and anxiety of our position kept us tongue-tied, and every one was on deck. The sailors fidgeted up and down, now and again shifting perfunctorily some of the heaped confusion of the decks, but stopping every minute to gaze inquiringly at the peak, as roar after roar and shock after shock swept down from it. We were like malefactors awaiting execution, but hoping desperately against hope for a reprieve.

Then a thunderous boom, fifty times louder than any that had preceded it, broke from the bosom of the hill. The pinnacles swayed, tottered, and bowed earthward; not one but was swept from its base. A red storm of lava surged boiling over the crater brim, swelled in a torrent down the channel through the heart of the glacier, and dashed in a cloud of steam into the far end of the lake. A vapor mist, impenetrable as a desert sandstorm, closed over the waters, but ere it fell we saw a huge threatening wave uprise and swing across at us in fury irresistible. Behind it was all the impact force of the fiery mass, but long ere it reached us the fog rolled down and shut us in in its warm gray veil.

A rending crash broke from the cliff in front, and the cold, hungry ocean came clamoring through, beating upon the outcharging tide. For some furious seconds our ship plunged and reared among the fighting billows like a restive horse. Then from the boat came a cry as the pursuing wave reached her and flung boiling spray upon the men. Like a toy she was raised and flung toward us. The wall of water struck with a thud below our stern, and thrust us, how forward, at the gap. Swifter than paddle or screw could have borne us we sped upon the crest, driving straight into the new reft opening.

A gasp went up from every throat, and not one of us but breathed a prayer. Two seconds more and the dark walls were flashing by on each side. Then with a dying effort the great wave flung us far out into the ice-bestrewed main, diffusing itself up the long lanes of floating berg, roaring and clanging amid the splinters of the floe.

Spinning on yet before that mighty impulse, lopsided, with ballast adrift, with fore-topmast gone and propeller-shaft broken, we fled forth from our prison, dragging the boat astern with her bows out of the water, and from boat and ship alike went up a mighty cheer of deliverance as the great crags faded into the steam-cloud behind us. And so did we accomplish our marvellous escape.

As the great surge sank to ripples, we sprang to work, full of the energy of relief and gratitude. Some set to right our littered decks, some descended into the hold to replace the shifted ballast, while Eccles, debarred from work by his broken collar-bone, stood over his subordinates and admonished them with many a good Glasgow expletive to seek drills to rivet a collar on the split propeller. Rafferty from between his oily compresses roared curses and commands at the deck-hands, and all, crew and passengers, were busy as best they knew how. And behind the deck-house my love and I found time to seal with a kiss the promise of new life that had had its birth under the very Shadow of Death.

The red glow of the fire-pillar was beginning to pale into the tints of dawn before we had cleared our deck into any similitude of tidiness. All night long we toiled, relieving each other in crews of eight at the towing. For the heat ashore made the breeze beat landward with aggravating steadiness, and but for persistent effort we should have drifted back on to the sheer cliffs of the wall, and pounded our timbers into matchwood on its iron face.

So wearily the oarsmen toiled and drew the unwilling ship by slow by-ways amid the herding pack-ice. And down in the engine-room Eccles sat to swing his sound arm upon the gearing and spit imperious blasphemy at his underlings, who drilled and drilled again with stiffening fingers, while forward the carpenter wrestled with a spare spar to raise anew a topmast. Both on deck and below Rafferty's nimble tongue reached and drove the lagging crew.

Finally with morning came a fair breeze off the land, and getting sail upon the mizzen we lurched easily along, and the weary towers came aboard, full of thankfulness and dropping with sleep. Then leaving two volunteers to steer—Janson and Parsons to wit—we one and all sank down upon our berths and slept as only those sleep who have labored through four-and-twenty hours of surpassing terror and excitement.

It was late in the afternoon ere I reached the deck again, washed, changed, and looking rather less like a sweep's apprentice than I had done twelve hours before. Gwen was pacing to and fro forward, and delicious it was to watch her from the companion, and to note, with all the inward glow of love's proprietorship, the golden curls flutter against her white forehead.

She turned as I stepped out into the sunlight, and came and gave me good-morning with such happy shyness that I entirely lost my head in the exuberance of my feelings, and took thrice as much as I was offered. Which sweet felony I might have continued in spite of my lady love's admonishings, but for the audible titterings of Gerry and Vi, who were conducting a similar function on the other side of the deck-house.

It was not an altogether cordial interview I had with Lady Delahay, but on my part it was a very determined one. And she was in no condition to face me boldly. The stress of the last few days had worn her down, and she made but half-hearted defence of her devious dealings with me, and after my explanation that the dignity of the Heatherslies was not to be kept up on an Irish rent-roll alone, was almost kind. At any rate she saw that further opposition was useless, and wisely considering that it was well to agree with her son-in-law while she was in the way with him, gave a consent that was not entirely a grudging one. As yet the desperate proposals of Vi and Gerry remained untold, and her temper had not been strained beyond its furthest limits. So I retreated with the honors of victory thick upon me, and in great peace my love and I went back to sit together behind the deck-house, and what we said to each other is no one's concern but our own.

For three days the flap of a two-knot breeze was upon our canvas, and we met occasional berg. But on the fourth morning we woke to an ice-free horizon, and to the hissing of steam in the boilers; this welcome sound being soon followed by the sight of a pale wake of screw-churned foam. Neither Eccles, nor any man who called him master, had had four consecutive hours of sleep in the last eighty, but thanks to this and to his Scotch determination, we thenceforward swept our way regardless of resisting winds. Ten days of half-speed, lest we should strain our new-spliced shaft, brought us through constant sunshine to within sight of the Falklands.

With the R. Y. S. pennant afloat, and black smoke curling from our funnel we breasted the billows into Port Lewis. As we drew near the land we were aware of a gallant ship standing out toward us; she too had fires new-stoked, and her cutwater spurned the foam. At her peak the white ensign floated, and we knew her for a man-of-war. Suddenly upon her decks commotion was visible, and the jangle of her engine-room bells came distinctly across the stillness. As she slowed, a stentorian hail came from a gesticulating figure on her bridge.

"*Raccoon*, ahoy! Is it yourself then, or a new *Flying Dutchman*? In the name of heaven, m' lord, how did you get away?"

It was poor old Waller, and across the intervening sea-lane his face showed white as the lashed hammocks he stared across. His eyes were starting from his head.

A cheer went up in answer from our assembled crew, and joyously I bade him come aboard to hear our news. In three minutes he was on our decks, exchanging heartiest of hand-shakings with us all as we pressed round him, and pouring out question on question as he surveyed the ship again unbelievingly. I left him to the care of Gerry and Denvarre, while I attended to the blue uniformed naval captain who had accompanied him. This individual I could see was under the impression that Waller had grossly and impertinently deceived him with a cock-and-bull story of our sad plight in the desolate regions of the South.

I gave a hasty *résumé* of our adventures, leaving detail till the evening, which we spent with the man-of-war's men in much jollification. Waller had been fortunate enough to arrive two days before us, and to find H. M. S. *Bluebell* paying her annual visit of inspection. Her gallant captain had promised to start directly Government stores were landed, and this promise we had found in the early stages of fulfilment.

We pledged this good purpose in champagne, and gave him thanks worthy of the accomplished deed. In the morning we coaled anew, and from the warship received help of engineers and artificers, who strengthened our patched propeller and battened down more firmly our ballast.

In the evening we parted with much esteem and desire for future foregatherings—we to turn northward and home by the south seas, the *Bluebell* setting her course for Buenos Ayres.

As the day died in the crimson of the sunset, my darling and I stood beside the taffrail and watched the ruby glories fade. We had just interviewed Lady Delahay on behalf of Vi and Gerry. With artful devices had I pictured the latter's probable career in his profession with my influence at his back, and desperately had I exaggerated the possible worth of his share of the Mayan treasure. Denvarre, too, had magnanimously promised that the whole patronage of the family should be exerted to gain him *attachéships* and like lucrative posts. The result had been a tardy and unwilling, but official, benison of Gerry's aspirations, and in the stern the young couple sat hand-in-hand with the more or less complacent assent of the lady's mother.

So in perfected content my love and I stood together in the bow, and saw the sun sink into the main and the stars rush out into soft splendors above us. A thousand miles behind us were the terrors of the land of fire—terrors forgiven, in that they had knit our lives and now loomed shadowy through a mist of happiness. Our prow was pointing to the islands of eternal summer; and in our hearts love's endless summer reigned.

Coachwhip Publications

CoachwhipBooks.com

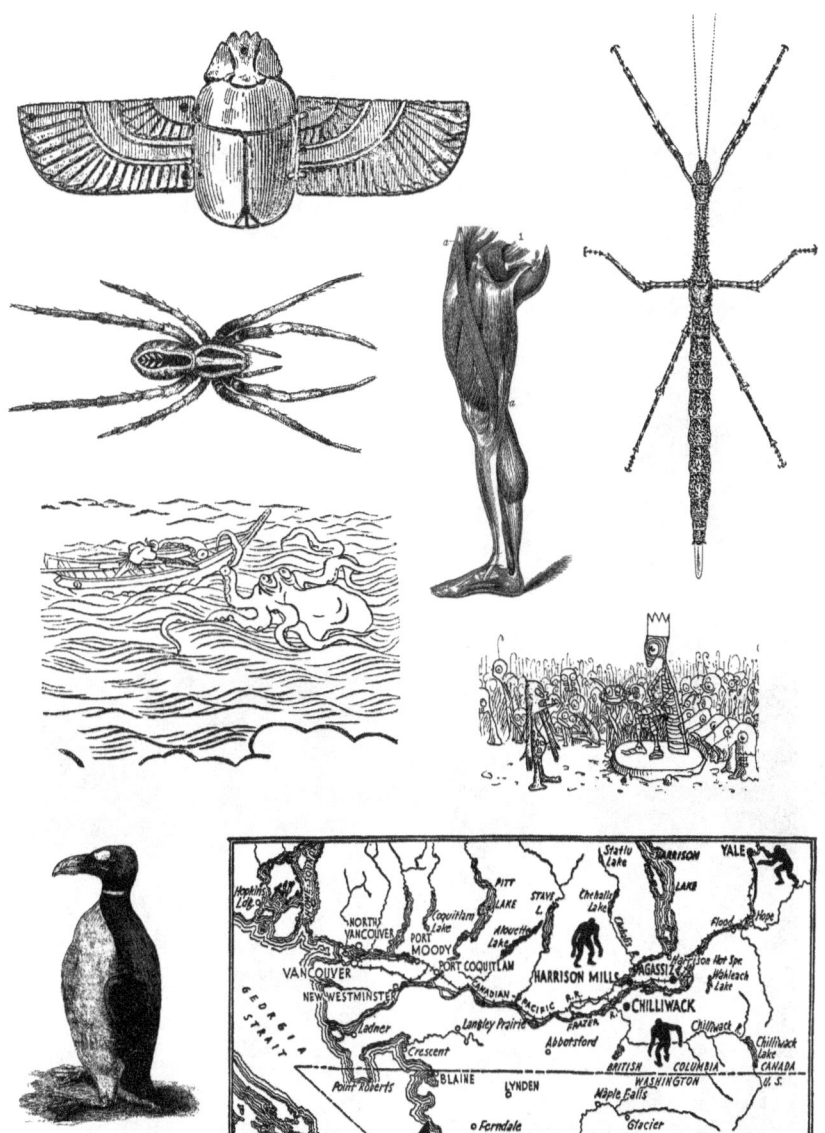

Cryptozoology Books
@ CoachwhipBooks.com

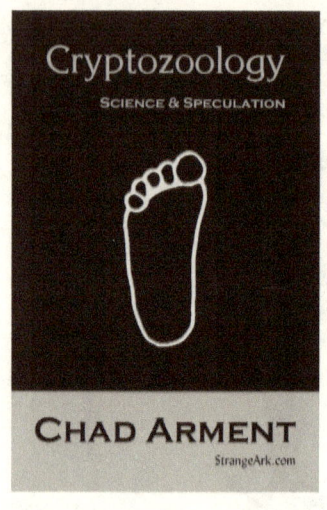

More Classic Cryptofiction
@ CoachwhipBooks.com

www.ingramcontent.com/pod-product-compliance
Lightning Source LLC
Chambersburg PA
CBHW020840260626
47169CB00003B/1073